Journey by Moonlight

Antal Szerb

Translated by Peter V. Czipott

ALMA CLASSICS
an imprint of

ALMA BOOKS LTD
Thornton House
Thornton Road
Wimbledon Village
London SW19 4NG
United Kingdom

Journey by Moonlight first published in Hungarian in 1937
This translation first published by Alma Classics in 2016
This new edition first published by Alma Classics in 2021

Cover design: Leo Nickolls

Printed in Great Britain by CPI Group (UK) Ltd, Croydon CR0 4YY

ISBN: 978-1-84749-582-2

Contents

Journey by Moonlight

Part One

THE HONEYMOON

I'm factious, yet in general I obey;
What else? I'd take my pledges back again;
Made welcome, and by all men turned away.

—FRANÇOIS VILLON

1

THERE HAD BEEN NO TROUBLE at all on the train. It began in the back alleys of Venice.

Taking the water taxi from the train station, Mihály* noticed the alleyways opening to the right and left as soon as they left the Grand Canal to take a short cut. He didn't yet bother with them, however, because at first he was completely taken by how Venetian Venice was: the water between the houses; the gondolas; the lagoon; and the city's brick-red-and-pink sheen. For Mihály was now seeing Italy for the first time – at the age of thirty-six, on his honeymoon.

He had covered the map in the course of his long-extended years of wandering. He'd spent years in England and France, but he had always avoided Italy, sensing that the time was not yet ripe: he wasn't prepared for it. He assigned Italy, along with siring offspring, to the category of grown-up matters, and in secret he even feared it: he feared it the way he shied away from strong sunlight, the scent of flowers and extremely pretty women.

If he hadn't got married and if his intention hadn't been to begin his wedded life with the standard Italian honeymoon, he might have postponed the Italian journey until his death. Even now, he had come to Italy not on a visit but on a honeymoon, which is a different matter altogether. He could come now, in any case, because he was married now. By this point, so he thought, the danger that Italy represented could no longer threaten him.

The first few days passed peacefully amid honeymoon pleasures and leisurely sightseeing that didn't tax the couple overmuch. As befitting highly intelligent people possessed of enormous self-awareness,

Mihály and Erzsi* strove to find the proper middle way between snobbery and anti-snobbery. They didn't exhaust themselves attempting to accomplish everything Baedeker demanded, but even less did they seek to belong to those who return home and boast: "The museums... well, of course we didn't visit any museums!" – and then look smugly at each other.

One night they went to the theatre; and when they returned to the hotel lobby afterwards, Mihály felt that he'd very gladly have something more to drink. He didn't know what, exactly – perhaps what he most longed for was some sweet wine; and the unusual, classical flavour of Samos wine came to mind, and how he'd often spent time tasting it in a small wine shop in Paris, at number 7, Rue des Petits-Champs; and then it occurred to him that Venice is more or less Greece anyway, and assuredly one could obtain Samos wine, or maybe Mavrodaphne, because he was not yet au fait with Italian wines. He asked Erzsi to go up to their room alone; he'd come along soon, but he just wanted to have a drink – "Really, just one glass," he said with affected seriousness – for Erzsi urged him towards moderation with an identical affectation of gravity, as befitting a young lady.

Leaving behind the Grand Canal, upon whose banks their hotel stood, he arrived in the streets around the Frezzeria,* where many Venetians still promenaded at this time of night, with that unusual, ant-like behaviour typical of this city's residents. People walk only along certain paths here, like ants setting out on journeys across the garden path; the other streets remain empty. Mihály, too, stuck to the ant highways, thinking that surely the bars and *fiaschetterie** would open off the bustling streets and not in the uncertain shadows of the empty ones. And indeed he found many places selling drinks, but somehow, not one of them was what he was seeking. Each had some flaw. The customers would be too elegant in one and too shabby in another, and he couldn't associate the beverage he sought with either one: somehow, the drink he had in mind had a more clandestine taste. Slowly he sensed that this drink would, without doubt, be sold at precisely one place in Venice, and that he must find that spot by instinct alone. That's how he ended up in the back alleys.

Impossibly narrow streets branched into impossibly narrow streets, and wherever they led, every one of these streets became still narrower and darker. If he extended both arms, he could simultaneously touch the opposing rows of buildings, those silent houses with large windows behind which, so he thought, mysteriously intense Italian lives must be slumbering. They were so near that it felt, indeed, like an intrusion to be walking these streets at night.

What was this strange spell and ecstasy that seized him here in the alleyways? Why did he feel like someone who had come home at last? Maybe a child might have dreamt of such things – the child, Mihály, who lived in a detached garden villa but was afraid of open spaces. Perhaps this adolescent wanted to live in such narrow confines that every half a square metre has separate significance, ten paces already mean a border violation, decades pass next to a rickety table and human lifespans in an armchair; but we can't be certain about this.

He meandered along the alleys this way until he realized that dawn was already breaking and he was on the far side of Venice, on the Fondamente Nove, from which one could see the cemetery island* and, beyond it, the mysterious islands – among them San Francesco del Deserto, which at one time had been a leper colony – and the houses of Murano in the far distance.* Here lived the poor of Venice, at the fringe of the tourist trade where its benefits trickled down only in lesser measure; the hospital was here, and the funerary gondolas set out from here. At this hour, some residents were waking up and heading to work; and the world was as immeasurably barren as the feeling one has after a sleepless night. He found a gondolier who took him home.

Erzsi had already been worried sick and dead tired for a long time. Only at half-past one did it occur to her that, all appearances to the contrary, one undoubtedly must be able to telephone the police even in Venice. And so she did, with the help of the night porter – and naturally, without result.

Mihály was still behaving like a sleepwalker. He was dreadfully fatigued and unable to produce intelligible answers to Erzsi's questions.

"The back alleys," he said, "I had to see the back alleys at night, just once – the way, I might add, that others also used to do."

"But why didn't you either tell me or take me with you?"

Mihály had no reply to offer, but crept into bed with an offended expression and fell asleep, feeling most bitter.

"So this is marriage," he thought. "Can she really misunderstand so badly – is every attempt at explanation really so hopeless? I admit I don't understand it, myself."

2

But Erzsi didn't fall asleep: she lay with furrowed brow and arms crossed under her head for a long time, thinking. Women can generally sustain wakeful vigils and thinking better than men. Erzsi found it neither novel nor surprising that Mihály should do and say things that she didn't understand. She concealed this incomprehension successfully, for a while; wisely, she refrained from making enquiries and behaved as though from time immemorial she'd had no doubts at all about everything to do with Mihály. She knew that this silent show of superiority, which Mihály regarded as a woman's innate, instinctive wisdom, was the most powerful means to keep hold of him. Mihály was full of fears, and Erzsi's role was to reassure him.

Yet there's a limit to everything; and besides, they were a married couple now, on a proper honeymoon, and to be out all night on such an occasion is unusual, no matter how you look at it. For an instant, the natural female suspicion arose that perhaps Mihály had been entertaining himself in another woman's company, but she rejected it instantly as an utter impossibility. Even aside from the absolute impropriety of such behaviour, she well knew how shy and cautious Mihály was with every unfamiliar woman, how much he feared diseases, how much he hated to spend money and, in any case, how little women interested him.

But in actual fact it would have been most reassuring to know that Mihály had merely been with a woman. This uncertainty, this completely blank darkness, the utter impossibility of imagining where and how Mihály had spent the night, would cease. And Zoltán Pataki came to mind: her first husband, whom she'd left for Mihály. Erzsi always knew which girl from the office's pool of typists was his lover of the moment, even though Zoltán was compulsively, blushingly, touchingly discreet – and the more he tried to keep something secret, the more Erzsi could see right through it. Mihály was just the opposite: he strove to explain his every action with painstaking conscientiousness; he sought maniacally to enable Erzsi to know him completely; and the more he explained, the more muddled things became. Erzsi had long realized that she didn't understand Mihály, because Mihály had secrets that he kept even from himself – and Mihály didn't understand her because it never even occurred to him to take an interest in the interior life of anyone besides himself. And nevertheless, they got married, because Mihály decided that they understood each other perfectly, so that their marriage would stand upon entirely rational foundations and not on transient passions. "How much longer," she wondered, "can this fiction be sustained?"

3

One evening a few days later, they arrived in Ravenna. The next morning, Mihály rose very early, got dressed and went out. He wanted to see the famed Byzantine mosaics, Ravenna's main attractions, alone, because by this point he knew that there were many things he couldn't share with Erzsi, and this was one of them. Erzsi was much more educated and sensitive than he was as far as history of art was concerned; she had even been to Italy before, so Mihály generally let her decide what they would see – and what they would think, having seen it. Paintings interested him only rarely, randomly, like a flash of lightning: one in a thousand. But the mosaics of Ravenna… these were the monuments of his own past.

One time on a Christmas Eve, they were looking at these mosaics together: Mihály, Ervin, Tamás Ulpius and Éva, Tamás's younger sister. They gazed at these images, in a big French tome at the Ulpius home, with nervous and inexplicable fear. Father Ulpius was alone in the enormous adjoining room, pacing up and down. They stared at the pictures, propping their elbows on the table, and the gold background of the images glimmered at them like some light from an unknown source at the deep end of a mineshaft. There was something in the Byzantine images that stirred up the dread sleeping in the very bottom depths of their souls. At a quarter to twelve, they put on their greatcoats and, with benumbed hearts, headed off to midnight Mass. That was when Éva fainted; that was the only occasion when Éva's nerves gave her any trouble. After that, everything was Ravenna for a month, and even up until this day, Ravenna remained an archetype of indefinable fear for Mihály.

All of this – that entire, now deeply submerged month – now emerged within him as he stood there in the basilica of San Vitale, in front of the fabulous mosaic with its light-green tonality. His youth struck him with such intensity that he reeled and had to lean against one of the columns. But it only lasted an instant, and then he became a serious man once again.

The other mosaics didn't even interest him any more. He returned to the hotel, waited for Erzsi to get ready, and then they went to see and discuss every sight together, dispassionately. Of course, Mihály didn't tell her that he'd already been to San Vitale that morning. He sidled into the church a bit sheepishly, as though something might betray him, and he declared that the place wasn't even all that interesting, in order to compensate for his morning shock.

The following evening they were sitting on the small piazza, outside one of the cafés; Erzsi was eating a gelato; Mihály sampled some bitter drink he didn't recognize but disliked, and he was racking his brains trying to decide what might wash the bitter taste away.

"This smell is awful," said Erzsi. "You can smell this odour wherever you go in this town. This is what a gas attack must be like."

"It's no wonder," said Mihály. "This town stinks of corpses. Ravenna is a decadent city, decaying steadily for more than a thousand years. Even the Baedeker says so. It had three golden ages, the last one in the eighth century after Christ."

"Really, you silly boy," said Erzsi, smiling. "You're always thinking about corpses and their smell. Whereas this stink arises precisely from life and plenty: it's the chemical-fertilizer plant that causes this odour, the factory that provides all Ravenna its livelihood."

"Ravenna lives on chemical fertilizer? This town, where the tombs of Theodoric the Great and Dante stand, this city, compared to which Venice is a parvenu?"

"Absolutely, my boy."

"Revolting."

At this moment a thunderous motorcycle rumbled into the piazza, and the begoggled and extraordinarily bikerishly clad man sitting on it sprang off it as though leaping off a steed's back. He looked around, saw Mihály and his bride, and headed straight in their direction, leading the motorbike beside him like a horse. Reaching their table, raising his goggles like a helmet's visor, he said: "Hello, Mihály. You're the man I'm looking for."

To his utmost surprise, Mihály recognized János* Szepetneki. Caught off guard, he could think of nothing to say, but: "How did you know I was here?"

"At the hotel in Venice they said that you'd come to Ravenna. And where else can one be after dinner in Ravenna than on the piazza? It wasn't hard at all. I came straight here from Venice. But now I'll sit down for a bit."

"A-a-ah, I say… let me introduce you to my wife," said Mihály nervously. "Erzsi, this gentleman is János Szepetneki, my former classmate, about whom… I think, I've never yet spoken to you." And he blushed violently.

János looked Erzsi up and down with undisguised distaste, bowed, shook her hand and, from that point on, took no notice of the woman's presence. He spoke not a word except to order some lemonade.

After a very long time, Mihály finally spoke up. "So, tell us. You must have some reason to find me here in Italy."

"I'll tell you later. Mainly, I wanted to see you because I heard that you'd got married."

"I thought you were still angry with me," said Mihály. "The last time in London, when we met at the Hungarian embassy, you left the room." Seeing that János wasn't going to respond, he continued: "But of course, now you no longer have reason to be angry. One becomes serious. Everyone becomes serious and slowly forgets why they'd been angry at someone for decades."

"You talk as if you knew why I was mad at you."

"Well, of course I know," said Mihály, and blushed again.

"If you know, then say it," said Szepetneki pugnaciously.

"I don't want to, here… in front of my wife."

"She doesn't bother me. Just be brave and tell me. What do you think is the reason I wouldn't speak to you in London?"

"Because it occurred to me that at some point I thought you had stolen my gold watch. Since then, I've learnt who stole it."

"See what an ass you are. *I* stole your gold watch."

"What, you stole it, after all?"

"Of course it was me."

Erzsi had already been fidgeting uneasily in her seat because, thanks to her knowledge of human character, she had long since read János Szepetneki's face and hands and deduced that he was indeed the sort of person who would occasionally steal a gold watch. She anxiously held her reticule – which contained their passports and traveller's cheques – tight to her body. The fact that Mihály, otherwise so tactful, would bring up this watch business astonished and aggrieved her, but the silence that now set in – the sort of silence that occurs when one man tells the other that he'd stolen his gold watch, and then both remain without speaking – was unbearable. She stood up and said:

"I'm going back to the hotel. The gentlemen have certain matters to discuss, that…"

Mihály glared at her in exasperation.

"Just stay right here. You're my wife now, so now everything concerns you too." And with that, he turned on János Szepetneki and shouted at him: "Well, then, why did you refuse to shake my hand in London?"

"You know perfectly well why. If you didn't, you wouldn't be so furious now. But you know I was right."

"Please be so kind as to talk some sense!"

"You understand how *not* to understand people just as well as you understood how not to find those who'd disappeared from around you, and whom you didn't even bother to look for. That's why I was angry with you."

Mihály was silent for a while.

"Well, if you wanted to meet me... seeing that we met in London..."

"Yes, but only by accident. That doesn't count. Besides which, you know very well that it's not about me."

"If it's about the others... I would have looked for them in vain."

"And that's why you didn't even try, right? Yet, maybe, all you would have needed to do is extend your hand. But now you have one more chance. Listen here. Say, I think I've found Ervin."

Mihály's expression changed instantly. Anger and consternation gave way to joyful curiosity.

"You're joking! Where is he?"

"I don't know yet, exactly, but he's in Italy, in one of the cloisters in Umbria or Tuscany. I saw him in Rome: he was in a procession with a lot of monks. I couldn't go up to him: I couldn't disturb the ceremony. But there was a priest I knew there, from whom I learnt that these monks are from an Umbrian or Tuscan monastery. This is what I wanted to tell you. Now that you're here in Italy, you could help me look for him."

"Yes. Thank you. But I don't know if I should help. I don't even know how to. And besides, I'm on my honeymoon now: I can't traipse through every cloister in Umbria and Tuscany. And I don't even know if Ervin has any interest in meeting me. If he'd wanted to see me, he could have informed me of his whereabouts a long time ago. And now go away, János Szepetneki. I hope not to see you for another few years."

"I'm going, all right. Your wife is a most disagreeable woman."

"I didn't ask for your opinion."

János Szepetneki mounted his bike. "Pay for my lemonade," he shouted over his shoulder, and he vanished into the darkness that had fallen in the meantime.

The couple remained where they were and said nothing for a long time. Erzsi was annoyed, and at the same time she found the situation comical. "So this is what happens when classmates meet… It seems that these matters from his student years touch Mihály deeply. Some day I should ask him who this Ervin and this Tamás are… even though they're so unpleasant." In general, Erzsi disliked the young, and anything that was half-baked.

But in fact, it was something entirely different that irritated her. Naturally, it bothered her that János Szepetneki had found her so displeasing. Not that the opinion of someone like him was of the slightest importance… such a dubious creature. Yet there's no more fateful thing in the world for a woman than the opinion of her husband's friends. Men are unbelievably suggestible when women are the topic. True, this Szepetneki was no friend of Mihály's. Or rather, he was not his friend in the word's conventional meaning, but they nevertheless seemed to share some very strong connection. And in any case, even the most scurrilous man can influence another in such things. "The devil take it, why didn't he find me pleasing?"

Fundamentally, Erzsi was totally unaccustomed to this. She was a wealthy, attractive, well-dressed, good-looking woman; men found her alluring – or at the very least, appealing. Erzsi knew that the fact that every man spoke appreciatively about her played a major role in Mihály's devotion. Often, she had gone so far as to suspect that Mihály didn't even look at her with his own eyes, but with the eyes of the others. As if he were saying to himself: "How much I'd love this Erzsi, if I were like other men." And now this cad showed up and didn't find her attractive. She couldn't resist bringing it up.

"Tell me, please: why didn't your friend the pickpocket care for me?"

Mihály's face broke into a smile.

"Oh please! It's not you that he didn't like. What he doesn't like is the fact that you're my wife."

"Why?"

"Because he thinks you're the reason I've betrayed my youth, our shared youth. That I've forgotten about those, who... And that I've constructed my life on the basis of other connections. Yet, well... And now you'll probably also say what fine little friends I have. I could reply to this by saying that Szepetneki is no friend of mine, which of course is merely evading the issue. But... how should I put it... people like this exist too... Stealing the watch was merely a childish exercise, a warm-up. Since that time, Szepetneki has become a highly successful con man; at a certain point he even had tons of money, and at that time he forcibly thrust various amounts on me that I couldn't repay because I had no idea where he was spending his time; and he's done time in prison already, writing to me from Baja to send him five pengős.* And he pops up from time to time, and he always has something terribly unpleasant to say. But I tell you, there are people like this too. In case you didn't know before, now at least you've seen it for yourself. Tell me, please, it is possible for us to get a bottle of wine somewhere around here that we could drink back in our room? I've grown bored with this public spectacle we're performing here on the piazza."

"You can get some in our hotel, since it has a restaurant too."

"And won't they object if we drink it in our room? Is that allowed?"

"Mihály, you'll drive me to the grave with your fear of waiters and hoteliers."

"I've already explained. I told you that they're the most grown-up people in the world, and that I particularly don't want to break the rules when abroad."

"Fine. But why this need to drink again?"

"I simply must have something to drink. Because I want to tell you who Tamás Ulpius was, and how he died."

4

"I HAVE TO TELL YOU THESE THINGS that happened long ago, because they're so important. Important things generally happened very long ago. And until you know them, forgive me, but you'll always remain – to a certain extent – just a newcomer in my life.

"Walking was my main pastime in my high-school days. Or rather, perhaps, rambling. This word is closer to the mark, since we're talking about an adolescent. I explored every district of Budapest one by one, systematically. Every district – indeed, every stretch of every street – had its own particular emotional value to me. For that matter, I can entertain myself with buildings just as much today as back then. I haven't changed with age in this respect. Buildings say a great deal to me. For me, they're the equivalent of what nature – or what they called nature – meant to poets in the past.

"But I loved the Buda* Castle district best of all. I never got tired of its ancient streets. Even back then, old things appealed to me more than new ones. The only things that attained deeper reality in my eyes were those into which many, many human lifetimes had seeped: things that the past had made to last, like Stonemason Kelemen's wife did for the high fortress of Déva.*

"Did you notice how eloquently I just expressed myself? Maybe it's the effect of this fine Sangiovese wine.

"I'd often see Tamás Ulpius up in the Castle district, because that's where he lived. This already struck me as very romantic, by itself, but I also liked the blond, archducal melancholy of his face, and many other things as well. He was formally courteous, wore dark suits and held aloof from his classmates. From me too.

"And now, once again, I have to talk about myself. You got to know me as a muscular, broad-shouldered, older young man with a calm, smooth face: the sort of face they call a poker face in Pest; and you know me as someone who's always more or less sleepy. Well, believe you me, I was entirely different in my high-school days. I've shown you a portrait photo from those days: you might have noticed how thin, hungry, restless and ecstatically radiant my face was. I suppose that I was very ugly – but nevertheless, I prefer my face as it was back then. And imagine it connected to a corresponding adolescent body: that of a thin, angular boy stooped from his growth spurts. And a correspondingly spindly, hungry character.

"Thus, you can imagine that I was healthy neither in body nor in spirit. I was anaemic and tormented by horrific depressions. Following a bout of pneumonia when I was sixteen, I began to experience hallucinations. When I was reading, I would often feel as though someone were standing behind my back, peering over my shoulder. I'd have to turn around to convince myself that no one was there. Or at night, I'd start awake in terror that someone was standing by my bedside, looking at me. Of course, there was nobody there. And I was constantly ashamed of myself. My position in the family slowly became unbearable because of my constant humiliation. I'd continually blush scarlet during dinner, and for a while even the slightest cause was enough to bring me to the very precipice of tears. At such times I'd dash out of the room. You know what normal people my parents are; you can imagine how astounded they were and how outraged, and how much my older brother and Edit made fun of me. Things finally got to the point that I was forced to lie, pretending I had a supplementary hour of French at school at half-past two, and this way I was able to dine by myself, earlier than the others.

"Later, I was gradually able to arrange for them to set supper aside for me.

"And then to top all this came the most awful symptom: the whirlpool. The whirlpool, exactly as I've put it. From time to time, I'd feel as if the earth were opening up next to me and I was standing at the edge of a terrifying whirlpool. You really shouldn't take the whirlpool literally after all: I never actually saw this whirlpool; I didn't have a vision; I just knew that the whirlpool was right there. What I mean is that I also knew that it wasn't there, I was just imagining it, since you know how complicated these things are. But the fact remains that when this whirlpool sensation took hold of me, I didn't dare budge, I couldn't even say a word, and I thought that everything was coming to an end.

"Having said that, this feeling didn't last long, and I didn't have many such attacks. The most uncomfortable occasion took place during natural-history class. The earth had just opened up next to me when they called on me to answer a question. I couldn't even move, but continued sitting in my seat. The teacher kept calling on me for a while, but when he saw that I wouldn't move, he got up and came over to me. 'What's your problem?' he asked. Of course I didn't reply. At that, he looked at me for a bit, then returned to the dais and called on someone else. He was such a sensitive priestly soul that afterwards he never said so much as a word about the incident. My classmates talked about it all the more. They thought I hadn't risen to answer out of rebellious defiance, and that the teacher had taken fright. At a stroke I became renowned as a fine fellow and enjoyed unimagined popularity throughout the school. A week later, the natural-history teacher called on János Szepetneki. The same János Szepetneki you saw today. Szepetneki adopted his most swashbuckling expression and remained seated. Whereupon the teacher rose, went over to Szepetneki and gave his face a resounding slap. From that moment on, Szepetneki was convinced that I had tremendously influential connections.

"But let's talk about Tamás Ulpius. One day came the first snowfall. I could hardly wait for school to be over, and I wolfed the luncheon set aside for me, then raced up into the Castle. Snow was an unusually strong passion of mine, and the fact that city quarters are utterly transformed in the snow – so much so that you can get lost even in familiar streets. I meandered a long time and then went out to the Bastion Promenade to gaze out towards the Buda hills. Suddenly the earth opened up beside me again. This time the whirlpool was even more plausible, since I was standing on a promontory. Given that I'd encountered the whirlpool several times before, I wasn't so terrified; indeed, I waited with a certain composed nonchalance for the earth to seal itself and the whirlpool to disappear. I waited this way for a while – I couldn't tell you how long, because at such times you lose a sense of time, just like whilst sleeping or making love. But what's certain is that this time the whirlpool lasted much longer than previously. And then I noticed, in terror, that the whirlpool was slowly expanding, that by now only ten centimetres separated me from its edge, and that the whirlpool was slowly, slowly nearing my feet. Another few minutes, and it'd be the end of me: I'd plummet. Desperately, I hung onto the railing.

"And then the whirlpool indeed reached me. The ground slipped out from under my feet and there I hung over the void, clinging to the iron railing with my hands. If my hands get tired, I thought, I'll fall in. And quietly, with resignation, I began to pray, preparing to die.

"Then I became aware that Tamás Ulpius was standing next to me.

"'What's your problem?' he asked, and put his hand on my shoulder.

"At that instant, the whirlpool vanished and I would have collapsed from exhaustion, had Tamás not grasped me. He helped me to a bench and waited for me to recover. When I was feeling better, I briefly told him about the whirlpool thing – the first time in my life I had told anyone. I can't even tell you how it happened: within moments, he'd become my best friend. The friend about whom adolescent boys dream no less intensely, but more deeply and seriously, than they do about their first love.

"And then we'd get together every day. Tamás didn't want to visit me, because he said he didn't like to introduce himself; on the other hand, it didn't take long before he invited me to his place. This is how I found myself in the Ulpius house.

"The Ulpius family lived on the heights, in a very old and dilapidated house. But the house was old and decrepit only from the outside: on the inside, it was lovely and homey, like these old Italian hotels. Mind you, it was also eerie in many respects, with its huge rooms and objets d'art – it was like a museum. For Tamás Ulpius's father was an archaeologist and museum director. His grandfather had, for his part, been a watchmaker at some point, and his shop had been there in the house, some time ago. By the time I met him, he just played around at his own whim with very old clocks and all sorts of unusual clockwork toys that he invented himself.

"Tamás's mother was no longer alive. Tamás and his younger sister Éva loathed their father, accusing him of having driven their mother to her death at a young age with his cold dourness. This was my first astonishing experience in the Ulpius house, right on my first visit. Speaking of her father, Éva said that his eyes were like shoe buttons – about which she was completely correct, by the way – and Tamás said, in the most natural tone in the world: 'For you know, my father is an extraordinarily revolting brute' – about which he too was correct. I, as you well know, grew up in a tight-knit family circle; I loved my parents and siblings dearly, I always adored my father and I couldn't even imagine parents and children not loving each other, or children condemning their parents' behaviour just as they would the behaviour of strangers. This was the first great primordial rebellion I'd ever encountered in my life. And oddly, I found this rebellion infinitely sympathetic, even though I hadn't the slightest inclination to rebel against my own father.

"Tamás Ulpius couldn't stand his father, but he loved his grandfather and sister all the more. He loved his sister so much that it seemed like a rebellion in itself. I too loved my siblings, I didn't quarrel with them very much and I took family solidarity seriously – to the extent that my withdrawn and distracted nature allowed. But our family custom held it to be improper for siblings to display their affection for each other: we considered any tenderness between us to be risible, indeed, even shameful. I think that's how it is in most families. We didn't buy presents for each other at Christmas; if one of us departed home or returned, he didn't greet the others, and if we went away on travel, we only wrote polite letters to our parents, signing off with 'I greet Péter, Laci, Edit and Tivadar'.* It was entirely different at the Ulpius family. The two siblings spoke to each other with exquisite courtesy, and in farewell they'd kiss each other with moving intensity, even if they were leaving for only an hour. As I realized later, they were extraordinarily jealous of each other, and this was the main reason they didn't befriend anyone.

"They were together, day and night. At night too, I say, because they shared a room. This was what struck me as the most unusual thing. At home, they separated Edit from us boys when she turned twelve, and afterwards, a separate female residence evolved around her: girlfriends would visit her, and indeed, male friends too, whom we didn't even know, and they pursued pastimes of which we disapproved deeply. The fact that Éva and Tamás lived together occupied my adolescent fantasies to a fair extent. I imagined that this situation somehow blurred the sexual difference between them, and they both acquired a slightly androgynous aspect in my eyes. In general, I spoke to Tamás in a tactful, refined manner, as is customary with girls, but on the other hand, with respect to Éva, I never felt the bored unease I experienced on encountering Edit's girlfriends, those beings officially declared as girls.

"I found it hard to get used to the grandfather, who would shuffle into the siblings' room at the most unlikely times – often in the middle of the night – and in the most unlikely clothes: robes and hats. The siblings always bestowed ceremonious ovations on him. At first I was bored by the old fellow's stories and I didn't even understand them clearly, because the old man spoke German, and moreover with a slight Rhine valley accent, since he had immigrated to Hungary from Cologne. But later I grew to understand both the meaning and the savour of his tales. The old man was a living encyclopaedia of old Pest. For me, the household friend, it was the grand prize. He could relate the history of every Castle District house and its owners. In this way, the Castle's houses, which until then I had known only by sight, slowly became intimate personal acquaintances.

"But I too loathed their father. I can't recall even a single time when we might have spoken to each other. Whenever he'd see me, he'd just growl something and turn away. The two Ulpius children suffered horribly when they had to dine with their father. They ate in a large hall, and not one of them would utter a single word during supper. Then the two siblings would sit down and their father would pace up and down the large room, lit by a single floor lamp. As their father reached the far end of the chamber, his figure would disappear in the murk. If they spoke to each other, their father would approach: 'What are you talking about?' he'd ask aggressively. But luckily, he was rarely at home. He'd drink himself under the table, alone, in pubs, with brandy, the way bad people do.

"Tamás was just working on a paper on the history of religion when we got to know each other. The study discussed his own childhood games. But he analysed the theme using the methods of comparative religion. It was a highly unusual study, in part a parody of religious history, and in part a deadly serious self-analysis.

"Tamás was just as maniacally obsessed with old things as I. And it was no wonder in his case: not only was it his paternal inheritance, but also, their house was like a museum. Antiquity represented the natural condition to Tamás, and it was modernity that was odd and alien. He constantly longed for Italy, where everything was ancient and suited to him. And behold, here I sit now, and he never made it here... My attraction to old things is mostly mere passive enjoyment and intellectual longing for knowledge; for Tamás the attraction was an active fantasy pursuit.

"He'd constantly re-enact history.

"What you have to visualize is that the two siblings' life in the Ulpius house was constant theatre, constant *commedia dell'arte*. The least thing was enough to start them off, for Tamás and Éva to enact something, or just to play, as they put it. Grandfather would talk about a countess in the Castle District who was in love with her coachman, and right away Éva became the countess and Tamás the coachman; or he'd tell how Lord Chief Justice Majláth* was killed by his Romanian lackeys, and Éva became the Lord Chief Justice and Tamás the Romanian lackeys; or they'd simply develop much longer, more complicated serialized historical tragedies. Naturally, the plays only followed historical events in their broad contours, the way *commedia dell'arte* does: they suggested the historical dress with one or two pieces of clothing, mainly from their grandfather's inexhaustible and astonishing clothes collection, followed by a not too long but extraordinarily baroque, convoluted dialogue and finally, the murder or suicide. Because as I now think back on it, these improvised dramas always led to denouements in death by violence. Tamás and Éva strangled, poisoned, stabbed or boiled each other in oil on a daily basis.

"They could not imagine their future in any other way than connected with the theatre, insofar as they thought about their future at all. Tamás was preparing to become a playwright, and Éva a great actress. But the word 'preparation' isn't entirely correct, because Tamás never wrote a play, and not even in her dreams did it occur to Éva that she ought to attend a drama school. Instead, they attended the theatre all the more passionately. Only the National, however: Tamás found light theatre as revolting as modern architecture; he preferred classical drama, which has plenty of murder and suicide.

"In order to attend the theatre, however, they needed money, but their father, I believe, gave them absolutely no pocket money. The old cook, the Ulpius's slovenly provincial ward, represented some small income: she'd set aside a few pennies from the household expenses on behalf of the youths. And the grandfather, who came up with a few crowns here and there from mysterious sources; I think he might have made a little money as a black-market watch dealer. But all this was naturally insufficient to satisfy the Ulpius children's theatrical passion.

"It was Éva who had to take care of the money. It was forbidden to utter this word – money – in Tamás's presence. And Éva indeed took care of it; she was extraordinarily resourceful in matters of making money. She could sell every saleable item of theirs, and at a good price; from time to time, she'd sell one of the house's museum-piece valuables too, but this was highly risky because of their father, and Tamás also took it ill if some familiar antique went missing. Sometimes Éva took out entirely surprising loans, from the green grocer, from the sweet shop, from the chemist – indeed, even from the electricity company's cashier too. And if all this wasn't enough, then she'd steal. She stole from the cook; she stole with death-defying courage from her father, taking advantage of his inebriation. This was still their most reliable and, from a certain point of view, most honourable source of income. But on one occasion she succeeded in lifting ten crowns out of a sweet shop's till, which made her very proud. And undoubtedly there were also instances that she never admitted to. And she stole from me too. When I noticed it later and objected bitterly, then, instead of stealing, she levied a proper tax on me: I had to contribute a certain sum to the family fund, on a weekly basis. Of course, Tamás was not allowed to know about this."

Here Erzsi interrupted: "*Moral insanity.*"*

"Yes, it is," continued Mihály. "Such technical terms are extraordinarily reassuring. And to a certain extent, they also provide exoneration. She's not a thief, but mentally ill. But Éva was neither mentally ill nor a thief. She merely lacked any moral sense in matters related to money. The two Ulpius siblings stood so far apart from the world, from the world's economic and social order, that they had no idea which ways to make money were allowed and which ones were forbidden. Money didn't exist as far as they were concerned. All they knew was that they were able to attend the theatre at the expense of certain pieces of paper – not even very pretty ones – and silver discs. The great abstract mythology of money, the foundation of modern man's religious and moral sense, and the rites of sacrifice to the money god – 'honest labour', thrift, turning things to account and such matters – were unknown concepts to them. Such things are inborn, but not in them; or you learn about them at home, as I did, but in their home, at most their grandfather taught them about the histories of the Castle District's houses.

"You can't even imagine how unrealistic they were, and how much they recoiled from any practical reality. They never held a newspaper in their hands; they had no idea at all of what was happening in the world. For this all took place during the World War; but that didn't interest them. One day at school, when he had to answer a teacher's question, we found out that Tamás had never heard of István Tisza.* When Przemysl fell,* Tamás thought that they were referring to some Russian general, and politely expressed his pleasure; they almost beat him to a pulp. Later, the more intelligent boys were already debating the merits of Ady and Babits;* Tamás had the theory that everyone was talking about generals, and for a long time thereafter he thought Ady was a general. The more intelligent boys considered Tamás stupid, just as his teachers did. His unusual genius, his historical knowledge, remained entirely unknown at school: something that he, in any event, didn't regret one bit.

"They stood outside the accustomed order of life in every other respect as well. Perhaps it would occur to Éva at two in the morning that she had inadvertently left her French notebook on Sváb Hill the week before; then both would get up, get dressed, go up Sváb Hill and wander about up there until dawn. The next day Tamás would miss school with regal indifference: Éva would fabricate a sicknote for him, complete with the elder Ulpius's signature. Éva didn't go to school at all, and she had no occupation of any kind, but even when alone, she entertained herself as well as a cat.

"You could pop in at any time at all; you never disturbed them. They'd carry on their own lives as if you weren't even there. They'd gladly see you even at night, but in my high-school days I couldn't visit them late at night because of the rules at our house, except perhaps for a short stay after the theatre – and I constantly fantasized about how wonderful it would be to sleep over at their place. After graduation, I often stayed there overnight.

"Later, I read in a famous English essay that the fundamental characteristic of the Celts was their revolt against the tyranny of facts.* Well, from this standpoint, the two Ulpius siblings were Celtic. I note in passing that both Tamás and I were mad for the Celts, the Grail legend and Perceval. Probably this is why I felt so good in their company: because they were such Celts. I discovered my own nature in their company. I came to realize why I'd always felt myself to be a shameful alien in my family home. Because there facts ruled. I was at home at the Ulpiuses. I went there every day, and I spent all my free time at their place.

"When I entered the atmosphere of the Ulpius house, my constant feelings of shame disappeared, and so did my nervous symptoms. I encountered the whirlpool for the last time when Tamás Ulpius pulled me out of it. Nobody peered over my shoulder any longer, and nobody stared at me in the dark of night. I slept soundly, and life provided me what I expected of it. I pulled myself together physically as well; my face smoothed out. This was the happiest period of my life, and if some scent or play of light awakens its memory in me, even now that excited and dizzying happiness courses through me: the only happiness I ever knew.

"Of course, this happiness didn't come without a price either. In order to be in the Ulpius house, I also had to tear myself away from the world of facts. Either-or: I couldn't conduct a life in both camps at once. I too abandoned reading the newspapers, and I broke off relations with my intelligent friends. Gradually they grew to consider me just as stupid as Tamás; this hurt a great deal, since I was vain and knew I was smart – but there was no helping it. I broke off from the family at home entirely; I spoke to my parents and siblings with the measured courtesy that I'd learnt from Tamás, and I haven't been able to repair the rupture that then developed between us ever since, no matter how much I've tried, and I've had a guilty conscience regarding my family ever since. After all this, I tried to correct this emotional distance with acquiescence, but that's another story entirely...

"Taking notice of my transformation, the people at home were dumbfounded. They convened an anxious family council at my uncle's, and they decided that what I needed was a woman. And indeed, my uncle, greatly flustered, informed me of this, using numerous metaphorical expressions. I listened to him with interest, but displayed no inclination to go along whatsoever; all the less so, because by that time Tamás, Ervin, János Szepetneki and I had sworn not to touch women, so that we could become the new knights of the Grail. So 'the woman' gradually went by the wayside, and my parents took cognizance of the fact that I am the way I am. I believe that, even to this day, my mother carefully warns new household staff and new acquaintances to be careful, because I'm not your ordinary man. But, well... how many years have already passed since not even a microscope could reveal anything within me that isn't ordinary.

"I couldn't even tell you what was at the heart of this transformation that my parents observed with such consternation. It's true that the two Ulpiuses demanded that one accommodate them in every respect, and I accommodated them willingly – happily, in fact. I dropped the habit of being a good student. I revised my opinions and found a bunch of things revolting that had pleased me until then: soldiering and battlefield glory, my classmates, Hungarian cuisine: everything that would have been described as 'ripping' or 'jolly good' in school. I abandoned football, which I'd pursued passionately until then; fencing was the only permitted sport, and all three of us practiced it all the more assiduously. I read a tremendous amount to keep up with Tamás, but this was no sacrifice. My interest in the history of religion dates from this time – an interest I later abandoned, like so many other things, when I became serious.

"Yet despite all that, my conscience was guilty with respect to the Ulpiuses. I felt as if I were hoodwinking them: for what was natural freedom to them was difficult, obstinate rebellion for me. I'm a bourgeois, too bourgeois in fact, and I was raised to be excessively so at home – but of course you know that. I had to take a deep breath and make a serious commitment to flick my cigarette ash on the ground; the two Ulpiuses couldn't even imagine doing otherwise. When, on occasion, I'd heroically commit to skipping classes with Tamás, I'd suffer stomach cramps all day. My nature is such that I wake up early in the morning and am sleepy at night; I'm at my hungriest at noon and supper time; I like to eat off plates and I don't like to begin with the pasta course; I like order, and I'm unutterably terrified of policemen. I had to hide these characteristics, my entire order-loving and conscientious bourgeois being, from the Ulpiuses. Of course they knew all about it – and they even had their opinion about it – but they were polite and never brought it up: when I'd burst out in a fit of normality or thriftiness now and then, they'd simply look away magnanimously.

"The hardest thing was that I had to participate in their plays. I absolutely lack even the slightest hint of theatrical inclination: I'm incurably bashful, and at the outset I almost died when they set grandfather's red vest on me so I could be Pope Alexander VI in a serial drama about the Borgias. Later I learnt this art too; but I could never improvise baroque speech as beautifully as they. On the other hand, I turned out to be a splendid victim. I was the best at being poisoned and boiled in oil. Often I was merely the masses who fell victim to Ivan the Terrible's atrocities, and I'd have to rattle and die twenty-five times in a row, differently each time. I enjoyed particular success with my death-rattle technique.

"And I also have to tell you, although it's hard for me to talk about it even after so much wine, but my wife must know this too: I dearly loved being the victim. I'd already be thinking about it in the morning, and I'd wait for it all day, yes…"

"Why did you love being the victim?" asked Erzsi.

"Hmm… well, for erotic reasons, if you understand what I mean… yes. Later, I myself would invent the stories in which I could be the victim according to my taste. For instance, stories like this (by that point, the movies had already begun to direct my imagination): that Éva, let's say, is an Apache girl – this was big in the movies at the time – and she lures me to an Apache encampment and makes me drink myself into a stupor; then they rob and kill me. Or the same thing, in more historical setting: to act out the story of Judith and Holofernes* – I adored that one. Or I'm a Russian general, Éva is a spy, she lulls me to sleep and then steals the battle plans. Tamás is, perhaps, a very clever adjutant who pursues Éva and recovers the secret document, but often Éva would render him harmless too, and the Russians would suffer a terrible defeat. This sort of thing would develop on the spot, in the middle of the play. Interesting that these plays also pleased Tamás greatly, and Éva too. But it's just that I was always ashamed of them, and I'm very ashamed today too, as I speak about it; but they: never. Éva enjoyed being the woman who seduces, betrays and kills the men; Tamás and I enjoyed being the men who are seduced, betrayed, killed or degraded…"

Mihály fell silent and drank. After a while, Erzsi asked him: "Tell me, were you in love with Éva Ulpius?"

"No, I wouldn't think so. If you want me to have been in love with someone at all cost, then it was more likely Tamás. Tamás was my ideal, and Éva rather merely a supplement and an erotic object in these plays. But neither would I willingly say that I was in love with Tamás, because the expression can be misunderstood; you might even think that there was some perverse homoerotic connection between us, while in fact that was out of the question. He was my best friend, in the great adolescent meaning of the word, and what was perverse about the situation, as I said before, was entirely different and of a deeper nature."

"But tell me, Mihály… it's so hard to imagine… you were together constantly for years, and no innocent flirtation developed between you and Éva Ulpius?"

"No, nothing."

"How can that be?"

"How?… Indeed… Apparently we were so intimate that we couldn't flirt, and we couldn't fall in love with each other. Love requires distance in order for the lovers to cross it as they grow close to each other. Growing closer is, of course, mere illusion, because in reality, love increases the distance. Love is polarization – the two lovers are the world's two oppositely charged poles…"

"You're saying very clever things, so late at night. I don't understand the whole situation. Was the girl ugly, perhaps?"

"Ugly? She was the most gorgeous woman I've ever seen in my life. No, that's not quite right either. She was *the* beautiful woman, and ever since she's been the standard to whom I compare all beauty. Every lover I've had since resembles her in some respect: the feet of one, the way another lifts her head, the voice of a third on the telephone."

"Me too?"

"You too... yes."

"How do *I* resemble her?"

Mihály blushed and said nothing.

"Tell me... I'm begging you."

"How should I put it... Stand up, please, and come here next to me."

Erzsi came over and stood next to Mihály's chair. Mihály put his arms around her waist and gazed up at her. Erzsi broke into a smile.

"Right now... that's it," said Mihály. "When you smile at me from above, this way. This was how Éva smiled when I was the victim."

Erzsi extricated herself and sat back down in her chair.

"Interesting," she said moodily. "You must be hiding something. That's not a problem. I don't consider it your duty to tell me everything. I don't have any pangs of conscience, either, that I haven't spoken to you about my adolescence. I don't even consider it important. But tell me... you were in love with that girl. This is merely a matter of semantics. People like me would call it love."

"No. I tell you, I wasn't in love with her. Only the others."

"What others?"

"I was just going to talk about them. For years, the Ulpius home had no other guest apart from me. The situation changed when we entered the eighth form.* That's when Ervin and János Szepetneki joined us. They came to visit Éva, not Tamás as I'd done. The way it came about was that the school, as it did every year, produced a stage play, and since we were the eighth-formers, we took the lead roles in the entire production. It consisted of an occasional piece; it was lovely, but the problem was that it contained a rather extensive female role. For this purpose, the boys brought over their little darlings from the ice rink and dance school, but the teacher who was directing the production, a very wise young priest who thoroughly loathed women, found none of them suitable. I somehow brought the matter to Éva's attention. From that point on, Éva found no peace: she sensed that this was the opportunity to launch her theatrical career. Tamás, of course, didn't even want to hear of such a thing: he found it spine-chillingly beneath his dignity to come into such an intimate, so to speak familial, association with the school. But Éva terrorized me until I mentioned it to the teacher in question, who was most fond of me and entrusted me with bringing Éva to him. And bring her I did. Éva had only to open her mouth, and the teacher instantly said: 'You'll play the part, you and no one else.' Upon which Éva drew herself up, citing her father's severe and anti-thespian world view, and made the teacher beg for half an hour before she finally relented.

"I don't want to talk about the production itself right now, of course; I'll merely mention in passing that Éva had no success whatsoever in the role. After close consultation, the parents, my mother included, found her too forward, not feminine enough, a bit ordinary, somewhat odd in other words, and so forth; or rather, they sensed her rebelliousness and, although there was nothing objectionable in Éva's performance, costume or manner, they sensed an affront to their morals. But neither did she garner success among the boys, despite being so much prettier than their little ice-rink and dance-school darlings. The boys acknowledged that she was beautiful, 'yet, somehow...' they said, and shrugged their shoulders. Their parents' attitude towards the rebel was already present in embryo in these bourgeois boys. Only Ervin and János, who by this point were rebels themselves, recognized the enchanted princess in Éva.

"You met János Szepetneki today. He was always that way. He was the best orator in the class; he stood out particularly as Cyrano in the school's literary society. He carried a revolver, and in his still younger years, he'd shoot dead several burglars a week who were in search of his mother's mysterious documents. He'd already had sensational affairs with women, back when the rest of us had, with great effort, only reached the point of stepping on our dance partners' feet. He went to military training every summer until he attained the rank of lieutenant. He'd tear his new clothes within minutes, because he was always in the process of plummeting off something. His chief ambition was to prove to me that he was my superior. I think this started at the age of thirteen, when we had a teacher interested in phrenology who established, on the basis of the bumps on our heads, that I was talented but János was not. I was never able to hear the end of it; many years after our graduation, he'd still bring it up tearfully. He sought to outdo me in everything: in football, schoolwork and intellectual pursuits. Then, when I gave up on all three, he became confused and didn't know what to do next. And so he fell in love with Éva, because he thought Éva was in love with me. Yes, that was János Szepetneki."

"And who's Ervin?"

"Ervin was a Jewish boy, recently converted to Catholicism, perhaps under the influence of our priest teachers, but I think more likely following his inner path. Earlier, at the age of sixteen, he'd been the most intelligent of all the intellectual and conceited boys: Jewish boys mature earlier. And indeed, Tamás detested him for his intelligence, and whenever the subject was Ervin, he'd become instantly anti-Semitic.

"It was from Ervin that we first heard about Freudianism, socialism and the March Circle;* he was the first among us to be affected by the odd world that would later become the Károlyi revolution.* He wrote beautiful poems in the manner of Endre Ady.

"And then, so to speak, he changed from one day to the next. He distanced himself from his classmates and only maintained contact with me, but I didn't understand his poems – at least, not with the understanding I had at that time – and I also didn't care for the fact that he began to write in long, unrhymed lines. He withdrew, he read, he played the piano, and we didn't know much about him. Afterwards, one day we saw him in the chapel, as he went up to the altar with the other boys to partake of the Eucharist. That's how we knew that he'd converted.

"You ask, why did he convert? Apparently because he was drawn to the beauty of Catholicism, which he found alien. And he was drawn to the implacable severity of its articles of faith and its commandments. I think there was something in him that ached for asceticism the way other people pine for pleasure. In other words, he became a fervent Catholic for all the same reasons that others also used to convert. And then there was something else besides – something I didn't yet see too clearly at the time. Like everyone in the Ulpius house except me, Ervin also had an inclination towards acting. When I think back upon it now, I see that from his early schoolboy days, he was constantly performing some part. He played the intellectual and the revolutionary. He wasn't spontaneous and natural, the way one ought to be, far from it. His every word and gesture was stylized. He used old-fashioned words; he was withdrawn; he was constantly seeking after large roles. But he didn't play-act like the Ulpiuses, who'd forget their parts in an instant and launch into another play: he wanted to play a single role with his entire life, and at last in Catholicism he found the great, worthy and demanding role. Indeed, he no longer changed his attitude thereafter, and the role grew ever inward, ever deeper.

"He was the sort of fervent Catholic that Jews occasionally become: in whom the inheritance of centuries hadn't yet worn off the great shock of Catholicism. He wasn't Catholic like his devout classmates of humble origin who took Communion daily, participated in the congregation and prepared for ecclesiastical careers. To them Catholicism meant acquiescence, but for him it was a rebellion, a confrontation with the entire unbelieving or indifferent world. He had a Catholic opinion about everything: about books, war, our classmates and the buttered rolls we had for our ten-o'clock snack. He was much more intransigent and dogmatic than our most severely pious teachers. 'Whoever puts his hands to the plough, let him not look back'* – this biblical saying was his motto. He eliminated everything that was not purely Catholic from his life. He stood guard over the salvation of his soul with a revolver.

"The only thing that he retained from his previous life was his passion for tobacco. I can't remember ever having seen him without a cigarette.

"And despite this he had his share of a great many temptations. Ervin loved women with extraordinary intensity. His schoolmates saw him as the class lover with the same comical single-mindedness that made János Szepetneki the class liar. The entire class knew about his loves, since he'd spend the whole afternoon strolling on Gellért Hill with the girl of his affections, and he'd write poems for her. The class respected Ervin's loves because it could sense their intensity and poetic quality. But when he became Catholic, naturally, he renounced love as well. That was about the time the other boys began visiting brothels.* Ervin turned away from them in disgust. However, the others – so I believe – went to those women mainly just for the hell of it, or for bragging rights: Ervin was the only one who already knew what physical lust was all about.

"That's when he met Éva. No doubt, it was Éva who set her sights on him, for Ervin was positively beautiful, with his ivory-coloured face, high forehead and glowing eyes. And he radiated singularity, defiance and rebelliousness. And furthermore, he was amiable and refined. I only became aware of the whole thing when Ervin and János showed up at the Ulpius house.

"That first afternoon was ghastly. Tamás was reserved and archducal; he'd just say something completely inappropriate from time to time, *pour épater les bourgeois*.* But Ervin and János weren't astonished, because they weren't bourgeois. János talked the whole afternoon, about his experiences hunting whales and about his great commercial plans to optimize the production and processing of coconuts. Ervin was silent; he smoked and watched Éva; and as for Éva, she was completely different from her usual self. She whined;

she was finicky; she became feminine. I felt worst of all. I felt like a dog who comes to the realization that, from this day forward, he'll lose his monopoly on sitting beneath the table at family mealtimes: he'll have to share with two other dogs. I growled, but I would have preferred to cry.

"Then, I indeed became a less frequent guest; I strove to come at times when Ervin and János weren't there. Furthermore, we were just about to graduate; I had to take it seriously, and in addition I tried to hammer the mandatory minimum information into Tamás as well. And somehow we managed to make it through the final exams. I succeeded in dragging Tamás to them by force, despite the fact that he didn't even want to get up that day. And then, afterwards, the high life resumed in the Ulpius house.

"But by this time everything had taken a turn for the better. The Ulpiuses had the upper hand. They assimilated Ervin and János completely into their company. Ervin yielded in his severity, adopting a sort of very amiable, though affected manner; he'd always speak as if in quotation marks, emphasizing that he didn't fully identify with what he was saying and doing. János became quieter and more sentimental.

"Gradually we also resumed our play, but it became much more intricate, enriched by János's adventurous and Ervin's poetic imaginations. János, naturally, revealed himself to be an outstanding actor. He constantly out-orated and out-wept everybody (because he preferred to play the part of hopeless lovers), so much so that we'd have to pause the performance and wait for him to calm down. Ervin's favourite role was that of the wild beast; he appeared with outstanding effect as the bison defeated by Ursus (that's me), and he proved to be a most talented unicorn. He was able to slice every obstacle – curtains, bedsheets and the like – apart with his tremendous single horn.

"At this time, the boundaries of the Ulpius house gradually expanded. We began to take long walks in the Buda hills; we also went to the baths, and then we also took up drinking. It was János who had that idea; he'd already been regaling us with tales of his tavern exploits for years. Besides him, Éva was the best drinker among us: she too would betray no sign at all of her drunkenness, except that she'd somehow become more Éva-like. Ervin threw himself into drinking just as passionately as he had into smoking. I don't mean to confirm any racial theories, but you know just as well as I do how odd it is when a Jew drinks too much. Ervin's drinking was just as unusual as his Catholicism. It was an embittered headfirst leap, and it was as if it weren't even simple Hungarian wines that were making him drunk, but something much more monstrous: hashish or cocaine. And by the same token it was always as if he were bidding farewell: as if he had just taken his last drink, and generally as if he were committing his last act of any sort in this world. I quickly became accustomed to wine, and the emotional release and shedding of inhibition that it brought about became essential to my life; but at home the next day, I'd be dreadfully ashamed of my hangovers, and I'd always swear never to drink again. And then I would drink again, and inexorably the awareness of my own weakness grew, as well as the sense of being doomed, which was my dominant feeling during this second half of the Ulpius years. I felt that I was 'racing towards self-destruction', especially when I was drinking. I felt that I'd irrevocably fall out of the proper life that proper people led and that my father would expect from me. Despite all the horrible pangs of conscience, I loved this feeling very much. During this period I also went into hiding from my father.

"Tamás drank little, and became ever more silent.

"This is when Ervin's piety began to influence us. We'd already begun to see the world, the reality from which we'd always withdrawn in the past, and it struck us with terror. We sensed that man necessarily becomes corrupted, and we listened in awe to Ervin, who said that this must not be allowed to happen. We too began to be severely and dogmatically judgemental about the entirety of contemporary life, like Ervin. For a time he became our hegemon: we listened to him in all things and János and I strove to outdo each other in devotional activities. Every day we discovered new unfortunates needing our assistance, and new immortals of Catholic literature whom we had to save from undeserved oblivion. St Thomas and Jacques Maritain, Chesterton and St Anselm of Canterbury* went flitting around the room like flies. We went to church, and János, naturally, had visions. One morning before dawn, St Dominic looked in his window and, raising his index finger, said: 'As for you, we're paying special attention to you.' I think János and I must have been irresistibly comical in our attitude. The two Ulpiuses took little part in Catholicism.

"This period lasted for perhaps a year, and was followed by the disintegration phase. You couldn't say precisely how it started, but everyday reality began to flood in somehow, and so at the same time did death. The Ulpius grandfather died. He suffered for weeks, choking and rasping. Éva nursed him with surprising patience, keeping vigil by his bed every night. When, later, I once mentioned to her that it was a lovely thing on her part, she smiled distractedly and said that it was very interesting to watch as someone dies.

"Then their father decided that something had to be done with the children; things couldn't continue as they had been. He wanted to marry Éva off urgently. He sent her away to a rich country aunt of his, who ran a grand manor, so that she could make her debut at a ball there, and who knows what else. Of course, Éva returned after a week with marvellous stories, and she stoically pocketed the paternal blows to her face. Tamás didn't have such a fortunate temperament. His father secured him an office job. It's awful to think of it: even today, my eyes fill with tears when I think about how much Tamás suffered in that office. He worked in the City Hall, among ordinary petit bourgeois who didn't consider him sound of mind. They entrusted him with the dullest, most mechanical tasks, because they couldn't imagine that he might be capable of doing anything that might require a bit of thought or initiative. And maybe they were right after all. He was subjected to countless humiliations at the hands of his colleagues: not that they insulted him – on the contrary, they felt sorry for him and were trying to spare him. Tamás never complained to us, only to Éva on occasion – or so I understand. Tamás would merely go pale and fall silent when we'd mention the office.

"This was when Tamás committed suicide for the second time."

"The second time?" Erzsi asked.

"Yes. I should have already mentioned the first. That one was actually both more important and much more terrible. It happened back when we were sixteen, so right at the beginning of our friendship. One day, as usual, I popped over to see them. I found Éva alone, drawing something with unaccustomed absorption. She said that Tamás had gone up to the attic and I should wait for his imminent return. In those days, Tamás would often go up to the attic on exploratory expeditions; he'd find all sorts of things in the old chests to occupy his antiquarian fantasies and serve as props for our theatrical activities – and besides, the attic of such an old building is a very romantic place. So I wasn't surprised and waited for him patiently. Éva, as I've said, was unusually quiet.

"All of a sudden she simply went pale, jumped up and, screaming, called for me, saying we had to go up to the attic and see what was the matter with Tamás. I had no idea what it was all about, but her dread was infectious. It was already fairly dark in the attic. I tell you, it was an enormous, old attic with many alleys and crannies, and in places there were boards and chests blocking the pathways; I'd also hit my head on low beams, and we had to race up and down unexpected stairs. But Éva ran in the dark without hesitation, like someone who knew where Tamás might be. There was a low-ceilinged and very long alcove at the very end of the hallway, and the light of a small, round window shone at the back. Éva stopped short and, screeching, clung to me. My teeth were chattering too, but even back then I was already the sort who found unexpected courage just at the moment of greatest fear. I entered the dark alcove first, dragging Éva, still clinging to me.

"There dangled Tamás next to the small, round window, perhaps a metre above the floor. He'd hanged himself. 'He's still alive, he's still alive,' screamed Éva, and pressed a small knife into my hand. It seems that she knew perfectly well what Tamás had been up to. A chest stood there; evidently, Tamás had stood on it to fasten the noose onto the beam. I leapt onto the chest, cut the rope and with my other arm caught Tamás, then lowered him slowly to Éva, who undid the noose around his neck.

"Tamás recovered his senses soon; it must have been only a couple of minutes earlier that he'd hanged himself, and he was unharmed.

"'Why did you betray me?' he asked Éva. Éva was deeply ashamed, and didn't reply.

"After a while I cautiously asked him why he'd done it.

"'I was curious to know what it felt like,' said Tamás indifferently.

"'And what was it like?' asked Éva, her eyes wide with curiosity.

"'It was very good.'

"'Are you sorry we cut you down?' I asked, by this time feeling a few pangs of conscience myself.

"'No. I'm in no hurry. Later, sometime.'

"At the time, Tamás could not yet explain what it was all about. But he didn't need to: I understood anyhow; I understood, thanks to our plays. We were constantly killing and dying in the tragedies we put on. Dying preoccupied Tamás constantly. But understand, if it's at all possible to understand it: not death, extinction, annihilation. No. Rather, the act of dying. There are people who commit murder after murder 'by irresistible compulsion', in order to enjoy the glowing beauty of murder. The same sort of irresistible compulsion drew Tamás towards the final great ecstasy of his own dying. Clearly I can't explain it to you, Erzsi: it's just as impossible to explain this sort of thing as it is to explain music to the tone-deaf. I understood Tamás. For years, we spoke no more about this matter; each of us just knew that we understood each other.

"The other attempt, in which I too participated, happened when we were twenty years old. Don't be frightened: after all, you can see that I'm alive.

"At the time I was deeply depressed, mainly because of my father. After graduation, I enrolled at the university, in liberal arts. On several occasions, my father asked what I wanted to become, whereupon I answered: to become a historian of religion. 'And what do you intend to live on?' asked my father. I couldn't answer the question, and I didn't even want to think about it. I knew that my father wanted me to work at the firm. He didn't have any weighty objection to my university studies, since he thought that it could only reflect glory on the firm if one of its senior partners had a doctorate. In the final analysis, I too regarded university as merely a few years' reprieve. To gain some time before becoming an adult.

"Zest for life was not my strong suit at the time. The foreboding sense of being doomed grew ever stronger within me, and during this period even Catholicism offered no consolation: indeed, it just reinforced my sense of my own weakness. I had no talent for self-deception, and at that time I already saw clearly just how far both my life and my being fell incurably short of the Catholic ideal.

"I was the first to abandon our group's Catholicism; this too is one of my numerous betrayals.

"So one beautiful spring afternoon I popped in at the Ulpiuses' and invited Tamás to join me for a walk. We got as far as Óbuda and sat down in an empty small tavern, under a statue of St Florian. I drank too much, and meanwhile moaned on about my father, about my prospects and about the entire horrible sorrow of youth.

"'Why are you drinking so much?' asked Tamás.

"'Cause it's good.'

"'Do you enjoy being dizzy?'

"'Of course.'

"'Do you like being unconscious?'

"'Of course. It's the only thing I enjoy.'

"'Well then... I don't understand you. Imagine how much more enjoyable it must be to die completely.'

"And I could see his point. One thinks much more logically when drunk. My only objection was that I recoil from all pain and violence. I have no desire to hang myself or to leap into the cold Danube.

"'You don't need to,' said Tamás. 'I've got thirty centigrams of morphine right here; I'm told it's enough for two, although just one can also die from it. As a matter of fact, I'm going to die shortly anyway; the time has come. But if you come with me, then it'll be much better still. Naturally I don't want to influence you. I'm just saying. Should you happen to be in the mood.'

"'Where did you get the morphine?'

"'From Éva. She cadged it from the doctor, saying she had trouble sleeping.'

"Both of us held it to be of decisive significance that we'd received the poison from Éva. This also derived from our plays, those sick games that we'd been forced to modify strongly since Ervin and János joined us. The thrill always resided in the fact that we died because of Éva or for her sake. The fact that Éva had provided the poison was what convinced me that I had to take it. And so it happened.

"I can't even describe how simple and self-evident it was to commit suicide at that time. I was drunk, and at the time drink always evoked a mood of 'oh well, it's all the same anyway' in me. And that afternoon, it liberated the chained demon inside me, the one that I believe sleeps in the depths of every person's consciousness and draws him towards death. Think it over: it's much easier and more natural to die than to keep living..."

"I'd rather you carried on with the story," Erzsi said uneasily.

"We paid for the wine and went on our walk with great serenity, deeply moved. We told each other how much we loved each other and that our friendship was the most beautiful of our lives. We sat for a while on the Danube bank, out there in Óbuda, next to the train tracks, as the sun set on the Danube. And we waited for the morphine to take effect. For the moment we felt nothing.

"All of a sudden I felt an irresistible, tearful longing to bid Éva farewell. At first, Tamás wouldn't even hear of it, but then the feeling that bound him to Éva won him over. We boarded the tram and then raced up the narrow stairs into the Castle.

"Today I know that the moment I wanted to see Éva, I'd already betrayed both Tamás and suicide itself. Unwittingly I counted on the fact that if we returned to be among people, they'd save us somehow. At a subconscious level, I was in no mood to die. I was dead tired, as tired as only someone in his twenties can be, and I too longed for the secret, dark intoxication of dying, but as soon as the wine-induced sense of foredoom began to dissolve, I was no longer in the mood to die, after all...

"There sat Ervin and János in the Ulpius house. I cheerfully related to them how we'd taken fifteen centigrams of morphine apiece, and now we'd shortly die, but first we wanted to say our goodbyes. Tamás had already gone totally white and was staggering, but my only visible symptom was that I'd drunk a lot of wine and was speaking thickly, the way drunks do. János raced off at once and phoned the medical emergency service, reporting that there were two young men here who'd taken fifteen centigrams of morphine per head.

"'Are they still alive?' asked the emergency worker.

"Hearing János reply in the affirmative, they instructed him to bring us in at once. János and Ervin stuck us in a taxi and took us to Markó Street. I still didn't feel a thing.

"I felt it all the more at the emergency room, where they pumped out my stomach mercilessly and removed all my interest in suicide.

As a matter of fact, I can't free myself of the thought that it wasn't even morphine that we'd poisoned ourselves with. Either Éva had tricked Tamás, or the doctor Éva. Tamás's symptoms might even have been autosuggestion.

"Éva and the boys had to stay up all night and make sure we didn't fall asleep, because in the emergency room they said that if we fell asleep we'd never wake up again. It was an unusual night. We were embarrassed in front of each other; I was even happy to have been a suicide, which is hugely sensational, and I was happy to have remained alive; I felt a remarkably comfortable fatigue. We all loved each other a great deal; their vigil was a great, self-sacrificing gesture of friendship and it accorded splendidly with our religious and brotherly ardour. We were all deeply shaken, and we had Dostoevskian conversations, drinking one espresso after another. That was the sort of youthful night that, as a grown-up, one typically looks back upon only with a sort of queasiness. But God knows, it seems that I've already grown old, because I feel no nausea when I think back on it, just enormous nostalgia.

"Only Tamás didn't say so much as a word, but allowed us to pour cold water on him and pinch him to prevent him falling asleep. Tamás was indeed in bad shape, and he was also shattered to have failed yet again. When I spoke to him, he turned away and didn't respond. He considered me a traitor. And afterwards we were indeed no longer truly good friends. He never mentioned this incident later; he was just as amiable and courteous as before, but I know that he never forgave me. He died with me no longer his closest intimate..."

Here Mihály fell silent and buried his head in his hands. Then he rose and stared out of the window into the darkness. He returned and stroked Erzsi's hands with a distracted smile.

"Does it still hurt so much?" asked Erzsi softly.

"I haven't had a single friend ever since," said Mihály.

Again, they fell silent. Erzsi brooded on whether Mihály was feeling so sorry for himself merely out of wine-induced sentimentality, or whether something had indeed snapped inside him in the Ulpius house and made him so indifferent and distant with people.

"And what happened to Éva?" she asked at last.

"At the time, Éva was in love with Ervin."

"And weren't the rest of you jealous?"

"No, we found it natural. Ervin was our hegemon: we considered him the most exceptional of us and felt it right for Éva to love him. In any case, I wasn't in love with Éva, and as for János, one really couldn't tell. At that time, the group was drifting apart. Ervin and Éva were all the more self-sufficient in each other's company, and they sought opportunities to be alone together. As for me, the university and history of religion began genuinely to interest me. I was filled with scholarly ambitions; the first encounter with scholarship is just as intoxicating as love.

"But to return to Ervin and Éva... Éva became much quieter at that time; she went to church, to the Sisters of Loreto,* where she had once been a pupil. I've already told you how Ervin had an entirely unusual disposition to be in love: love belonged to him the way swashbuckling belonged to Szepetneki. I could understand how even Éva couldn't remain aloof next to him.

"It was a touching love, a love saturated with poetry, the Buda Castle and being twenty years old. You know, the sort of love that makes one expect crowds to part respectfully before the two of them as they stroll down the street, as if they were carrying the Host in procession. Somehow, the entire meaning of our group was fulfilled in their love. And how short was its duration! I never learnt precisely what happened between them. It seems that Ervin asked for Éva's hand, and old Ulpius threw him out. According to János, he even slapped him. But Éva just loved Ervin all the more, and she undoubtedly would have gladly become his lover, but for Ervin the Sixth Commandment was an implacable reality. He became even paler and more silent than before; he didn't visit the Ulpius house, and I saw him more and more rarely; and that's when the great transformation may have taken place within Éva, later rendering her so inscrutable to me. And after this, one fine day, Ervin disappeared. It was Tamás who informed me that he'd become a monk. Tamás had destroyed the farewell letter in which Ervin told him of his decision. Whether he knew Ervin's monastic name, and which monastery and which order he entered, is a secret that he took with himself into the grave. Maybe he only revealed it to Éva.

"Without a doubt, the fact that he couldn't marry Éva was not the only reason Ervin became a monk. After all, we'd spoken a great deal about the monastic life before, and I know that Ervin's piety was much deeper: it's impossible for him to have become a monk without some definitive sign of an inner calling, but merely out of despair and romantic inclination. He indubitably saw it as a sign from above when he couldn't take Éva as wife. But the suddenness of his departure, as if in flight, must have been determined in large part by the fact that he wanted to flee Éva, the temptation that Éva represented to him. In this fashion, although perhaps a bit in the manner of Joseph, he nevertheless accomplished what we'd fantasized about so much in those days: he offered his youth as an undefiled sacrifice to God."

"The only thing I don't understand," said Erzsi, "is that if, as you say, he was so predisposed to love, why did he make this sacrifice?"

"Darling, contradictions sit side by side in the soul. It's not cold and dispassionate people who become great ascetics, but the fieriest ones, the ones who have something to renounce. This is why the Church doesn't allow castrated men to become priests."

"And what did Éva say to all this?"

"Éva was left to herself, and from this point on, she became unbearable. At the time, Budapest was in the hands of profiteers and the Entente's officers.* Somehow or other, Éva wound up in Entente officer circles. She spoke languages, and in her manner there was something not provincially Hungarian but genuinely cosmopolitan. As far as I know, she was tremendously popular. This is when from one day to the next, the little adolescent girl became a beautiful woman. This is when that other gaze found its way into her eyes, which had been so open and chummy in expression: now she always looked at you as if she were meanwhile paying attention to some distant, soft voices.

"During this last period, the hegemony of János followed the hegemonies of Tamás and Ervin. That is to say, Éva needed money to be able to appear elegant among the elegant men. Although she could sew elegance for herself extremely cleverly out of nothing, even that nothing required a bit of money. And here began the role János played. He was always able to conjure money for Éva. Where from was his business. Often he'd sting precisely those Entente officers with whom Éva was dancing. 'I've collected the companionship fee,' he'd say cynically. By that point we too were talking cynically, because we always adapted to the hegemon's style.

"I greatly disliked the unscrupulous methods János used. For example, I disapproved of the way, one day, he looked up Mr Reich, the old bookkeeper at my father's firm, and used a horribly convoluted story about my gambling debts and attempted suicide to tap him for a pretty serious sum. Later, of course, I had to confess to having run up debts at the card table, even though I'd never held a card in my hand all my life.

"And I particularly didn't appreciate the fact that he stole my gold pocket watch. This happened on the occasion of a big party, somewhere outdoors in a summer garden restaurant that was highly fashionable back then; I don't even recall its name any more. There were a lot of us, Éva's companions, two or three foreign officers, some young men made rich by inflation and peculiar women clad in the exceptionally brazen dress and manners of the time. My sense of foreboding was already heightened by the fact that Tamás and I had wound up in company so utterly inappropriate for us: among people with whom we had nothing else in common but the feeling that by now it was all the same anyhow. For at that time not only did I sense the prospect of doom, but so did the entire city: it was in the air. People had loads of money and they knew that, despite everything, it would disappear from one day to the next: catastrophe hung above the garden restaurant like a chandelier.

"They were apocalyptic times. I don't even know if we were sober when we sat down to drink. In my memory, it seems I was drunk from the first instant. Tamás hardly drank at all, but this general end-of-the-world atmosphere corresponded so well to his own psychological state that he circulated with unusual ease among the clientele and the gypsy musicians. I spoke a lot with Tamás that night – that is, with few words, but the words we uttered had frightful emotional import, and once again we got on with each other splendidly; we understood each other in the shadow of doom. And we also got on well with the odd girls; at least, I felt that my mild religious-historical disquisitions on the Celts and their isles of the dead elicited a lively response from the drama student sitting next to me for most of the time. Then Éva and I sat apart, just the two of us, and I paid her court as though I hadn't known her since her skinny and large-eyed adolescence, and she too received my attentions with utter womanly seriousness, in half-sentences and looking into the distance, in the full brilliance of her pose at the time.

"As dawn began to break, I became very sick, and as I sobered up a bit, I noticed that my gold pocket watch had disappeared. I was horribly thunderstruck, in an ecstasy of despair. You have to understand: the loss of a watch isn't such a great misfortune, in and of itself; not even when one is twenty years old and has no other valuable in the world than this gold pocket watch. But when you're twenty, and at dawn you sober up to find that they'd stolen your gold watch, you're likely to endow the loss with a deep symbolic significance. I'd received the watch from my father, who is not generally inclined to give gifts. I tell you, it was my only valuable, my only piece of private property worth speaking of, and while in my eyes its bulky, ostentatious philistinism represented everything I so despised, its loss, now that it appeared to me in its symbolic form, filled me with abject terror. I felt that now I'd been irrevocably consigned to the infernal powers: they'd stolen the possibility that I'd ever be able to recover my senses and return to the bourgeois world.

"I staggered over to Tamás and announced to him that they'd stolen my gold pocket watch; I said I'd telephone the police and alert the restaurateur to lock the gate and have every guest frisked. Tamás calmed me down in his usual manner: 'It's not worth it. Let it go. Of course they stole it. They'll steal everything from you. You'll always be the victim. This is what you like.'

"I looked at him in astonishment, but indeed, I didn't speak to anyone about the watch's disappearance. As I stared at Tamás, all of a sudden it became perfectly clear that only János Szepetneki could have stolen the watch. There had been some sort of clothes-swapping game going on during the evening, and Szepetneki and I exchanged coats and neckties: evidently, when I got my coat back, the pocket watch was no longer in it. I began to look for János to question him, but he was no longer there. I didn't see him the next day, nor the day after.

"And on the fourth day, I no longer demanded the return of the watch. I realized that, if it was indeed he who'd taken it, then he'd done so because Éva needed the money. And he likely took it with Éva's knowledge, since it was Éva who'd initiated the entire clothes-exchange game – and the tête-à-tête with Éva might have been intended for me not to notice the watch's disappearance straight away. As soon as this possibility came to mind, I resigned myself to the matter. If it happened for Éva, then it was for a good cause. In that case, this was also part of the performance, the old play in the Ulpius house.

"From then on I was in love with Éva."

"But until this moment, you've denied in the most forceful terms that you'd ever been in love with her," Erzsi interrupted.

"Of course. And I was right. I'm only calling what I felt for Éva 'love' for lack of a better word. This feeling doesn't resemble my love for you, and for one or two of your predecessors, in any respect – don't be angry. It's somehow the exact negative of that. I love you because you belong to me, and I loved her because she didn't belong to me – the fact that I love you instils self-confidence and strength; the fact that I loved her humiliated and annihilated me... of course these are mere rhetorical antitheses. At that time, I felt as if the old play-acting were becoming reality, and that I'd slowly perish in its magnificent fulfilment. I'd perish because of Éva, through her agency, the way we'd played it out in our adolescence."

Mihály rose and paced the room uneasily. Now, just now, it began to bother him that he'd revealed himself this way. To Erzsi... a stranger, and a female one at that...

Erzsi spoke up: "Before, you said something to the effect that the reason you couldn't be in love with her is that you knew each other too well, and the distance love requires didn't exist between the two of you."

("Good: she doesn't understand," thought Mihály. "The only bit of it she grasps is what her utterly primitive jealousy can comprehend.")

"It's good that you bring it up," he said, relieved. "Until that memorable night, there had indeed been no distance. That's when I discovered, as we sat there alone together, as a lady and a gentleman, that Éva had become an entirely different woman, a stranger, a magnificent and beautiful woman, and that at the same time she remained the old Éva, forever bearing within herself the sick and dark sweetness of my youth.

"In any case, Éva couldn't care less about me. I was able to see her only on rare occasions, and she didn't concern herself with me then either. Her restlessness had already become pathological, in some sense. Especially ever since the serious suitor came on the scene. A famous, wealthy, not exactly young collector of antiquities had turned up at the Ulpius house once or twice with the old man, and he'd occasionally seen Éva, and he'd long since occupied himself with plans to marry her. Old Ulpius announced to Éva that he'd accept no objections whatsoever. Éva had lived at his expense long enough. Let her get married or go to the devil. Éva requested a two-month postponement. The old man, at the suitor's request, agreed.

"The less Éva paid attention to me, the stronger the feeling became that, for lack of a better term, I called love. It seems that I had a most peculiar inclination to hopelessness at the time: to loiter outside her gate at night to spy her returning home laughing loudly with company; to neglect my studies; to spend all my money on stupid gifts that she didn't even really notice; to go all soft and soppy and make an unmasculine display when encountering her – that was my style; that's when I was truly alive; no joy that has befallen me since has reached such true depths as the pain, the happy shame that I must lose myself because of her and that she didn't even care about me. Could it be that this is what they call love?"

("Why am I saying this, why?... I've drunk too much again. But I just had to say it out loud, once, and Erzsi won't understand it anyhow.")

"Meanwhile, the postponement granted Éva was approaching its end. Old Ulpius occasionally burst into the room and made awful scenes. By that time he was never sober. The fiancé also appeared, with grey hair and an apologetic smile. Éva asked for one more week. So that she could travel away quietly with Tamás for a week, for them to say their goodbyes. She had even found the travel money somehow.

"And so they went away: to Hallstatt.* It was late autumn, and aside from themselves, there wasn't another soul there. There's nothing more deadly than such old, historical spa towns. Because it's perfectly natural for a fortress or a cathedral to be very ancient, completely outmoded, and crumbling here and there: that's its function. But when a place designed for the pleasures of the moment shows its age, for instance a coffeehouse or the promenade of a health spa… there's nothing more terrible."

"Fine," said Erzsi, "carry on. What happened to the Ulpiuses?"

"Darling, the reason I've delayed and philosophized is that from here on, I don't know what happened to them. I never saw them again. Tamás Ulpius poisoned himself in Hallstatt. This time he succeeded."

"And what happened to Éva?"

"You mean, what part did Éva play in the death of Tamás? Maybe none. I don't know. She didn't come back again. They say that after Tamás's death, a high-ranking foreign military officer came for her and took her away.

"Perhaps I could have still met her. I might have had one or two opportunities in the following years. János showed up from time to time, dropping obscure hints that he might be able to manage my seeing Éva and would welcome my honouring his offer of assistance. But I no longer wanted to meet Éva by then; this is why János said, earlier, that I severed the connection to my youth intentionally, when all I needed to do was to reach out my hand… He's right. When Tamás died, I thought I'd go mad – and then I decided to change, to wrench myself free of this spell: I didn't want to go the way of Tamás, but rather be a proper man. I left the university, learnt my father's profession, went abroad to gain a better understanding of the business and then returned home and tried to be like other men.

"As for what belonged to the Ulpius house – I wasn't wrong to feel it was foredoomed – everything perished, and nothing from it has remained. Old Ulpius didn't live long after that. They beat him to death as he was heading home, drunk, from a pub on the city outskirts. A wealthy man by the name of Munk, a business friend of my father's, had already purchased the house. I even visited them there once: awful… They decorated it beautifully, making it look much older than it was. A genuine Florentine well stood in the centre of the courtyard. The grandfather's room had become an antique German dining room, panelled in oak. And our room… my God, they decorated it to be some ancient Hungarian country inn or whatnot, with tulip-decorated chests, pitchers and knick-knacks. Tamás's room! Such is transience… St Stephen,* look how late it is! Don't be angry, dear, but I had to tell someone, just once… no matter how stupid it might sound from the outside… well, now I'll go to bed."

"Mihály… you promised to tell me how Tamás Ulpius died. And you didn't, nor did you say why he died."

"I didn't say how he died, because I don't know. And as for why he died? Hmm. Well, maybe he was tired of living, wasn't he? One can get dreadfully sick of life, no?"

"No. But let's go to sleep. It's very late already."

5

THEY HAD NO LUCK IN FLORENCE. It rained throughout their stay. They were standing in their raincoats in front of the Duomo when Mihály abruptly broke out in laughter. He had suddenly comprehended the Duomo's entire tragic aspect: the fact that it stood here in its unequalled beauty, and nobody at all was taking it seriously. It had become a touristic and art-historical attraction, and nobody would think – nobody at all would believe any more – that the reason for its existence is to proclaim God's and the city's glory.

They went up to Fiesole and watched as a thunderstorm raced across the mountain with self-important haste to catch up to them in time. They took refuge inside the cloister and took a look at the many oriental trinkets that the humble friars had brought home from their missions over the past centuries. Mihály admired a series of Chinese paintings at length, whose subject he could only determine after some time. The upper portion of every picture depicted a fierce and alarming Chinese man enthroned, a huge book before him. What gave his face a particularly frightening aspect was the hair above both temples that was shocked straight upright. And in the lower portion of the pictures, all sorts of spine-chilling things were happening: they were using iron pitchforks to toss people into some uncomfortable liquid; they just happened to be sawing others' legs; they were shown taking great care to pull out the rope-like intestines of another; and in one place, a contraption resembling an automobile, driven by a monster with the hair on his temples combed upwards, plunged into a crowd, and spinning cleavers fixed on the machine's nose were slicing the people to bits.

He realized that this was Judgement Day as seen by a Chinese Christian. What expertise and objectivity!

He began to feel dizzy and went outside into the square. The landscape between Bologna and Florence, which had seemed so marvellous from the train, was now soaked and unfriendly, like a weeping woman with the mascara running off her face.

When they'd come back down from Fiesole, Mihály went to the main post office; this is where he'd had their letters forwarded ever since they'd left Venice. On the envelope of one of the letters addressed to him he recognized the handwriting of Zoltán Pataki, Erzsi's first husband. "Maybe there's something in it that Erzsi oughtn't read," he thought, and sat down with the letter in front of a coffeehouse. "Behold male solidarity," he thought with a smile.

Here is how the letter read:

Dear Mihály,

I know perfectly well that it's a bit nauseating for me to write you a long and friendly letter after you've "lured my wife away and eloped with her", but you were never a slave to convention, and this is why you might not even be shocked if I – although you always called me an old conformist – for once also don't bother with the rules that govern our conduct. I'm writing to you because I can't be at peace otherwise. I'm writing to you because, to tell the truth, I don't know why I shouldn't, since we both know that I'm not angry at you. Let's just keep up appearances to the world, because the romantic notion that we're mortal enemies because of her will certainly flatter Erzsi's self-esteem; but just between us, my dear Mihály, you well know that I've always held you in high regard, and the fact that you lured my wife away and eloped with her doesn't change a thing. Not as though your "deed" hadn't broken me up completely, since I also don't need to hide from you how much I still adore Erzsi – but of course let's keep this between us too. But

I'm perfectly aware that you can't help it at all. I believe – don't be angry – that you can't help it about anything on earth.

And this is precisely why I'm writing to you. To tell the truth, I'm a bit worried for Erzsi's sake. You see, I've got used to thinking about her over so many years, keeping her constantly in mind, supplying her with everything she needs and, above all, with things she doesn't need, making sure she's dressed warmly enough when she goes out at night: now I can't get out of the habit of worrying about her, day in, day out. This worry is the connection that binds me so closely to Erzsi. I'll confess to you that, not long ago, I had a stupid dream: I dreamt that Erzsi was leaning very far out a window, and that if I didn't hold her she'd fall out. And then it occurred to me that I'm not sure whether you'd notice if Erzsi were to lean too far out a window, being such a distracted and introverted man as you are. This is why I thought I'd ask you to do a few things, to pay particularly close attention, so I wrote everything up in a note, just as it came to me. Don't be angry, but it's an undeniable fact that I've known Erzsi much longer than you, and that confers certain rights.

1. Make sure that Erzsi eats. Erzsi (perhaps you've come to realize this already) is terrified of gaining weight; this fear sometimes besets her like a panic, and at such times she won't eat for days, and afterwards she has serious stomach acid that, in turn, is bad for her nerves. It occurred to me that your unberufen* *hearty appetite might inspire her to eat. Regrettably, I've long suffered from stomach trouble and was unable to set a good example for her.*

2. Beware of manicurists. If Erzsi wants a manicure while on travel, take it upon yourself to select a manicurist, and consider only the very best firm. Ask the hotel concierge for information. Erzsi is extraordinarily sensitive in this respect, and it has already happened several times that a manicurist's clumsiness has led to an infection of her fingers. Something whose consequences you will also surely not enjoy.

3. Don't let Erzsi get up early. I know that the temptation to rise early is strong when on travel; when we were last in Italy, I too fell into this error, because the Italian intercity buses leave very early. Let the buses go to the devil. Erzsi goes to sleep late and rises late. Rising early does her great harm, and she can't get over it for days.

4. Don't let her eat scampi, frutti di mare or other aquatic monsters, because it makes her skin break out.

5. This is such a touchy subject, I don't even know how to put it. Maybe I should assume that you're clear about it too, but I don't know whether a man so withdrawn and philosophical by nature is typically clear about such things: the immeasurable fragility of the feminine character, and the extent to which bodily things dominate her. I ask you to take careful note of Erzsi's times of the month. A week before the start of the business, be infinitely lenient and patient. Erzsi is not entirely predictable at these times. She picks fights. The wisest thing is, in fact, to bicker with her: that dissipates her temper. But don't argue seriously. Keep in mind that it's just a physiological process, or whatever. Don't get carried away, don't say something that you'll regret later and, above all, don't let Erzsi say that sort of thing, because she'll regret it deeply later, and it will do harm to her nerves.

Don't be angry with me. There are a thousand other things I should write, a thousand little details to be careful about – these are just the most important – but I can't think of them this way, I have no imagination. Nevertheless, why deny it, I'm terribly worried, not only because I know Erzsi, but primarily because I know you. I beg you, don't misunderstand me. If I were a woman and had to choose between the two of us, I'd choose you without a moment's hesitation, and Erzsi assuredly loves you precisely because you are as you are, so infinitely distant and withdrawn that you have nothing to do with anyone or anything, as though you were a foreigner travelling through, or a Martian on this globe; that you can't take precise note of anything, that you can't be truly angry at anyone, that you can't pay attention when others are speaking, that you behave as if you were also a human mainly out of goodwill and courtesy. I tell you, all this is very lovely, and I could also hold it very dear if I were a woman; the only thing that worries me is that now, after all, you're also Erzsi's husband. And Erzsi has grown accustomed to her husband taking care of her in every respect, even protecting her from the wind, so that she needn't think of a thing except her intellectual and spiritual life, and – not least – about maintaining her body. Erzsi's nature is fundamentally that of a lady of luxury – that's what they raised her to be at home, and that's what I respected her for – and I don't know whether, by your side, she might not be forced to look the sorts of reality in the eye which her father and I had conscientiously concealed from her.

I have one more delicate matter to touch upon here. I know very well that you, and your dear father, in whose firm you work, are well-to-do people, and your wife won't suffer for lack of anything. Yet I still sometimes worry, because I know how spoilt Erzsi is, and I'm afraid that a man as withdrawn as you might not keep due account of Erzsi's needs. You yourself, I know, are of an endearing, bohemian, undemanding nature; you've always lived a most solid life, a different living standard than that to which Erzsi has become accustomed. But now, one of you must make accommodation to the living standards of the other. If Erzsi accommodates to yours, sooner or later she'll resent it, because she'll feel déclassée the moment she encounters her previous milieu. What do I know, in Italy she might meet a girlfriend of hers who'll look down her nose when she hears that you're staying in a not-quite-first-class hotel. The other possibility is that you adapt to her standard; that will come with material consequences, sooner or later, because – don't be angry – I am probably better informed about the financial capacity of firms than you, who are so withdrawn, and besides which, you have three brothers, and your dear father is a bit conservative, a gentleman of fairly strict understanding, predisposed more to saving than to enjoying one's income... in other words, in brief, you're not in a position to maintain Erzsi's accustomed living standards on your own. And since it's a great concern of mine that Erzsi have everything she needs, I beg of you not to take it ill if I tell you that, in the event of need, I'll be at your service unconditionally upon your command, even in the form of long-term loans. I'll honestly confess that I'd most gladly pay a standard monthly sum, but I know that this would be an impertinence. But I must inform you of this much, in any event: if the need should ever arise, just count on me.

I beg you not to be angry with me. I'm a simple businessman, I have no other task but to make money, and this, thank God, I do surpassingly well. I think it's only fair if I like to disburse my money to whom I please, don't you agree?

So once more, nichts für ungut.* *Have a good time; with truly respectful, affectionate greetings,*

Zoltán

The letter really got under Mihály's skin. He was revolted by Pataki's unmanly "goodness", which in any case was not even goodness, just lack of masculinity; but would hardly have been more praiseworthy if it *had* been goodness, since Mihály didn't have a very high opinion of goodness. And all that obsequiousness! In spite of it all, Pataki remained a mere shop assistant, no matter how rich he'd become.

But all this was Zoltán Pataki's business, and it was his problem if he was still in love with Erzsi, who had behaved truly scandalously towards him. That wasn't what upset Mihály, but the parts of the letter referring to him and Erzsi.

First of all, the material issues. Mihály held "economic necessity" in immeasurable esteem. Perhaps precisely because he had so little feeling for it. Whenever someone told him, "material causes force you to behave thus and so", Mihály would fall silent right away and consider every underhandedness justified. This is exactly why that aspect of things had made him extraordinarily uneasy when it had come up before, but Erzsi always brushed it aside humorously, saying "oh, you…" Erzsi had made a very poor match with him: she had been the wife of a wealthy man before, and now she was with a middle-class bourgeois – she'd resent it sooner or later, as the sober Zoltán Pataki, so at home in material affairs, already saw clearly.

Suddenly a bunch of things occurred to him that had already, even on their honeymoon, highlighted the difference between their two standards of living. Immediately at hand, one did not have to look further than the hotel in which they were lodging. Mihály, having seen in Ravenna and Venice how much better Erzsi spoke Italian than he, and how much cleverer she was in dealing with the porters, from whom he recoiled in any case, left the hotel and other practical matters entirely up to Erzsi in Florence. Upon which, without further ado, Erzsi took a room in one of the old but exceedingly expensive small hotels on the Arno, with the observation that since they were already in Florence, they simply must live overlooking the Arno. The price of the room – as Mihály dimly sensed, being too lazy to calculate it – was completely at odds with the sum they'd set aside for their Italian sojourn; it was a good deal more expensive than their Venetian room, and for a moment this pierced Mihály's heart, used as it was to thrift. But then he drove this niggling sensation away with disgust. "After all, we're on our honeymoon," he said to himself, and thought no more about it. But now that he'd read Pataki's letter, this too loomed before him as a symptom.

But the biggest problem was not material, but moral… When, after six months of brooding, he reached the decision to separate Erzsi (with whom he'd already been having an affair for a year) from her husband and take her to wife, Mihály committed himself to this consequential step in order to "set everything aright", and further, to enter the ranks of grown-up, serious men via the haven of matrimony, so that he could be of equal status with, for precise example, Zoltán Pataki. This is just why he pledged to strive with all his strength to be a good husband. He wanted to make Erzsi forget what a good husband she'd left in order to be with him and, moreover, he wanted "to set everything aright" retroactively, all the way back to his adolescence. Pataki's letter now convinced him of the hopelessness of his undertaking. He'd never be able to be as good a husband as Zoltán Pataki, who could look after his admittedly faithless and absent wife, even across great distances, with greater consideration and understanding than he, who was right here with her, but so ill-suited to the role of protector that he loaded Erzsi down with even the choice of hotel and other practical concerns, with the utterly transparent excuse that she spoke better Italian.

"Perhaps Pataki's right," he thought, "that I am overly withdrawn and introverted by nature. Of course this is an oversimplification: people can never be reduced to words that way, but it's certainly true that I'm extremely clumsy and incompetent in practical matters; I'm not at all the type of man in whose calm superiority a woman can trust. Whereas Erzsi is the sort of woman who loves to entrust herself entirely to someone else, who loves to know that she belongs unconditionally to someone: she's not one of those motherly women – maybe this is why she has no children, in fact – but one of those who want to be their lover's child. My God, how unfortunate she'll be, sooner or later, at my side: I think I could sooner be a general than play the paternal role, the sort of quality that, among others, is completely absent in me. I can't bear it when someone depends on me, even if in the form of subordinate staff; this is why I always did everything alone in my youth. I can't bear responsibility, and in general I come to detest those who expect something from me…

"This whole thing is madness, madness for Erzsi, since she'd have done better with ninety-nine out of a hundred men than with me;

any average, normal man would have made a better husband than I, and now I'm looking at it not from my own viewpoint, but entirely from hers. Why didn't I think of all this before I got married – or rather, how can it be that Erzsi, who is so wise, didn't think things through better?"

But of course, Erzsi couldn't have thought it through, because Erzsi was in love with Mihály, and when it came to him, she wasn't so wise; she hadn't recognized Mihály's faults – not, it seems, right up until this moment. But this is just a consequence of being driven by her senses: Erzsi craves the happiness of love with a completely raw, uninhibited appetite, which she didn't find at Pataki's side; but what will happen once she's had her fill? After all, such sensuous passion doesn't usually last too long...

By the time he returned to the hotel after a long meander, he saw it as inevitable that one day Erzsi would leave him, and furthermore only after terrible crises and suffering, after ugly affronts to his manliness, "dragging his name through the mud", as they say. To a certain extent, he even resigned himself to the inevitable, and when they sat down to dinner, he could already begin to see Erzsi as a lovely part of his past, and a moving sense of solemnity seized hold of him. The past and present always played an odd game within Mihály, colouring and flavouring each other. He enjoyed placing himself, in his imagination, back at some point in his past, and rearranging his present life from that viewpoint – for instance: "What would I have thought of Florence if I'd come here at sixteen?" – and this re-emplacement in the past always endowed the present moment with richer emotional content. But one could play it the other way round too: to make the past out of the present – "What a lovely memory this will be in ten years' time, that I once went to Florence with Erzsi... what content will this memory have, what emotional resonance, which I can't even guess yet today?"

He expressed his celebratory feeling by assembling an enormous festive menu and ordering expensive wine. Erzsi knew Mihály and that a grand dinner meant a grand mood, and she too tried to rise to the situation. She directed the conversation cleverly, posing one or two questions regarding the Florentine past to focus Mihály's thoughts in a historical direction, because she knew that such associations would fire him with enthusiasm even more splendidly than wine; in fact, this was the only thing that could drag Mihály out of his indifference. Mihály indeed responded with passionate, colourful and, from a factual perspective, unreliable expositions, and then, his eyes glittering, he tried to analyse what the very word "Tuscany" meant to him, how many marvels and what ecstasy. For this land had not one particle that hadn't been trampled by historical armies, emperors and the splendidly costumed troops of French kings; here every woodland trail led to a very important place, and more history had befallen a single street in Florence than seven counties back home.

Erzsi listened to him with delight. Tuscany's historicity, mind, didn't interest her at all at the moment, but she loved Mihály very much when he was fired up like this; she loved how, precisely at such times, in his historical reveries – that is, when he wandered furthest from the world of the here and now – his indifference lifted and he became just like a man. Sympathy, in Erzsi, instantly transmuted into stronger feelings, and she thought of what the night had in store with joy, all the more since Mihály had been in a bad mood the night before, and had fallen asleep – or pretended to – as soon as he'd lain down.

She knew how easily she could redirect Mihály's fired-up mood from history to herself. It was enough to place her hand on Mihály's and look hard into his eyes: Mihály forgot Tuscany, and his face, blushing from the wine, went entirely pale from the sudden access of desire. Then he began to pay court and fawn on her, as if he were now battling for Erzsi's love for the first time.

"How odd," thought Erzsi, "after a whole year of intimacy, he still pays court in that tone of voice, with such inner unease, as if he were completely unsure whether I'd give him a chance. In fact, the more he entreats, the greater the distance gets from which he does so, and the more refined his manner becomes – as if to embellish his desire and confer the proper respect on it – and the greatest closeness, bodily intimacy can't bring him any closer. He can only love me when he feels distance between us."

And so it was. Mihály's desire spoke to the distant Erzsi, to the person whom he knew would leave him one day, and who already lived within him like a lovely memory. That is also why he drank so much: to stay in the mood, to make himself believe that it wasn't Erzsi he was with, but Erzsi's memory, Erzsi as history.

But Erzsi was also drinking in the meantime, and wine always affected her strongly: she became loud, good-humoured and very, very impatient. This Erzsi was relatively new to Mihály, because before their marriage, Erzsi had had few opportunities to behave so freely in Mihály's presence while in public. Mihály found this Erzsi exceedingly attractive, and they both hurried up to their room.

On this night, when Erzsi was the new Erzsi and historical, memory Erzsi in the same person, and when Zoltán Pataki's letter and the memory of the Ulpiuses swirling around him had shaken him so deeply, Mihály forgot his earlier commitment and brought elements into his married life that he'd always wanted to withhold from Erzsi. We allude to those certain, adolescent behaviours fashionable between young boys and virgin girls, with which release can be attained via circuitous routes and without responsibility. There are people who, like Mihály, prefer this responsibility-free release to the wholly serious, officially sanctioned pleasures. But Mihály was infinitely ashamed of this preference, even before himself, because he understood its essentially adolescent nature, and when he had entered the truly serious, grown-up intimacy of love with Erzsi, he decided that he'd only relate to Erzsi via the official forms of love, as befitting two serious, grown-up lovers.

This Florentine night was the first and only exception. Erzsi was astonished, but gladly accepted and returned Mihály's unaccustomed endearments; she didn't understand the matter, and afterwards, she understood neither Mihály's infernally bad mood nor his shame.

"Why?" she asked. "After all it was wonderful this way too – and besides, I love you."

And she fell asleep. Now it was Mihály who couldn't fall asleep for a very long time. He felt that now he'd definitively and demonstratively acknowledged the failure and collapse of his marriage. He acknowledged that he could not be an adult, even in his marriage, and, what was most dreadful, he had to realize that Erzsi had never given him as much pleasure as now, when he had loved her not as an adult and as his passionate lover, but as an immature adolescent girl, as if on a spring outing.

And now Mihály got out of bed. After assuring himself that Erzsi was still asleep, he stepped to the vanity on which her handbag lay. He found the cheques inside – for Erzsi was their treasurer. He found the two National Bank cheques denominated in lire, each for the same amount, one in his name and one in Erzsi's. He removed his own cheque and smuggled in a piece of paper of the same shape to replace it; then he put the cheque very carefully into his wallet, and lay down again.

6

THE FOLLOWING MORNING, they travelled on towards Rome. The train rolled out of Florence and entered the Tuscan landscape between green and spring-like hills. It proceeded slowly, stopping for ten minutes at every station; the passengers would disembark and then, with southern ease, take their time getting back on, chatting and laughing all the while as the train prepared to depart.

"Just look," said Mihály, "how many more things one can see looking out the window here, than in other countries. I don't know how they do it – the horizon is wider here, or the objects smaller – but I'll wager that looking from the train, one sees five times as many villages, forests, rivers, sky and clouds here as in, say, Austria."

"True," said Erzsi. She was sleepy, and Mihály's enthusiasm for all things Italian was already grating on her. "But Austria is still prettier. We should have gone there."

"To Austria?!" shouted Mihály. He was so offended that he didn't even continue.

"Put away your passport," said Erzsi. "You've left it out on the table again."

The train stopped in Cortona. Mihály, when he saw the small hill town, felt as though at some point he'd seen many such towns before, and now he enjoyed the delight of seeing one again.

"Tell me, why do I feel as though I'd spent part of my youth in hill towns?"

But Erzsi had nothing to say on the subject.

What she said was: "I'm already bored with all this travel. I'd like to be in Capri already. I'll be able to rest there."

"Capri, really? It'd be much more interesting to get off here in Cortona. Or anywhere. Off the itinerary. The next station, for instance, is Arezzo. Arezzo! It's fantastic that Arezzo even exists in the world and isn't just Dante's invention, when he compared its acrobats to devils who made trombones out of their nether parts.* Come, let's disembark in Arezzo."

"Oh, of course. I should get out because Dante writes such obscenities! Arezzo is a dusty little backwater; I'm sure it has a Duomo from the thirteenth century, a Palazzo Communale, a portrait of *Il Duce* on every corner with corresponding nationalist inscriptions, lots of coffeehouses and a hotel named Stella d'Italia. I'm not curious to find out. I'm bored. I want to be in Capri already."

"Interesting. Maybe because you've already been to Italy many times, you no longer swoon on seeing a Fra Angelico painting or a Bel Paese cheese. I still feel as though I'm committing a mortal sin at every station at which I don't disembark. There's no more frivolous thing than to travel by train. We should be going on foot, or at least by stagecoach, like Goethe. It's horrifying to think that I've both been in Tuscany and not. That lo! – I went right past Arezzo, and over there somewhere lies Siena, and I didn't go there. Who knows if I'll ever get to Siena if I don't go there now?"

"Oh, come now. Back home, you never let on that you were such a snob. What harm will come of it if you don't get to see the Sienese Primitives?"*

"Who cares about the Siena Primitives?"

"Well then, what do you want to do in Siena?"

"What do I know? If I knew, maybe it wouldn't even excite me any more. But if I say this word, 'Siena', out loud, I get the feeling that I might see something there that would make everything all right."

"You're mad, that's the problem."

"Could be. And I'm also hungry. Do you have anything?"

"Mihály, it's awful how much you've been eating ever since we've been in Italy. After all, you just had breakfast."

The train arrived at a station by the name of Terontola.

"I'm going to get out here and have a coffee."

"Don't get out – you're not Italian. The train will leave without you."

"Of course it won't leave –it spends a quarter of an hour at every station. So long, God be with you."

"So long, you monkey. Make sure to write to me."

Mihály got off, ordered the coffee and, while the espresso machine hissed the wonderful, hot beverage out of its innards, drop by drop, he began to converse with a local about the sights of Perugia. Then he drank the coffee.

"Come quickly," said the local. "The train's leaving already."

And indeed, by the time they reached it, half the train was already beyond the platform. He was just barely able to grapple his way onto the last car. This was an old-fashioned, third-class carriage; it had no corridor, and every compartment was a separate world.

"Never mind, I'll run ahead at the next station," he thought.

"Is this your first time visiting Perugia?" asked the friendly local.

"Perugia? I'm not going to Perugia. No, alas."

"Then you must be going on to Ancona. That's a mistake. Get out at Perugia: it's a very ancient city."

"But I'm travelling to Rome," said Mihály.

"To Rome? The gentleman must be joking."

"I must be what?" asked Mihály, thinking he'd misunderstood the Italian term.

"Joking," shouted the Italian. "This train isn't going to Rome. Well well, you're a funny one," he said, using the corresponding Italian expression.

"But why wouldn't this train be going to Rome? I boarded it in Florence with my wife, and it was announced as going to Rome."

"But this isn't that train," said the Italian with delight, as if he was hearing the best joke in his life. "The train to Rome had already left. This is the Perugia-Ancona train. The junction is at Terontola. Splendid! And the lady's calmly travelling towards Rome!"

"Sensational," said Mihály and, bewildered, looked out of the window at Lake Trasimeno, as if a solution might be out there rowing towards him.

When he'd got hold of the cheque and his passport that night, he thought – of course, not entirely seriously – that happenstance might separate them during the journey. When he got off in Terontola, it again crossed his mind that he might leave Erzsi to travel on with the train. But now that it had indeed happened, he was surprised and at a loss. But in any case – it had happened!

"And what will you do now?" the Italian pressed him.

"I'll get off at the next station."

"But this is an express. It won't stop until Perugia."

"Well then, I'll get off at Perugia."

"See, I told you right away that you're travelling to Perugia. Don't worry: it's worth it. A very ancient city. And take a look at the surrounding area too."

"Fine," thought Mihály. "I'm travelling to Perugia. But what will Erzsi do? She'll likely travel on to Rome and wait for the next train there. But it's also possible that she'll get off at the next station. She might return to Terontola. She won't find me there either. It probably won't occur to her that I left on the Perugia train."

Yes, that would be unlikely to occur to her. If he alighted in Perugia now, it was utterly certain that nobody would find him for a day or two. It would take even longer if he didn't remain in Perugia, but travelled on from there on some unlikely route.

"It's lucky I have my passport with me. And my luggage? I'll buy myself some shirts and other necessaries; Italian underwear is good and inexpensive, and I wanted to buy some anyhow. And the money... how are we doing for money, anyway?"

He took out his wallet and found the National Bank cheque, in lire, inside.

"Of course, since last night... I'll cash it in Perugia; there must be a bank in town where they'll accept it. Yes."

He sank back into the corner and slept deeply. The friendly Italian woke him when they arrived in Perugia.

Part Two

THE FUGITIVE

Tyger, tyger, burning bright
In the forests of the night...

WILLIAM BLAKE

1

WITHIN A FEW DAYS, the great Umbrian plain – in one corner of which stood Perugia on its clifftop table, while in the opposite leant glimmering pale Assisi against immense Monte Subasio – burst into bloom. In every direction, blossoming fruit trees – peculiar mulberries with twisted branches, pale Italian-green olive trees and those large purple-flowered trees whose name nobody could tell Mihály – erupted with the season's universal exultation. One could promenade in shirtsleeves during the day; the night-time was still cool, but not uncomfortably so.

Arriving in Assisi on foot from Spello, Mihály went up to the town's highest point, the Rocca, listened to the historical account of a pretty and smart little Italian boy, sat down on a wall of the ancient fortress ruins, gazed for hours at the Umbrian landscape – and was happy.

"Umbria is entirely different from Tuscany," he thought, "more rustic, more ancient, more holy – and just a shade more austere, it seems.

"The land of the Franciscans. Full of hill towns. Back home, people always built in the valleys, beneath the mountains, while here they built on the mountains, above the plain. I wonder what sort of ancient enemies the founders' nervous systems imagined: What sort of terror were they fleeing, constantly upward, into the shelter of steep cliffs? Wherever a hill grew out of the plain, they built a town right away.

"And every place here is a city. Spello, for instance, would be a miserable little village back home – here, on the other hand, it's a proper city with a cathedral and coffeehouse; it's much more of a city than, for example, Szolnok or Hatvan. And without a doubt, a great painter was born in Spello, or they lost a major battle nearby.

"The Italian landscape isn't as merely amiable, merely sweet, as I'd imagined. Not here in Umbria. Here there's something desolate, something dark and rough, like the laurel tree – and it's precisely this rugged side of Italy that's attractive. Maybe the large, bare mountains appeal. I'd never have believed that there would be so many high, bare mountains in Italy. There are still patches of snow on Subasio."

He broke a branch off a tree whose name he didn't know and, adorned with flowers, went down into the little city in good spirits. On the piazza opposite the ancient temple to Minerva, which was the first temple of antiquity that Goethe had seen on his Italian journey, he sat down in front of a small coffeehouse, ordered a vermouth and asked the waitress what they called this tree.

"*Salsifraga*," lisped the young lady after a bit of dithering. "*Salsifraga*," she repeated uncertainly. "At least that's what they call it where I come from, up in Milan. But here, everything has a different name," she added scornfully.

"The hell it's *salsifraga*," thought Mihály. "*Salsifraga* might be stonecrop. Let's say that this is a Judas tree."

But this aside, he felt marvellous. The Umbrian plain coursed with happiness, modest and Franciscan happiness. He felt, as so often in his dreams, that important things didn't happen here but elsewhere, maybe up there in Milan, whence this lisping young lady came in sad exile, or Rome, where Erzsi was now... but now he was also filled with happiness due to the fact that he didn't have to be where important things happen, but entirely elsewhere, in the back of beyond.

Coming to Assisi, he was hoping that he might find Ervin here. After all, in their youth, when Ervin was the hegemon, they'd read everything there was to be read about Assisi's great saint. Ervin surely must have become a Franciscan monk. But he didn't find Ervin, nor could the Franciscan churches evoke his youthful piety – not even Santa

Maria degli Angeli, inside of which stands the Porziuncola, where the saint died. He didn't stay the night here, because he was afraid that the people looking for him might find him in such a touristic centre. He travelled on and reached Spoleto by nightfall.

There he dined, but he didn't find the wine palatable at all; these Italian red wines were susceptible to acquiring a flavour of spirits or an odour of onions at times – God knows why – when at other times, and just as groundlessly, they were so magnificent. His mood worsened even more when, in paying, he realized that, despite all his thrift, the money he had obtained in Perugia would run out eventually, and he had no idea what he'd do then. The outside world, which he'd so happily forgot in Perugia and in the plains, here began to seep back in again.

He took out a cheap room in a cheap *albergo* – there wasn't much choice in this little place anyway – and before supper he set out on a short walk in Spoleto's alleys. Clouds hid the moon, it was dark and the black town's alleys constricted him suffocatingly, not embracing him as the pink byways of Venice had. Somehow he'd wound up in a part of town where the streets became darker and more threatening with each step; the open stairways led to ever more dubious doors; one could no longer see many people; and then he lost his way – and all of a sudden it became certain that someone was following him.

He turned around just as the figure rounded the corner, a very tall figure in dark clothes. An unnameable fear seized Mihály and he suddenly hurried into an alley that was narrower and darker than any until now.

But it was a blind alley; Mihály was forced to retrace his steps, and by that time the stranger was already standing there at the narrow street's entrance. Hesitating, Mihály took a few steps towards him, but when he got a better view of the stranger, he halted in terror. The stranger was wearing a short, black, round cape that had been fashionable in the previous century, and over it a white silk shawl, and on his old, oddly creased, soft, hairless face, some indescribable smile. He held his arms apart a little towards Mihály and in a thin eunuch's voice he piped: "Zacomo!" – or some similar name.

"That's not me," said Mihály, and the stranger realized this too; and he departed amid profuse apologies. Now Mihály was able to see that the indescribable smile on the old man's face was simply that of an idiot.

But the fact that his adventure had been based entirely on an unreasonable fear and had ended fairly comically didn't reassure Mihály; on the contrary, given his bent for seeing symbolism, he drew even from this stupid episode the conclusion that he was being pursued, that people were following his tracks. In a panic, he found the way leading back to his inn, hurried up to his room, locked it and braced the door with a chest. The room remained frightening even in this state. First of all, it was too big for one person, and second, Mihály still could not get comfortable with the fact that in Italy the smaller hotels have stone floors: he felt like he would have in his childhood if they had exiled him to the kitchen, which in any event would have been a horrible punishment – although, to be fair, it would have been unlikely. Third, the room was at the edge of the hill town, and a sheer cliff face dropped down two hundred metres directly beneath his window. And, utterly incomprehensibly, next to the window, a glass door was cut into the wall. At some time it might have led onto a balcony, but the balcony had either been removed in a bygone era, or it had collapsed on its own from dry rot, and now only the door remained, and it opened outward into the vertiginous void. This room would have meant certain death for people inclined to suicide: they wouldn't have been able to resist that door. And to top it all off, only a single picture hung on the huge expanse of wall, some illustration cut out of a picture magazine: an extraordinarily hideous woman, attired in the fashion of the 1900s and holding a revolver in her hand.

Mihály established that he had slept in more reassuring environments before, but even more disquieting than the surroundings was the fact that his passport was downstairs in possession of the simultaneously sullen and shifty-looking proprietor, who hadn't been willing to accept Mihály's clever offer to fill in the registration form himself, since his passport was written in an incomprehensible foreign language. The innkeeper insisted that Mihály's passport remain with him as long as Mihály stayed at the inn. Apparently he'd had bad experiences. Indeed, looking at the inn one could easily imagine that it had given its owner more than his fair share of sinister experiences. Apparently only down-on-their-luck travelling salesmen come this way during the day, thought Mihály, and at night the snickering ghosts of horse thieves play cards in the *sala da pranzo*, the dining room, stinking of the kitchen...

But in whatever fashion and in whoever's hands, his passport was a weapon aimed at himself, potentially revealing his name to his pursuers – although to sneak away leaving his passport behind would be just as uncomfortable as to run away in his underpants, as we do in our dreams. Mihály lay down anxiously in the bed, of dubious cleanliness, and didn't sleep much; sleep, half-sleep and anxious wakefulness merged together into the constant nocturnal feeling that people were on his tail.

He rose before dawn, slipped downstairs and, after a prolonged battle, roused the innkeeper, paid his bill and, retrieving his passport, hurried out to the train station. A sleepy woman brewed coffee for him at the bar, and then, after a while, sleepy Italian labourers arrived. Mihály's anxiety would not cease. He constantly feared that they'd catch him; he was continually suspicious about every person who resembled a soldier or policeman, until at last the train arrived. Breathing a sigh of relief, he prepared to toss his cigarette and board.

Just at this moment a very young and conspicuously handsome little Fascist stepped up to him and asked him not to throw his cigarette away, but to give him a light first.

"*Ecco*," said Mihály, and offered his cigarette. He didn't think anything might go wrong. In any case, the train was already there.

"You're a foreigner," said the little Fascist. "I recognized it from the way you said: *ecco*. I have an ear for it."

"*Bravo*," said Mihály in Italian.

"You're Hungarian!" said the little Fascist, looking up and beaming.

"*Sì, sì*," said Mihály, smiling.

At this instant, the Fascist seized him by the arm with a force that Mihály truly would not have expected from such a small man.

"Oh! You're the man they're looking for all over Italy! *Ecco!* Here's your photograph!" he said, drawing forth a paper with his other hand. "Your wife is looking for you!"

Mihály wrenched his arm free, took out a business card and quickly scrawled on it "I'm fine, don't look for me" and gave it, with a ten-lira note, to the little Fascist.

"*Ecco!* Send this telegram to my wife. *Arrivederci!*"

Again he tore his arm free of the Fascist's hand, which had meanwhile seized it again, leapt onto the moving train and slammed the door behind him.

The little train was going to Norcia, up in the mountains. When he got off, the Sibillini Mountains were already looming before him, with their peaks higher than two thousand metres, and to the right the Gran Sasso, the tallest massif in the Apennines.

Terror had driven Mihály to the peaks, as it once had the city-building Italians. They'd never find him up there in the snowy and icy wilderness. He no longer thought about Erzsi; indeed, he felt that with the telegram, he'd cleverly disengaged Erzsi, as an individual, from himself. But Erzsi was just one among the many, and it wasn't so much people who were hounding him, as institutions and the alarming terrorist hordes of his advancing years.

For what had his life been after all during the preceding fifteen years? At home and abroad, he'd been learning the ropes – not of his own life, but of his family, father and firm, which didn't interest him – and thereafter he'd installed himself in the business and then striven to learn the pleasures that suited a senior partner – learning to play bridge, to ski and to drive automobiles; he'd tried to get involved in the sorts of love affairs appropriate to a senior partner and finally succeeded in finding Erzsi; whereupon, in gentlemanly company, they gossiped as much about him in connection with her as is just fitting for the young senior partner of a distinguished firm; and at last he indeed married her as befits a senior partner, taking for a wife a beautiful, intelligent, wealthy woman who had risen to prominence thanks to their previous relationship. Who knows, maybe only one more year would be needed and he would indeed become a senior partner, and his inner attitudes would harden: one begins as so-and-so who happens to be an engineer, and with the passage of time one becomes the engineer who happens to be called so-and-so.

He set out up the mountains on foot. He wound his way past little upland villages; the inhabitants behaved reassuringly: they didn't pursue him. They accepted him as a mad tourist. But if a member of the bourgeoisie had encountered him on the third or fourth day of his wanderings, he would certainly not have considered him a tourist, just a madman. He no longer shaved and didn't wash up; he didn't undress before going to sleep; he was simply on the run. And everything became confused inside him, here among the rugged contours of the pitiless mountains, in the uninhabited solitude and desolation. Not even the faintest shadow of the thought of a purpose arose in his consciousness: all he knew was that there was no going back. The many individuals and issues hounding him, the years and institutions, all acquired a sort of tangible, monstrous form in his brain: he sensed the paternal firm as a gigantic steel rod lifted to strike, but he was also able somehow to see his own slow ageing, the slow but visible metamorphic processes of his own body, as if his skin were shrinking at the tempo of a clock's minute hand. These were all the early symptoms of a delirium caused by nervous fever.

Doctors later determined that the nervous fever was caused by exhaustion. And it was hardly surprising: after all, Mihály had been exerting himself continuously for fifteen years. He exerted himself to be someone other than he was, never to live according to his own inclinations but as others expected of him. His final and most heroic exertion had been his marriage. And after that, the excitement of travel and the marvellous process of coming undone that the Italian landscape had sparked in him, and the fact that he had been drinking almost continuously during his entire honeymoon and never got enough sleep, all had led to his collapse. And this above all: as long as we keep moving, we don't notice how tired we are, but only when we sit down. Similarly, in Mihály's case, the cumulative exhaustion of fifteen years only began to manifest itself in Terontola when – involuntarily but not unintentionally – he boarded the other train, the train that took him ever farther from Erzsi, towards solitude and into himself.

One evening or another, he arrived at a slightly larger mountain town. By that time, he was already in such an unhinged psychological condition that he didn't even enquire about the town's name, especially since he had noticed around noon that day that he couldn't think of a single word in Italian. Therefore we don't need to take note of the little township's name either. An *albergo* of rather amiable aspect stood on the town's piazza, and he entered and ate supper with exceptionally fine, healthy appetite – gnocchi in tomato sauce, local goat's cheese, oranges and white wine. But when the time came to pay, he thought the innkeeper's daughter was looking at him suspiciously and whispering conspiratorially with the two men who were also sitting in the room. He raced away at once and rambled uneasily on the mountain covered with brushy *macchia** above the town; but he couldn't stay up there, because a strong wind was blowing, so he picked his way down a steep mountainside.

He reached a deep, well-like valley where the wind wasn't blowing, but the ravine was so constricted and dark and bleak that he would not have been at all surprised to come across human bones and, among them, a royal crown or some other bloodstained symbol of ancient distinction and tragedy. He was extraordinarily sensitive to the mood of a landscape even when psychologically sound, and now his sensitivity grew tenfold. He fled the valley at a run, and by this time he was very spent indeed. A narrow path led him up a gentle hill. Arriving at the hilltop, he stopped at the foot of a short wall. It was a friendly, inviting area. Leaping over the wall, he found himself, as far as he could tell by the faint starlight, in a garden where lovely cypresses were growing. A small mound at his feet offered itself as a pillow. He lay down and soon sank into deep sleep.

Later, the light grew much stronger; the stars were burning as brightly as if some unaccustomed disquiet had taken over the heavens, and he awoke. Sitting up, he looked hesitantly around in the stars' frightful glimmer. Tamás stepped out from behind one of the cypresses, pale and in a bad mood.

"I have to go home," he said, "because I can't sleep in this horrible starlight." Then he left, and Mihály wanted to dash after him, but he couldn't stand up, no matter how hard he tried.

He awoke to the cold at the first light of dawn and looked sleepily around the garden. All sorts of grave markers stood beneath the cypresses; he'd been sleeping in the town's cemetery, its *camposanto*! Although this in itself was not necessarily horrible: the cities of the Italian dead are perhaps even friendlier and more inviting than those of the living, both in daylight and in moonlight. But for Mihály, this too had a terrifying symbolic significance. Again he fled at a run, and this is the moment that one might consider his illness to have broken out. Later, he could not recollect what happened to him next.

On the fourth, fifth or possibly sixth day, dusk caught him on a mountain path. The pink and gold shades of the setting sun enchanted him even now, in his fevered state – in fact, perhaps even more so than in his healthy days, because when sober he'd have disapproved of reacting so strongly to the old, familiar and completely pointless colours of the sky. When, however, the sun dropped behind a mountain, he was seized by a feverish fancy and suddenly hoisted himself up a cliff in the belief that atop the peak he might still see the sun for a while. But his clumsy hand gripped the wrong spot and he slipped down into the ditch by the side of the path, and then he hadn't the strength to get up. He remained lying there.

Luckily, towards dawn, itinerant pedlars were passing that way with their mules, saw the man lying there in the moonlight, recognized in him the distinguished foreigner and with tactful sympathy took him down to the village. From there the authorities transported him onwards, with many transfers, to the hospital in Foligno. But he knew nothing of this.

2

When he regained consciousness, he still didn't know a single word of Italian. He asked the nurse in Hungarian, in a tired and frightened voice, the usual questions: where am I; how did I get here? Since the nurse couldn't answer, he figured out by himself – it wasn't very difficult – that he was in a hospital. He also remembered how oddly he'd felt in the mountains, and then he relaxed. The only thing that he was curious about was the nature of his illness. He felt no pain: he was merely very weak and tired.

Luckily the hospital had a doctor who was half English, and they called him to Mihály's bed. Mihály had lived a long time in England, and the English language was in his blood to such an extent that he hadn't forgotten it, and they understood each other well.

"You have no illness," said the doctor, "just some sort of extreme exhaustion. What did you do to tire yourself out so much?"

"I?" asked Mihály thoughtfully. "Nothing. I lived."

And he fell asleep.

He felt much better when he awoke. The English doctor came to visit him again, examined him and informed him that there was nothing the matter with him: he'd be able to get up in a few days.

The doctor found Mihály intriguing and conversed a lot with him. He would have liked to find out what had made him so exhausted. Gradually, he noticed now uneasy Mihály was made by the thought that he'd regain his health in a few days and be discharged from the hospital.

"Do you have some business here in Foligno or the area?"

"Not at all. I didn't even know that Foligno exists."

"Where do you want to go from here? Will you return to Hungary?"

"No, no. I'd like to stay in Italy."

"And what do you want to do here?"

"I haven't the faintest."

"Do you have any relatives or associates?"

"No, I don't have anyone," said Mihály, and he broke down in tears in his weakened nervous state. The tender-hearted doctor took pity on this forlorn man, and from then on he dealt even more affectionately with him. Mihály, however, hadn't cried because he indeed had no one, but, on the contrary, because he had so many people and feared he couldn't much longer protect the solitude he so enjoyed here in the hospital.

He told the doctor that, all his life, he'd longed to lie in a hospital. Not, to be sure, as a critically ill or suffering patient, but just the way he was lying here now, in inert and involuntary fatigue, taken care of, without any goal or desire, far beyond human concerns.

"After all's said and done, Italy is giving me everything I've ever wanted," he said.

It turned out that the doctor loved thinking in historical terms just as much as Mihály. Gradually he spent all his free time at Mihály's bedside in idly rambling conversation. Mihály learnt a great deal about England and Foligno, and about the mystic saint, Foligno's most noted son, of whom even the residents of Foligno generally hadn't heard. And he learnt much about the doctor himself, who had adventure-filled family stories, like every English family. Some time ago, his father had been a naval officer; he contracted yellow fever one time in Singapore, terrible visions tormented him in his illness and, when he recovered, he converted to Catholicism, thinking it the only way to avoid the tortures of hell. His pious family, most of them Anglican priests, disowned him, whereupon the old man became a hater of the English, left the navy, entered the Italian merchant marine and later took an Italian woman for wife. Richard Ellesley – this was the doctor's name – spent his childhood in Italy. His Italian grandfather left them a considerable fortune, and his father had young Ellesley schooled at Harrow and Cambridge. During the Great War the old man rejoined the English Navy and fell in the Battle of Skagerrak;* their fortune dwindled away and, ever since, Ellesley had been earning his daily bread as a physician.

"The only thing I inherited from my father was a fear of hell," he said, smiling.

The roles thus became reversed. Of course, Mihály was afraid of a great many things, but not at all of hell; he had no feeling whatever about the afterlife, so he attempted to cure the doctor. For the need for treatment was urgent: the little English doctor would be seized with terror nearly every third day.

It wasn't a guilty conscience that brought about the fears: his was a pure and benevolent soul, and he couldn't even accuse himself of any sins worth noting.

"Well, then, why do you think you'll end up in hell?"

"Good Lord, I can't tell why I'll end up there. I'm not going there on my own; they're going to take me."

"Satan only has power over evil men."

"You can never tell about that. After all, as the prayer says (you know it too): 'St Michael, the Archangel, defend us in battle. Be our safeguard against the wickedness and snares of Satan. May God rebuke him, we humbly pray; and do you, O Prince of the heavenly host, by the power of God cast into hell Satan and all the evil spirits who wander through the world seeking the ruin of souls.'"

The prayer reminded Mihály of the time he spent in the school's chapel and the adolescent shivers that, back in the day, this prayer had always elicited in him. But it wasn't Satan and damnation that made him shiver, but the grim historicity, reaching back into antiquity, of the prayer – in other respects, the Catholic faith struck him as modern (or as both old and modern); but this prayer alone resembled a remnant of long-buried past ages.

Ellesley, when seized by the terrors of hell, would hurry to the priests and monks to be absolved of his sins. But not even this helped very much. In part because he didn't feel himself to be a sinner, and so forgiveness of sins didn't help him. And in part the problem was that his confessors were, by and large, primitive country priests who never passed up the opportunity to call his attention to the horrors of hell over and over again, thus only aggravating his condition. Amulets and similar magical implements seemed the most likely to help. On one occasion, an old holy woman made him breathe the smoke of some holy herbs, and then he remained calm for two months.

"Well, but what about you?" he asked. "Aren't you afraid at all? So what do you think happens to our souls after death?"

"Nothing."

"And don't you hope for immortality and eternal life?"

"The names of the great remain alive for ever. I'm not great."

"And can you bear life this way?"

"That's a different question."

"I don't understand how you can believe that someone who dies completely ceases to be. After all, there are a thousand proofs of the contrary. Every Italian can recite them to himself, and every Englishman. There is not a single person in these two nations who hasn't encountered the dead, yet these are the two most respectable peoples. I don't know what sort of people the Hungarians are."

"Have you, too, personally encountered the dead before?"

"Of course. More than once."

"How?"

"I won't tell you, because it might get you worked up. But one occasion was so straightforward that it can't possibly disturb you. During the War, I was studying at Harrow. One day I'm lying in my bed – because I had influenza – and staring out the window. Suddenly there's my father, standing on my window sill, wearing his naval uniform and saluting. The only unusual thing was that his officer's cap had two wings. The way they used to portray Mercury. I leapt out of bed and opened the window. But by then he was gone. This happened at noon. My father had died that morning. That's how long it took for his soul to reach Harrow from Skagerrak."

"And the other story?"

"That one's much more mysterious: it happened in Gubbio, and not that long ago either. But I really can't tell you that one now."

"Gubbio? Why's that name so familiar to me now?"

"Without a doubt because of the legend of St Francis, the *Fioretti*."*

"Of course, right, the wolf of Gubbio... with whom St Francis made a bargain, that he wouldn't threaten the town's residents, who in turn would see to his feeding..."

"And one could see the wolf each night, as he went from house to house in Gubbio, a little basket hanging from his neck, collecting the donations."

"And Gubbio still exists?"

"Of course: it's just nearby. Go for a visit, once you've recovered. It's most worthwhile, and not just in memory of the wolf..."

They conversed a great deal. About England too, Doctor Ellesley's other homeland, to which he greatly longed to return. Mihály also loved England dearly. He'd spent two very serious and dream-filled years there, before going on to Paris and then home. He had indulged in an orgy of solitude in London; weeks might pass without him speaking to a soul, except in working-class pubs on the city outskirts, and only a few words with the people there. He loved the terrible London climate, its wet, bloated, foggy softness into which he could sink, such a faithful companion to solitude and spleen.

"November in London isn't even a month," he said, "but a spiritual condition."

Ellesley agreed enthusiastically.

"You see, now it occurs to me," said Mihály, "that once, during a November in London, I too experienced something that would have reinforced the belief, for people such as you, in the dead's continued existence in some form. For me it merely confirmed that I have a problem with my nervous system. Listen. One morning I was working in the factory (in November, as I said), when they called me to the telephone. An unfamiliar female voice asked me to go, without fail, to such and such a place that afternoon on some extraordinarily important business; she gave me an unfamiliar address and name. I objected that there must be some misunderstanding. 'But no,' said the female voice, 'I'm seeking a Hungarian *gentleman* who works as a volunteer in the Boothroyd factory – is there more than one such there?' 'There isn't,' said I, 'and you have my name right. But tell me what this is about.' She couldn't say... We spoke at length, and finally I promised to be there.

"And I went there indeed, because I was curious. Does a man exist who isn't excited by the sound of an unfamiliar and pleasant female voice on the telephone? If women really understood men, they'd always ask them for things on the phone, anonymously. The street – Roland Street – lies in that unpleasant area of London behind Tottenham Court Road, north of Soho, where those artists and prostitutes live whose income doesn't even allow them to live in Soho itself or the Bloomsbury quarter. I'm not sure, but I believe it most likely that this is where the founders of new religions, Gnostics and the more downmarket mediums used to live in London. The entire quarter has an aura of obsolete religions. So this is where I had to go. You should know that I'm unbelievably sensitive to the atmosphere of streets and landscapes. As I went along the dark streets looking for Roland Street in the fog – it wasn't actually a *fog*, merely a *mist*, that sort of white, drizzling, milky fog, a proper November mist – the feeling of déclassé religion seized me so strongly that I almost became seasick.

"Finally I found the house and, on the sign next to the gate, the name given me by the unfamiliar telephonic voice. I rang. The sound of shuffling could be heard after a while, and a sleepy, slovenly maidservant opened the door.

"'What do you want?' she asked.

"'Well, I don't know,' I said, embarrassed.

"Then it seemed as though someone shouted down from a very great distance. The maid became contemplative, and for a while said not a word. Then she led me to a filthy little stairway and said, in the English manner, 'Just go straight ahead.' She herself remained below.

"Upstairs I found an open door and a half-lit room; there was no one in the room; on the contrary, the door opposite had just shut, as if someone had just left the room. Remembering the maid's instruction, I crossed the room and opened the door that had just been shut. Again I entered a half-lit, old-fashioned, dusty and tastelessly furnished room, in which nobody was present, and again the door opposite had seemingly shut an instant earlier, as if someone had just left. Again I crossed the room and entered the third, then the fourth room. In front of me, a door was constantly shutting softly, as if someone were walking in front of me. Finally in the fifth room... incidentally, it's an exaggeration to say 'finally', because there was nobody in the fifth room either, but here at least no door shut in front of me. This room had only one door, the one I'd entered. But whoever had been preceding me was not in the room.

"A light was on in the room, and there was no other furniture but two armchairs. Pictures, tapestries and all sorts of worthless and outmoded furnishings hung on the walls. Irresolutely, I sat down in one of the armchairs and began to wait. Meanwhile I looked around continually in my unease, because it was already clear that some very odd business was afoot.

"I don't know how long I sat this way, when suddenly my heart began to beat wildly, because I found what I'd been constantly, subconsciously looking for. From the moment I'd stepped into the room, I felt I was being watched. And now I found it. A Japanese tapestry was hanging on one wall, depicting dragons and unidentifiable animals, and the animals' eyes were set with coloured-glass spheres. Now I saw that the eyes of one animal weren't made of glass, but real, and they were watching me. Or rather, that someone was standing behind the tapestry and watching me.

"Under any other circumstances, something reminiscent of a detective novel would have come to mind, since one reads so much about foreigners disappearing without a trace in London, and my own story had begun by following precisely the conventions one expects from such stories of disappearances. I tell you, the natural thing would have been for me to get scared, suspect a criminal activity and assume a defensive posture. But this isn't what I did. I remained seated, motionless, benumbed. Because, my good sir, those eyes were familiar to me..."

"How so?"

"Those eyes were the eyes of a friend of my youth, one Tamás Ulpius, who'd died very young and in tragic, though unclear circumstances. After a few moments, my terror indeed passed, and a sort of pale, ghostly joy overtook me, like some spectre of happiness. 'Tamás!' I shouted, and wanted to hurry over to him. But in that instant the eyes disappeared."

"And then?"

"As a matter of fact, that's it. What happened next is completely meaningless. An older lady stepped into the room, an eccentric, old-fashioned, disagreeable woman with large eyes, and she asked me something with a fairly blank expression. I didn't understand it: she wasn't speaking English. I tried French, German and Hungarian, but the lady shook her head sadly. Then she said something in an unfamiliar language, by now with growing liveliness, and continually besieging me with questions. I listened intently so that I might at least determine what language she was speaking. I have a good ear for languages, including those I don't understand: I established that the language the woman was speaking was neither Romance, nor Germanic, nor Slavic, nor even Finno-Ugric, because once, at university, I'd studied Finnish. And then I was suddenly certain that she was the only person on Earth who spoke that language. I have no idea why I thought that. But I became so terrified that I sprang up and ran right through the rooms and out of the house."

"So what's the explanation?" asked Ellesley.

"I can't think of any explanation, other than that it was November. I must have ended up in this house as the result of some weird, random blunder. Our lives are full of meaningless coincidences..."

"And the eyes?"

"Without a doubt, I merely imagined the eyes, under the influence of the strange circumstances and the London November. For I remain steadfastly convinced that the dead are dead."

3

HIS STAY WAS COMING TO AN END. Mihály recovered and had to leave the hospital. A prisoner released after twenty years in captivity might feel as goalless and as disengaged from everything as Mihály did when, with his meagre belongings (for he had no other property than what he'd so thriftily amassed in Perugia on the day of his escape), he made his way among Foligno's low houses.

He felt he couldn't go home. His standing vis-à-vis his family was rendered impossible by his flight, which he neither could nor wanted to explain. Besides, he couldn't bear the thought of going to Pest, entering his office, attending to business dealings and playing bridge and chatting for relaxation.

He ought to tour many more Italian towns: they must surely have many more sights in store for him. He decided to write home and ask for money.

But he kept putting off composing the letter from one day to the next. And in the meantime he remained in Foligno, where lived the only person with whom he had even the faintest connection: Doctor Ellesley. He took a room and lived quietly, reading English novels the doctor loaned him and enjoying his luncheons and suppers. The taste of Italian food was the sole thing binding him to reality during these listless days. He liked the undisguised sentimentality of the Italian kitchen: Franco-European cuisine generally privileged fine, muted and limited flavours – it was as disciplined as the colours of a gentleman's wardrobe. The Italian loves very sweet, very sour and highly characteristic flavours that can put their sentimental stamp even on immense quantities of pasta.

One evening, he was sitting in front of the little town's main coffeehouse with Ellesley. As usual, they were conversing in English. Suddenly a young woman stepped up to their table, addressed them in American-accented English and then sat down with them.

"Please don't be angry at my intrusion," she said, "but I've been wandering round this damned town all day, and I haven't been able to find a single person to whom I can make myself understood. I must ask you for some information. That's why I approached you. It's very important."

"We're at your service."

"You see, I study art history in Cambridge."

"Oh, at Cambridge!" Ellesley cried out happily.

"Yes, in Cambridge, Massachusetts. Why? Could that be where you studied too?"

"No, I was at Cambridge, England. But how may we help you?"

"As I was saying, I'm studying art history, and now I've come to Italy because, as you might also know, there are a great many paintings here that don't exist elsewhere. And indeed, I've seen them all."

Taking a small notebook out, she continued: "I've been to Florence, Rome, Naples, Venice and a whole bunch of places whose names I can't read right now because the lighting's so poor. I was in Per… Perugia most recently. Did I say that right?"

"Yes."

"In the museum there I met a French gentleman. Even though he was French, he was a very polite man. He explained everything beautifully, and then said that I absolutely must go to Foligno, because it has a very famous painting by Leonardo da Vinci – you know, the one who painted the Last Supper. So I came here. And I've been searching for the painting all day, without success. And no one in this disgusting little burg has been able to point me in the right direction. Would you be so kind as to tell me where they've stuck this picture?"

Mihály and the doctor stared at each other.

"A Leonardo? There's never been one in Foligno," said the doctor.

"That's impossible," said the girl, taking offence. "The French gentleman said so. He said that there's a very lovely cow on it, and a goose, and a cat."

Mihály broke out in laughter.

"*My dear lady*, it's very simple: the French gentleman has tricked you. There is no Leonardo painting in Foligno; and though I'm no expert, my sense is that Leonardo never even made a painting containing a cow, a goose and a cat."

"But then why did he say he did?"

"Probably because cynical Europeans like to compare women to these animals. Only European women, of course."

"I don't understand. Surely you don't mean to say that the French gentleman was making fun of me?" she asked, blushing.

"Regrettably, one can put it this way too."

The girl brooded at length. Then she asked Mihály:

"You're not French, are you?"

"No. I'm Hungarian."

The girl waved dismissively: it was all the same to her. Then she turned to Ellesley:

"But you're English?"

"Yes. In part."

"And you are of the same opinion as your friend?"

"Yes," said Ellesley, nodding sadly.

The girl thought it over for another while, and then her hand curled into a fist.

"And I was so friendly towards him! If only I knew the crumb's name at least."

Her eyes overflowed with tears. Ellesley consoled her: "At least no great harm came of it. Now you can record in your notebook that you were in Foligno as well."

"I already have," said the girl, sniffling.

"There you go," said Mihály. "And tomorrow, you'll return to Perugia in fine fettle and continue your studies. I'll accompany you to the train, since I've already made the mistake of boarding the wrong one..."

"That's not the issue. The shame, the shame! To treat a poor, defenceless woman this way! They always warned me not to trust Europeans. But my character is so straightforward. Can you get whisky here?"

And so they sat together until midnight.

The girl's appearance had an uplifting effect on Mihály; he too drank whisky, and he became talkative – although he mainly encouraged the girl to talk. On the other hand, the little doctor became very taciturn, because he had a jealous disposition, and he found the girl rather attractive.

The girl, who was called Millicent Ingram, was astonishing. Astonishing primarily as an art historian. She knew that Luca della Robbia was a town on the Arno's banks, and she insisted that she had visited Watteau in his Paris atelier.* "He's a dear old gentleman," she said, "but his hands are dirty, and I didn't care for the fact that he kissed my neck in the ante-room." And besides this, she spoke about art history constantly, passionately and pompously.

Slowly it emerged that the girl was the child of very wealthy parents in Philadelphia, that back home she enjoyed the status of a most distinguished figure in fine society – or at least that was how she regarded herself – and it appeared that she was taken by some Rousseauist inclination to solitude and nature, which she associated with Europe. She spent semesters in Paris, Vienna and other good places; but nothing at all stuck. She preserved the American, unspoilt nature of her mind.

And yet, when Mihály went home, he hummed to himself in a good mood as he undressed for bed, and his apathy deserted him.

"Millicent," he said. That they should actually call someone Millicent! Millicent.

Millicent Ingram was not the sort of ravishing American beauty to make you weep, the sort one could see in Paris in the post-war years, when everything on this earth besides them was so ugly. Millicent belonged to the reserve team of American beauties. Nevertheless, she was also beautiful, although to call her that might be an exaggeration, because her face was entirely devoid of expression. But in any case she was very good-looking with her tiny nose, her healthy mouth – which was large and painted large – and her outstanding, athletic figure; her muscles seemed as elastic as rubber.

And she was American. After all, she was of the race that had exported all those marvellous beauties to Paris back in the day when Mihály was still young. The idea of the "foreign woman" is also central to youth and the years of wandering. And later, it leaves behind an eternal nostalgia, because in one's years of wandering, one is still clumsy and cowardly and lets the best opportunities slip. By this point, Mihály had already lived in Pest for many years, and his lovers had all been Pest natives. To an extent, foreign women represented his youth. And liberation, after Erzsi, after the serious marriage, after the many serious years. Finally, an adventure, something unexpected that gravitates towards an unexpected conclusion.

He also found Millicent's stupidity attractive. In utter vacuity, just as in death, there is something dizzying and attractive, like a whirlpool. The attraction of the vacuum.

It so happened that the next day, when he accompanied Millicent to the train but before they had purchased her ticket, he said: "Why are you going back to Perugia? Foligno is a town too. Stay here instead."

Millicent gazed at him with her vacantly serious eyes, and responded: "You're right."

And she stayed.

That day was fairly warm; they spent it all eating gelato and conversing. Mihály had the same ability that rendered English diplomats so feared among their colleagues: he could be extraordinarily stupid when the need arose. Millicent didn't notice any difference of intellectual level between the two of them: in fact, thanks to her art-historical expertise, she felt herself at an advantage, and this felt wonderful to her.

"You're the first European who has been able to value me intellectually," she said. "Most Europeans are very dull and lack a sense for artistic beauty."

He won Millicent's complete confidence. By nightfall, he already knew everything about Millicent; but there was nothing worthwhile to know.

That evening, they encountered Ellesley in the coffeehouse. The doctor was startled to find the girl still in Foligno.

"You know, I thought," said Millicent, "you can't occupy yourself with artistic issues constantly. A doctor friend of mine said that constant, intensive thinking is very harmful to your skin. Isn't that so? So I've decided to relax a little bit. I'm giving myself an intellectual break. Your friend has such a calming effect on me. He's such an amiable, simple, harmonious soul. Isn't that so?"

Ellesley took notice with resignation that his patient was courting the American girl, and he became yet more taciturn. For he still found Millicent attractive. She was so different from Italian women. Only the Anglo-Saxon race can be so pure, so innocent. *Millicent – innocent*: what a lovely rhyme it would make, if he were a poet. Ah well, no matter. The main thing was that this amusement, plopped down from the sky, was visibly doing his dear Hungarian patient a world of good.

The following day, Mihály and the girl took a long walk. They stuffed themselves with pasta at a small village inn, then lay down in a small, classical-looking clearing and went to sleep. When they awoke, Millicent said: "There's an Italian painter who paints trees just like these. What do they call him anyway?"

"Botticelli," said Mihály, and kissed her.

"O-o-oh!" said Millicent, terror on her face, and then kissed him back.

Now that he held the girl in his arms, Mihály established with joy that he had not been deceived. Her body was indeed as elastic as rubber. O the body of a foreign woman: what it means to someone who chases fantasies in love, and not physiological facts! Even during their preliminary and truly innocent kissing, he sensed that every least bit of Millicent's body was foreign, different, magnificent. Her healthy mouth was American (O the prairies), her neck with its tiny hairs was foreign, as were the caresses of her strong hands and the transcendental, inconceivable, just-washed cleanliness of her body (O Missouri-Mississippi, North against the South, *and the blue Pacific Sea!...*).

"Geography is the strongest aphrodisiac," he thought to himself.

But that evening a letter was awaiting Millicent at the post office, forwarded from Perugia. It was written by Miss Rebecca Dwarf, professor of medieval art history at the university in Cambridge (Massachusetts), Millicent's advisor and main intellectual mentor. Over supper, Millicent tearfully related that Miss Dwarf was very satisfied with Millicent's last letter, in which she'd given an account of the progress of her studies, but considered it absolutely necessary for her to proceed at once to Siena, to see the famous Siena Primitives.

"Although it was so good to be with you, Mike," she sniffled, putting her hand in Mihály's.

"So you must go to Siena without fail?"

"Of course. If that's what Miss Dwarf writes..."

"The devil take that old beast," Mihály broke out. "Look, Millicent, listen to me. Don't go see the Siena Primitives. The Siena Primitives are likely to be nearly identical to those Umbrian Primitives you saw in Perugia. And besides. Isn't it all the same, whether one sees ten paintings more or ten less?"

Millicent stared at him in astonishment and withdrew her hand.

"But, Mike, how can you say that? I thought you had a feeling for artistic beauty, despite being European."

And she turned away.

Mihály saw that he'd struck the wrong note. He was forced to retreat to the key of stupidity. But he could think of no stupid argument with which he might dissuade Millicent. He tried the sentimental approach.

"But I'd miss you infinitely if you were to leave now. We might never see each other again in this life."

"Certainly," said Millicent, "I'll miss you horribly too. And I've already written to Philadelphia, to Doris and Ann Mary, saying how marvellously you understand me – and now we must part."

"So stay here."

"That's impossible. But you should come to Siena. After all, you don't have any business here anyway."

"That's true. I could leave my work."

"Well then, why don't you come?"

After a fair amount of hemming, Mihály confessed: "Because I have no money."

Which was, in fact, true. His money had almost completely run out at this point. It had gone on the few items of quality clothing he'd purchased the day before, in Millicent's honour, and for Millicent's meals, which were remarkably ample and choice. True, in a couple of days he'd have no money to stay in Foligno either... but after all, you don't feel the lack of money as much when you stay in one place as when you are travelling.

"You have no money?" asked Millicent. "How can that be?"

"It ran out," said Mihály, smiling.

"And won't your parents send more?"

"Of course. They'll send some. Once I write to them."

"There you go, then. And until then, I'll make you a loan" – and she took out her chequebook. "How much do you need? Will five hundred dollars suffice?"

Mihály was dumbstruck by the offer, and dumbstruck by the amount. His every fibre of bourgeois honour and, simultaneously, his every romantic inclination protested against accepting money from his partner in the escapade, this foreign girl who had plopped from the sky and whom he'd kissed for the first time just that day. But Millicent insisted on her offer with enchanting innocence. She said she was always making loans to her friends, male and female. It's the natural thing to do in America. And besides, Mihály would repay her soon. They finally agreed that Mihály would think about it until the morrow.

Mihály would have loved to go to Siena, even aside from Millicent. He was already bored to tears by Foligno, while he longed intensely for Siena, because, now that his apathy had passed, the towns of Italy began again to demand, sweetly and painfully, that he see every one of them and experience their secrets before it was too late. As he had at the beginning of his honeymoon, once again he bore within himself that something that Italy represented, like a very fragile treasure he might drop at any moment. As for Millicent, she was much more desirable since he'd kissed her than she'd been before, and the nature of such an escapade is that one likes to pursue it to its conclusion.

But is it permitted for a grown-up, serious man, the senior partner of a well-known Budapest firm, to take a loan from a young girl? No: it's not allowed for a grown-up, serious senior partner. There can be no doubt. But was that what he still was? Hadn't he perhaps retreated, via his flight and hiding, to an older state, to a lifestyle in which money consisted merely of paper scraps and silver discs? To put it bluntly: hadn't he returned to the ethics of the Ulpius house?

Mihály was horrified by the thought. No, it was not allowed, since even his youthful paradise had foundered on this point, on reality, which they hadn't taken into account, and whose principal manifestation is money.

But it's easy to soothe one's conscience as long as one desires something intensely. After all, it was merely a matter of a very short-term loan, a small amount; he wouldn't even accept five hundred dollars, one hundred would be enough, or let's say two hundred, or maybe, after all, three hundred… He'd write home at once, right away, and he'd repay the money shortly.

And indeed, he sat down and finally wrote the letter. He didn't write to his father, but to his youngest brother, Tivadar. Tivadar was the bon vivant and wastrel of the family; he went to the horse races, and it was rumoured he'd even had an affair with an actress once. He might understand and forgive the matter.

He wrote to Tivadar that – as he assuredly knew already – he and Erzsi had separated, but in a completely amicable way, and that he'd shortly take care of everything as befits a *gentleman*. As to why they separated, he'd tell him later, face to face, as it would be a bit complicated to do so in a letter. He hadn't written until now because he had been confined, seriously ill, here in hospital in Foligno. He was healthy now, but the doctors said that he must still have absolute rest, and he'd like to spend his convalescence here, in Italy. For that, therefore, he must ask Tivadar to send money. And all the sooner and all the more. For his money had already run out, and he'd been forced to borrow three hundred dollars from a local friend and wanted to repay it as soon as possible. Tivadar should send the money straight to the address of his friend, Doctor Richard Ellesley. He hoped all at home were well, and that they'd see each other again soon. He also asked that letters be sent to Ellesley's address in Foligno, because he'd be travelling onward, but didn't yet know exactly where he'd be staying for an extended time.

The next morning, he posted the letter by airmail and hurried to Millicent's hotel.

"You've thought it over and you're coming, isn't it so, Mike?" asked Millicent radiantly.

Mihály nodded yes and, blushing terribly, accepted the cheque. Then he went to the bank, bought a nice suitcase, and they bade Ellesley farewell and departed.

The two of them were alone in the first-class compartment, and they kissed each other as conscientiously as the French. Each of them had retained this manner from their study years in Paris. Later, a distinguished elderly gentleman entered the compartment after all, but they didn't let this bother them, either, enjoying the privileges that come with being barbarian foreigners.

They arrived in Siena that evening.

"A room for the *Signora* and *Signore*?" asked the porter obligingly, at the hotel in front of which their old hansom cab had stopped. Mihály nodded affirmatively. Millicent, for her part, didn't understand what the topic was; it only dawned on her upstairs, but she didn't object.

In any case, Millicent was not nearly as innocent as Doctor Ellesley imagined. Nevertheless, in love she was just as fresh-tasting and quietly marvelling as always. Mihály found it most worthwhile to visit Siena.

4

SIENA WAS THE MOST BEAUTIFUL Italian city of those Mihály had seen so far. It was lovelier than Venice, lovelier than noble Florence and sweet Bologna and its arcades too. Perhaps it helped that he'd come here not with Erzsi, officially, but with Millicent, fortuitously.

The entire city with its steep pink streets undulated haphazardly over its serried hills in the shape of a star; one could also read on the faces of its residents that they were very poor, but very happy, happy in their own inimitable Latin fashion. What gave the town its storybook – happy storybook – character was that from its every point one could spot the Duomo atop the town, seeming to float above it like some comical, zebra-striped, towered Zeppelin.

One of the cathedral's walls stands apart from the bulk of the church, a good two hundred paces away, grotesquely and magnificently, as one of the largest-scale spatial symbols of failed human ambition. Mihály adored the bohemian manner with which these old Italians set about building their cathedrals. "If Florence has one, we need one too; in fact, let it be the biggest one possible," they said, and built the most widespread walls first, to make the Florentines quake at the scale of the Sienese church to be. Then the money ran out, the builders naturally downed tools and didn't cast another glance at the cathedral. "Yes, yes," thought Mihály, "this is how to build a church; if the residents of the Ulpius house had built a church, this is surely how they'd have gone about it too."

Afterwards they descended to the Campo, the city's shell-shaped main square, which was – even judging by its shape alone – like the city's smile. Mihály could scarcely tear himself away, but Millicent insisted: "Miss Dwarf didn't write anything about this," she said, "and it's not even primitive."

In the afternoon, they walked to all of Siena's city gates in sequence, stopped before each gate and Mihály inhaled the view, the constricted sweetness of the Tuscan landscape.

"This is the human landscape," he said to Millicent. "Here, a mountain is just the size that a mountain should be. Everything has its scale here; here everything is of human scale."

Millicent thought it over.

"How do you know what size a mountain has to be?" she asked.

The inscription on one of the gates read: *Cor magis tibi Sena pandit*, "Siena will open your heart wider"... Here, even the gates spoke wisdom and truth: Siena opens your heart wider so it may be filled with life's simple and easy intoxication and desire, as was only appropriate to the season's veiled beauty.

Mihály awoke at dawn the next day, rose and stared out the window. The window looked out of the city towards the mountains. Fine lavender mists swam over the Tuscan land, and the golden light slowly and timidly prepared for the day. And there was nothing at all but this lavender-golden glimmering beneath the distant mountains.

"If this landscape is reality," he thought, "if this beauty really exists, then everything I've done until now is a lie. But this landscape *is* reality."

And he spoke the Rilke poem aloud:

Denn da ist keine Stelle,
*Die dich nicht sieht. Du musst dein Leben ändern.**

Then, alarmed, he turned towards Millicent, who was still sleeping sweetly. And he realized that Millicent had no reality. Millicent was no more than a simile that accidentally comes to mind. And – nothing. Nothing.

Cor magis tibi Sena pandit. All of a sudden, a deadly longing seized him, a longing such as he'd only known when very young, but this was a more reflected, burning longing: for he was longing for the longing he'd known in youth, so sharply that he had to shout.

At this point, he knew that this escapade, this return to his years of wandering, was merely a transition, merely a step on a stairway he'd have to descend still farther, still farther back, into his past, into his own history. The foreign woman remained foreign, just as the years of wandering had been merely time spent in useless vagrancy, but he had to return home, to those who are not foreign. Except that they... were long since dead, and the world's errant winds had swept them to the four corners.

Millicent awoke when she felt Mihály burrowing his head into her shoulder, crying. Sitting up in the bed, she asked in fright: "What's wrong? Mike, for God's sake, what's wrong?"

"Nothing," said Mihály, "I dreamt that I was a little boy and a big dog came and ate my buttered bread."

He embraced Millicent and drew her to him.

That day, they no longer had anything to say to each other. He left the girl to study the Sienese Primitives by herself, and at noon he only gave half an ear to the idiocies that she related about her experiences.

In the afternoon, he didn't even budge from the room but lay, fully clothed, on the bed.

"...My God, what is all civilization worth if we've forgotten what even the most godforsaken Negroes know: to conjure up the dead..."

This was the state in which Millicent found him.

"Do you have a fever?" she asked, and placed her large, lovely hand on his forehead. The touch made Mihály come to his senses a bit.

"Come for a walk, Mike. It's such a lovely evening. And every Italian is out on the streets, and each one has six children with wonderful names like Emerita and Assunta. There are some this tiny, and they already call them Annunziata."

Mihály clambered to his feet with great difficulty, and they went out. Mihály's strides were heavy and uncertain; he saw everything as if through a veil; he heard the sounds of the Italian evening as if through ears full of wax. His legs were heavy as lead. "Where do I know this feeling from?" he wondered.

They got down to the Campo, and Mihály gazed at the Torre della Mangia, the city hall's tower, more than a hundred metres tall, piercing the night sky like a needle. His gaze slowly followed the tower upward into the dizzying heights, and it seemed as though the tower were also growing continually towards the heavens' resounding, dark blue lands.

That's when it happened. There, by the fountain, the earth opened and there was the whirlpool at his feet again. It lasted only an instant before disappearing. Everything was in its place. Once again, the Torre della Mangia was just like a very tall tower. Millicent hadn't noticed a thing.

But that night, when their sated bodies separated and Mihály remained alone in that oppressive solitude a man feels when he'd made love to the sort of woman with whom he has nothing in common, the whirlpool opened again (or did it just come to mind?), and this time it lasted a very long while. He knew that he'd only have to extend his hand to feel the wholesome reality of that other, dear body, but he couldn't extend so much as his hand, and he suffered in isolation, seemingly for hours.

His head ached the next morning, and his eyes burned terribly from sleeplessness.

"I'm ill, Millicent," he said. "I've had a relapse of the condition that had me in bed in Foligno."

"What sort of illness do you have?" asked Millicent uncertainly.

"One can't be certain. A sort of sporadic cataleptic-apocalyptic thing," he jabbered.

"Oh, that."

"I have to return to Foligno, to the good Doctor Ellesley. Maybe he can do something. And I know him after all. What will become of you, Millicent?"

"Well, I'll come with you too, naturally, if you're sick. I wouldn't dream of leaving you alone. Besides which, I've already looked at every Sienese Primitive."

Touched, Mihály kissed her hands. They were already in Foligno by late afternoon.

They took separate rooms, at Mihály's initiative. After all, he said, Ellesley doesn't need to know.

Ellesley came to see Mihály towards evening. He listened to Mihály's symptoms, and just hemmed and hawed about the whirlpool sensation. "A type of agoraphobia. Rest, for the time being. Then we'll see."

Mihály spent days in bed. The whirlpool sensation indeed didn't return, but he had no desire at all to rise. He felt that if he did, the whirlpool would seize him again. He slept as much as possible. He took every tranquillizer and mild sleeping aid that Ellesley brought. When he slept, he succeeded in dreaming about Tamás and Éva.

"I know what's wrong with me," he said to Ellesley. "I have acute nostalgia. I want to be young. Is there a cure for that?"

"Hmm," said Ellesley. "There certainly is, but one mustn't speak of it. Think of Faust. Don't long to be young again: God grants us adulthood and old age too."

Millicent visited him diligently, but was bored. Ellesley popped in towards evening, and they left together.

"Tell me honestly," said Ellesley when he was sitting alone by Mihály's bed one day, "tell me honestly: do you have someone dear who's deceased?"

"Why, yes."

"Have you been thinking a lot about that person lately?"

"Yes."

From this point on, Ellesley's methods corresponded ever less to the rules of medical science. Once he brought a Bible with himself, once a rosary, once a Virgin Mary of Lourdes. On one occasion, Mihály noticed that, while he was chatting with Millicent, Ellesley drew a cross on the door. And one fine day he entered with a garland of onions.

"Place this round your neck before you go to sleep. The scent of onions strengthens the nerves."

Mihály broke out in laughter.

"Doctor, I've read *Dracula* too. I know what the onion garland is for. To repel the vampire who sucks one's blood at night."

"Just so. I'm glad that you know. You refuse to believe that the dead continue to exist, but it's no use. You're sick because of your dead. They come to visit and draw off your life force. Medical science is of no use here."

"In that case, take the onion garland home. You can't repel my dead this way. They're inside me."

"Naturally. These days, even the dead use psychological tactics. But that doesn't change their essence one bit. You just have to defend yourself against your dead."

"Leave me in peace," said Mihály, mildly irritated. "Say that I've got poor circulation in the brain, and prescribe Chinese *vinum ferri** and bromide for my nerves. That's your business."

"Of course it is. There's nothing more I can do. Medical science is helpless against the dead. But there are more powerful, supernatural means…"

"You know I'm not superstitious. Superstition only helps those who believe in it."

"That viewpoint is long obsolete. Besides which, why not try it? You're not risking anything."

"Of course I am. My sense of self, my self-respect and my self-awareness as a rational being."

"Those are long and meaningless words. You have to try it. You have to go over to Gubbio: a miracle-working monk lives there, up in the Sant'Ubaldo cloister."

"Gubbio? You've already spoken to me about that place once. If I remember correctly, you said that something very eerie happened to you there."

"Yes. And now I'll tell you, because maybe this story will convince you. And in any case, it involves this very monk."

"Let's hear it."

"You know, the thing was that I was the town doctor in Gubbio before I came here to the hospital. One time they called me to a patient who, it seems, suffered from a severe nervous disease. The individual lived in the Via dei Consoli, in this utterly medieval street, in a dark, old house. She was a young woman, not a Gubbio native, not even Italian; I don't even know what nationality she might have been, but she spoke good English. She was very beautiful. The house residents said that the woman, who lived there as a paying guest, had been suffering hallucinations for some time. Her *idée fixe* was that the gate of the dead wasn't locked at night."

"What?"

"The gate of the dead. You should know that in Gubbio, these medieval houses have two gates. An ordinary gate for use by the living and, next to it, a second, narrower one for the dead. They only open this gate when they carry the deceased out in a coffin. Then they wall the gate up again so that the dead can't return. According to them, the dead can only re-enter where they'd left. This gate isn't even at street level, but about a metre higher, so that they can pass the coffin out to people standing in the street. The lady of whom I speak lived in such a house. One night, she awoke to the noise of the gate of the dead opening, and someone entering: someone she had loved very much, and who had long since died. And from that time on, the dead came to visit every night."

"Well, it would've been easy to help in this case. The lady should simply have moved out."

"That's what we said too, but she didn't want to leave. She was very glad that the deceased visited her. She just lay abed all day, like you, and waited for nightfall. Meanwhile she wasted away rapidly, and the house residents were terribly concerned for her. Nor were they glad that a dead man was visiting the house every night. It was a patrician family of exceedingly strict morals. As a matter of fact, the reason they called for me was to use my status as a doctor to convince the lady to move out."

"And what did you do?"

"I tried to explain to the lady that she was experiencing hallucinations and she needed to seek a cure; but she just laughed me off. 'How could they be hallucinations?' she said. 'He's here every night, as truly and indisputably as you are here now. If you don't believe me, stay here for a night.'"

"The issue wasn't entirely my cup of tea, perhaps because I'm a bit too susceptible to things of such nature; nevertheless, I had to remain there out of my duty as a physician. As it happened, the waiting wasn't uncomfortable at all; the woman was neither terrified nor ecstatic, but amazingly sober; in fact, without wanting to boast about it, I can aver that she behaved flirtatiously towards me... Indeed, I even forgot why I was there, and that midnight was approaching. Before midnight, all of a sudden she took me by the hand, took up a candle in her other hand and led me to the ground-floor room into which the gate of the dead opened."

"I have to admit that I didn't see the dead man. But that was my mistake: I didn't dare await his arrival. I just felt it become extremely cold, and the candle's flame fluttered in the draught. And I sensed – somehow felt it in my entire body – that there was someone else in the room. And I'll be candid, this was more than I could bear. I rushed out of the room, raced back home, locked the door and pulled the duvet over my head. Of course, you'll say that I fell under the influence of the lady's suggestion. Perhaps..."

"And what happened to the lady?"

"Oh, that's just what I want to tell you. When they saw that a doctor, or at least, the sort of doctor I am, was no help, they called for Pater Severinus from the Sant'Ubaldo cloister.* This Pater Severinus is a most unusual and holy man. He wound up in Gubbio from some distant country – nobody knows where. One didn't much see him in town, just on major feast days or funerals; otherwise, he didn't come down from the mountain, where he lived a life of strict self-denial. Now they succeeded somehow in convincing this Pater Severinus to come down and visit the sick lady. Their encounter, so they say, was most harrowing and dramatic. As soon as she saw Pater Severinus, the lady screamed mightily and collapsed. For his part, Pater Severinus went pale and staggered. It seems that he felt just how difficult the matter was. But then he succeeded, nevertheless."

"How?"

"That, I don't know. It seems that he exorcised the ghost. After he had spoken to the lady for an hour in some unknown tongue, he returned to the mountain; for her part, the lady calmed down and left Gubbio, and no one has seen either her or the ghost ever since."

"Interesting. But tell me," asked Mihály, seized by a sudden suspicion, "this Pater Severinus, did he truly arrive from some foreign country? And that you really don't know where?"

"Unfortunately, I don't. Nor does anyone else."

"What sort of man is he – I mean his external appearance?"

"Fairly tall, gaunt... the way monks used to be."

"And he's still up there in that cloister?"

"Yes. He's the one you ought to seek out. He's the only one who can help with your problem."

Mihály pondered the matter deeply. Life is full of unmotivated coincidences. What if this Pater Severinus were indeed Ervin, and the lady were Éva, haunted by the memory of Tamás...

"You know what, Doctor, I'll go to Gubbio tomorrow. Just to please you, because you're such a dear man. And as an amateur historian of religion, I'm curious about the gate of the dead."

Ellesley rejoiced at this result.

The next day, Mihály packed his belongings. To the visiting Millicent, he said:

"I have to go away to Gubbio. The doctor says that that's the only place I can be cured."

"Really? I'm afraid that in that case, we have to say goodbye. I'm going to stay here in Foligno for a while. I've fallen in love with this town. And remember how furious I was initially at that Frenchman who tricked me into coming here? But I no longer mind. The doctor is also a very nice man."

"Millicent, unfortunately I still owe you. I'm infinitely ashamed, but you know, in our country, the National Bank handles all foreign-currency transfers, and it's a very complicated mechanism. I beg you to be a bit indulgent. By now the money should really be here within days."

"Not even worth mentioning. And if you see some beautiful painting, write me about it."

5

TO REACH GUBBIO, one must take a narrow-gauge railway that shuttles between Fossato di Vico and Arezzo. The journey is decidedly long despite the short distance and, furthermore, it was hot, and Mihály was deeply fatigued by the time he arrived. But the moment the town appeared before him on the short uphill route from the station, it thrilled him instantly.

The town draws itself up against the side of an enormous, barren, typically Italian mountain as if it had collapsed while fleeing uphill in terror. Immediately at first glance, one can tell that there's not a house in it less than many centuries old.

In the centre of the streets twisting this way and that towers an unbelievably tall building: a building of which one cannot fathom who would have built it in the middle of this godforsaken, remote place, and why. It's an immense and melancholy medieval skyscraper. This is the Palazzo dei Consoli; from here the consuls administered the small city-state of Gubbio up until the fifteenth century, when the town fell under the ownership of the princes of Urbino, the Montefeltri. And above the town, almost at the tip of Monte Ingino, lies a great, expansive white block of buildings, the cloister of Sant'Ubaldo.

Down below, on the road leading from the train station into town, is a small *albergo* of better-than-average appearance. Mihály took a room here, dined, rested a bit, and then set out to discover Gubbio. He looked at the interior of the Palazzo dei Consoli, reminiscent of a gigantic, gaping artist's studio, and in it the ancient copper tablets of Iguvium that still remained from pre-Roman times and preserved the sacred texts of the Umbrii. He also took a look at the old cathedral. There wasn't much else to see, in fact; here the town itself was the attraction.

Most of the Italian towns in this region evoke the impression that their buildings are in the process of disintegrating: just a few more years, and annihilation will swallow them, as it has so many other ancient cities. This is because where the Italians build with rough quarry stone, they don't plaster the walls and, on seeing it, a Central European thinks that the plaster has peeled off the entire house, or the entire town, and they've abandoned it as it is, to perish in utter desolation. Gubbio is much more unplastered, much more crumbling than the other Italian towns: Gubbio is indeed desolate. It falls by the touristic wayside; it has hardly any industry or commerce; how the couple of thousand people squeezed within its walls make their living is a mystery.

Leaving the cathedral, Mihály turned onto the Via dei Consoli. "This is the street Ellesley was referring to," he thought. One could indeed believe any number of things about this street. In its blackened, ancient, bleak, medieval houses with their air of down-at-heel respectability, one imagines residents who've been living on the memories of their glorious past for centuries already, subsisting on bread and water...

And indeed, right at the third house, there was a gate of the dead. Next to the proper gate and a metre above ground level was a narrow, walled-in gothic gateway. Nearly every house on Via dei Consoli had one; there was nothing else at all on the entire street; in particular, there were no people.

He went down a narrow alley onto the parallel street, which was no less ancient, merely somewhat less grim in its distinction: as if there were still living beings residing there after all. And, it seems, dead ones too. For in front of one of the houses a startling group of people appeared before his eyes. If he hadn't known instantly what it was all about, he'd certainly have thought he was seeing things.

Men, their faces hidden by cowls and candles in their hands, were standing in front of the house. It was a funeral, and here, still following the ancient rites, cowled members of the *confraternita* were taking out the dead.

Mihály removed his hat and went over to get a closer look at the rite. The gate of the dead was open. One could see into the house, into a dark chamber in which stood the catafalque. Priests and acolytes stood with censers around the coffin, singing. Soon they raised the coffin and passed it through the gate of the dead to the street, where the cowled men hoisted it onto their shoulders.

Now the surpliced priest appeared in the Gothic gateway. He tilted his pale face, the colour of ivory, with its sad and unseeing gaze, towards the sky, turned his head to one side and, with an inexpressibly endearing gesture, reminiscent of ancient ways, he put his hands together.

Mihály didn't race over to him. After all, he was a priest now, a serious and pale monk, in the middle of performing his ecclesiastical function… no, he couldn't race over to him like a high-school student, like a boy…

The procession set into motion with the coffin, trailed by the priest and the mourners. Mihály also took a place at the rear and, hat in hand, he proceeded to the distant *camposanto*, up the mountainside. His heart was pounding so strongly that he had to stop from time to time. Could they still talk to each other after so many years of following such divergent paths?

He asked one of the men in the procession what the priest was called.

"That's Pater Severinus," said the Italian. "He's a very holy man."

They reached the *camposanto*; they lowered the coffin into its grave; the funeral reached its conclusion and the people dispersed. Pater Severinus, with his companion, headed for town.

Mihály still couldn't bring himself to go over to him. He felt that Ervin, who'd become such a saintly man, must certainly be ashamed of his worldly youth, recalling it with noble disgust, like St Augustine.* He must certainly have re-evaluated everything, and perhaps he had even expunged Mihály from his memory. Maybe it would be better if he just left immediately, satisfied with the miracle of having seen Ervin.

This is when Pater Severinus left his companion and turned around. He headed straight for him. All his adulthood sloughed off Mihály, and he ran to Ervin.

"Mischi!" shouted Ervin, and embraced him. Then he held his right cheek, followed by his left, to Mihály's, with priestly tenderness.

"I'd already seen you at the gravesite," he said softly. "What brings you here, where not even the birds go?"

But he only enquired to be polite: his tone revealed that he wasn't a bit surprised. Rather, he seemed like someone who'd been expecting this encounter long since.

Mihály couldn't say a single word. He just gazed at Ervin's face, how long and thin it had become, and his eyes, in which the youthful fire had burnt itself out, and from which the same deep sorrow looked out from behind the momentary joy as the sorrow that shone from Gubbio's houses. Until now, "monk" had only been a word to Mihály, but now he understood that Ervin was a monk indeed, and his eyes brimmed with tears. He turned his face away.

"Don't cry," said Ervin. "You too have changed since then. Oh, how much I've thought about you, Mischi, Mischi!"

Mihály was seized by a sudden impatience. He must tell Ervin everything, everything, even things he hadn't been able to tell Erzsi... Ervin would know of a balm for everything, since this halo, this radiance was descending on him from another world entirely...

"I knew you must be here in Gubbio – that's why I came. Tell me, when and where could I speak with you? Could you come to my *albergo* right now? Could we have supper together?"

Mihály's naivety made Ervin break into a smile.

"That's not possible. And even now, at this moment, I unfortunately don't have any time, my dear Mihály. I have non-stop commitments until night-time. I really need to hurry off immediately."

"What, you have that much work to do?"

"Heaps. You people can't even imagine. I'm behind on a whole bunch of prayers today."

"In that case, when will you have the time, and where can we meet?"

"There's only one way, Mischi, but I'm afraid that you'll find it most uncomfortable."

"Ervin! How can you think that something would be uncomfortable for me if it means that I can talk with you?"

"Because you'd have to come up to the cloister. We are not permitted to leave, except for pastoral duties, for example the way I just came out for this burial. And up in the cloister, every single hour comes with its strict duties. There's only one way for us to converse without interruption. You know, we go to church at midnight to chant the evening office. We usually go to bed at nine and sleep until midnight. But this sleep is not mandatory. Our *regula* doesn't govern this period, nor is silence enforced. This is the time when we could speak with each other. The wisest course is for you to drop by the cloister after dinner. Come as a pilgrim: we receive pilgrims as guests. Bring some small gift for St Ubaldo, and for the benefit of the brothers too. A few candles, perhaps: that's the usual custom. And ask the gatekeeper brother to give you a place in the pilgrims' hall for the night. Well, you know, it's not very comfortable – that is, by your standards – but I can't offer anything else. I wouldn't want you to leave at midnight and return to town: you need to know the mountain well for that. It's a very unfriendly region for those who don't know it. Hire a boy to show you the way up. Will that do?"

"It'll be fine, Ervin; it will be splendid."

"Well then, God be with you until then. I must hurry – I'm already late. I'll see you this evening. God be with you."

And he left with very rapid strides.

Mihály strolled down into town. He found a shop next door to the cathedral and bought a few lovely candles for St Ubaldo, then went to his hotel, had supper and tried to figure out what gear he should take with himself as a pilgrim. At last he made a clever little pack of the candles, his pyjamas and his toothbrush; if one were being generous, it might even be regarded as a pilgrim's backpack. Then he commissioned the waiter to find a guide for him. The waiter returned promptly with a youngster, and they set off.

On the road, Mihály enquired about the local notables. He asked what happened to the wolf that St Francis of Assisi had tamed and that had struck a bargain with the town.

"That must have been a long time ago," mused the boy. "Even before Mussolini. Because there haven't been any wolves since he's been the *Duce*." But he dimly recalled having heard that the wolf's head was buried in one of the more distant churches.

"Do pilgrims go up to the cloister often?"

"Of course, very often. St Ubaldo is highly effective against chronic knee and back pain. Does the gentleman's back ache too, perhaps?"

"Not my back, so much…"

"But he's also very good against anaemia and nervous complaints. A lot of people come here on 16th May, which is St Ubaldo's Day. Then they carry the *ceri*, the wax figures, from the cathedral down below up to the cloister in a procession. But it's not the same sort of procession as Easter or Corpus Christi. The *ceri* have to be transported at a run…"

"What do the *ceri* depict?"

"Nobody knows. They're very old."

The former historian of religion in Mihály was resurrected. He must enquire about the *ceri*. "Most interesting, that they carry them up to the cloister at a run… like the bacchantes who raced up the mountain during the festival of Dionysus in Thrace. This Gubbio is miraculously ancient: the copper tablets of the Umbrii, the gates of the dead… And, maybe, that wolf tamed by St Francis had been some ancient Italian deity, a relative of Romulus and Remus's wolf-mother, who lives on in this way in the legend. How odd for Ervin to have arrived precisely here…"

After an hour of strenuous clambering up the mountain, they reached the cloister. A strong stone wall surrounded the buildings; the small gate cut into the wall was locked. They rang. After a long time, a small window opened in the gate and a bearded monk looked out. The helpful lad explained that the gentleman was a pilgrim who wanted to see St Ubaldo. The gate opened. Mihály paid his guide and stepped into the cloister's forecourt.

The gatekeeping brother looked Mihály's attire up and down in surprise.

"Is the gentleman a foreigner?"

"Yes."

"That is not a problem: there is a pater here who's a foreigner himself and speaks foreign languages. I'll let him know."

He led Mihály into one of the buildings where some light was still glimmering. After a few minutes, Ervin arrived, no longer in a surplice but in the brown habit of the Franciscans. Only now did it strike Mihály how very Franciscan Ervin was. The tonsure gave his face a completely different character: it was enough by itself to eradicate every trace of worldliness on his face, everything of this world, and elevate it into the atmosphere of the Giottos and Fra Angelicos – and yet, Mihály felt that this was Ervin's true face: he'd been preparing for this face from the beginning, the tonsure had always been there on his head – except that back then it had been concealed by Ervin's curly black hair… No doubt Ervin had found himself, no matter how frightful it appeared. And before he even noticed, he was addressing Ervin the way he'd become accustomed to address ecclesiastical figures at school: "*Laudetur Jesus Christus.*"

"*In Æternum*,"* said Ervin. "So you found the way up here, where not even birds go? Come, I'll take you to the reception room. I'm not allowed to receive guests in my cell. We adhere very strictly to the rule of seclusion."

He lit a torch and led Mihály through enormous, whitewashed and utterly empty halls, corridors and small rooms, where not a soul passed by, and only their footsteps echoed.

"Say, how many of you live in this cloister?" asked Mihály.

"Six of us. We have plenty of room, as you can see."

It was most eerie. Six men in a house that could comfortably accommodate two hundred. And where at one time, there assuredly had been that many.

"Aren't you ever afraid here?"

Ervin smiled and didn't answer the childish question.

In this way they arrived in the reception room, a vaulted, gigantic, empty hall, in one corner of which stood a table and a few rickety wooden chairs. On the table, red wine in a pitcher and a single glass.

"Thanks to the benevolence of the Pater Prior, I am in the fortunate position to be able to offer you a bit of wine," said Ervin. Mihály was suddenly struck by the slight peculiarity of Ervin's speech. After all, he hadn't spoken Hungarian for so many years already... "I'll pour some right away. It will feel good after your long journey."

"And you?"

"Oh, I don't drink. Ever since I joined the order..."

"Ervin... can it be that you no longer even smoke?"

"No."

Mihály's eyes filled with tears again. No, he couldn't imagine this. He was willing to believe anything about Ervin. "Of course he wears a nail-studded hair shirt under his habit, and before he dies, he'll receive the stigmata – but that he doesn't smoke!..."

"I had to give up much more important things too," said Ervin, "so I didn't even notice this sacrifice. But go ahead and drink, and light up."

Mihály downed a glass of red wine. People have great illusions about their friends' wines, that they preserve them in spider-web-shrouded bottles in honour of rare guests. Well, this wasn't that. It was an ordinary, but very pure village wine, and its flavour accorded splendidly with the simplicity of the white empty rooms.

"I don't know whether it's a good wine," said Ervin. "We have no cellar. We're a mendicant order, and one must understand that in fairly literal terms. Well then, now tell me about yourself."

"Look, Ervin, between our two lives, yours is by far the more extraordinary. My curiosity is understandably greater than yours. You must go first..."

"What do I have to tell, my dear Mischi? We have no biography. The story of one of us is exactly the same as another's, and the whole thing blends into the history of the Church."

"But do tell me: how did you end up in Gubbio?"

"First I was back home in Hungary; that's where I was a novice, in Gyöngyös, and then I was in the monastery in Eger for a long time. Then the Hungarian province had to send a pater to Rome on some business and, well, they sent me, because I'd learnt Italian by then. After I took care of that matter, they called me to Rome again because they'd become very fond of me there, although I really didn't deserve it, and they wanted to keep me there at the Minister General's side. But I was afraid that this would eventually lead me... into a career – of course only in the Franciscan meaning of the word – to become the father superior somewhere, or to obtain some rank by the General's side, and I didn't want that. I asked the Father General to assign me here, to Gubbio."

"But why precisely here?"

"I can't even explain it. Perhaps because of the old legend, the legend of the wolf of Gubbio that we loved so much in our student days, remember? Once I came here from Assisi because of the legend, and this cloister pleased me very much. You know, this is the sort of place where even the birds don't go..."

"And do you feel good here?"

"Good. As the years pass, my inner peace keeps growing… but I don't want to 'preach'" (and with a peculiar, thin smile, he put this word in quotation marks) "because I know that you came to see not Pater Severinus but the person who once was Ervin: isn't that right?"

"I myself don't know… tell me… it's so hard to ask these sort of things… isn't it very monotonous here?"

"Not monotonous at all. Our lives contain joy and remorse just like lives outside, except that the scale is different and the emphasis is elsewhere."

"Why don't you want to pursue a monastic career? Out of humility?"

"That's not why. The ranks I could attain are reconcilable with humility, all the more so because they would provide one with opportunities to conquer one's pride. I avoided a career for an entirely different reason. Because my promotions could not be thanks to my being a good monk, but thanks to those characteristics I brought with myself from my previous worldly life – indeed, from my ancestors. My facility with languages and the fact that I can sometimes formulate certain things faster and better than some of my brethren. In other words, my Jewish characteristics. And I didn't want that."

"Tell me, Ervin, how do your fellow monks regard the fact that you were a Jew? Isn't that to your disadvantage?"

"No, on the contrary, it's entirely to my advantage. Because I've encountered individual fellow monks who made me aware of how averse they are to my race, and in this way they offered me the opportunity to practise mildness and self-abnegation. And in Hungary, furthermore, when I spent time on pastoral duties in the villages, somehow word always got around about this issue, and the upstanding village faithful regarded me like some queer fish – and so they'd listen to me with even greater attention. As for Italy, here nobody even bothers about it. Here even I hardly ever recall that I was once a Jew."

"Tell me, Ervin... what do you actually do all day? What work do you have to do?"

"A great deal. Mainly prayers and spiritual exercises."

"Don't you do any writing any more?"

Ervin broke into a smile once again.

"No, not for a very long time now. You see, it's true that when I entered the order, I imagined that I'd serve the Church with my pen, becoming a Catholic poet... but then..."

"Well? Did inspiration abandon you?"

"Not at all. I abandoned inspiration. I came to realize that it too is utterly superfluous."

Mihály reflected on that. Now he began truly to understand what worlds separated Pater Severinus from the person who used to be Ervin.

"How long have you been here in Gubbio?" he asked at last.

"Wait a moment... six years, I think. But it could be seven."

"Tell me, Ervin – I've pondered this question a lot, whenever you came to mind – do you also sense the passage of time, and the perception that every little instant is a separate reality? Do you and your brethren have a sense of chronology? If some event occurs to you, can you say whether it happened in 1932 or 1933?"

"No. Among the mercies pertaining to our condition is the fact that God has lifted us out of time."

Then Ervin began to cough violently. Only at this moment did it dawn on Mihály that Ervin had already been coughing earlier – a dry, nasty cough.

"Say, Ervin, isn't there something wrong with your lungs?"

"Well, my lungs are indeed not entirely sound... in fact, one might say that they're in very bad shape. You know, we Hungarians are spoilt. They heat the houses so well in Hungary. Yes, indeed, these Italian winters have worn me down, being constantly in unheated cells and cold churches... and walking the stone floors in sandals... and this habit doesn't keep me very warm either."

"Ervin, you're sick… and don't they treat you?"

"You're such a good man, Mihály, but you really needn't feel sorry for me," said Ervin, coughing. "You see, my sickness is also nothing but a blessing for me. It's why they accepted my departure from Rome and let me come here to Gubbio, where the air is so healthy. Perhaps I'll even get well. And then, bodily suffering belongs to the order of our lives. Others have to scourge their bodies, while my body takes care to scourge itself… But enough of this. You came here to talk about yourself, so let's not waste precious time on something that neither you nor I can do anything about."

"But Ervin, that's not the case… you've got to live differently, go away somewhere where they'll care for you and make you drink milk and lie in the sun."

"Don't worry about me, Mihály. Perhaps that will happen in due course. We too must defend ourselves against death, because if we just let sickness attain dominion over us it would be a form of suicide. When the problem gets serious, the doctor will come see me too… but we're still far from that, believe me. And now tell me about yourself. Tell me everything that's happened to you since I saw you last. And first of all, tell me how you found me."

"János Szepetneki said that you were somewhere in Umbria, but he didn't know exactly where either. And it was thanks to peculiar coincidences and events seeming to point the way that I guessed you were in Gubbio, and that you were the famed Pater Severinus."

"Yes, I'm Pater Severinus. And now tell me about yourself. I'm listening."

He placed his head in his palm in the classical attitude of the confessor, and Mihály began to talk: haltingly and reluctantly at first, but Ervin's queries were astonishingly helpful. He can't help it, thought Mihály to himself, it's his long experience in the confessional. Mihály couldn't resist the confessions that strove to erupt from him. As he talked, everything that he'd sensed instinctively since his flight came to the surface: how much of a failure he felt his adult – or mock-adult – life and marriage had been; how he had no idea what to do next and what to expect from his future; and how he might recover his true self. And mainly, how much he suffered from his nostalgia for his youth and the friends from his youth.

When he reached this topic, he was overcome by intense emotion, and his voice choked into silence. He felt sorry for himself, but at the same time he was ashamed of his sentimentality before Ervin, before Ervin's mountaintop serenity. Then, all of a sudden, he asked in astonishment:

"And you? Well, how do you stand it? Doesn't it hurt? Don't you miss it? How did you do it?"

That thin smile appeared once again on Ervin's face; then he bowed his head and did not reply.

"Answer me, Ervin, I beg you to answer: don't you miss it?"

"No," he said in a colourless tone, his face clouded, "I no longer miss anything at all."

They were silent for a very long time. Mihály tried to understand Ervin. "There's no other way, he must have exterminated everything from inside. Since he had to tear himself away from everyone, he even dug the roots out of his soul, the roots from which the feelings binding one to another might sprout. It no longer hurt, but he remains here, fallow, infertile, barren, on the mountain..." He shivered.

Then something suddenly occurred to him:

"I heard a legend about you... that you exorcised a woman who saw the dead here, in one of the palaces on the Via dei Consoli. Tell me, Ervin: am I right that the woman was Éva?"

Ervin nodded.

Mihály sprang up in excitement and downed the remaining red wine.

"Oh, Ervin... tell me... how was it... and what was Éva like?"

What was Éva like? Ervin thought it over. "Well, what should she be like? She was very beautiful. The same as ever..."

"How? Hadn't she changed?"

"No. Or at least, I didn't notice any change in her."

"And what's Éva doing now?"

"I don't really know that either. All she said was that she was doing well and travelling all over the western nations."

Had something perhaps still flared up in Ervin when they met? But he didn't dare ask that question.

"Don't you know where she is now?"

"How should I know? It's been a few years, I think, since she was here in Gubbio. Although, as I said, my sense of time is highly unreliable."

"And tell me... if you can... how was it... how did you send the dead Tamás away?"

Mihály's voice betrayed the terror that seized him when he thought about it. Again, Ervin broke into that thin smile.

"It wasn't hard. It's that building that made Éva see ghosts: the gate of the dead has undone others before. All I had to do was convince her to leave. And besides, I think she played the whole thing up a bit too: after all, you knew her... I'm afraid she never even saw Tamás, nor had visions, although it's possible that she did. I don't know. You know, I've had so many visions to address, and so many spirits over the years, especially here in Gubbio, the city with its gates of the dead, that I've become relatively sceptical on this matter..."

"Nevertheless... how did you cure Éva?"

"I didn't. As is generally the case in such situations. I spoke to her seriously, I prayed a bit, and she calmed down. She came to understand that the living belong among the living."

"Are you sure about that, Ervin?"

"Absolutely sure," said Ervin with great seriousness. "If one doesn't choose the path I did. Otherwise, among the living. But why am I preaching to you? After all, you know it yourself."

"Did she say nothing about how Tamás died?"

Ervin said nothing.

"Tell me: could you exorcise me of the memory of Tamás and Éva and all of you?"

Ervin thought about it.

"It's very difficult. Very difficult. And I don't even know if it's a good idea, because what would remain for you afterwards? It's very hard to say anything at all to you, Mihály. Pilgrims as desperate and as impossible to advise as you rarely come to Sant'Ubaldo. And in any case, you wouldn't accept what I might advise – what it's my duty to advise. The storehouse of grace only opens to those who seek grace."

"Then, nonetheless, what will become of me? What shall I do tomorrow, and the day after? It was you I turned to in the hope of a miraculous reply. Superstitiously, I trusted you to provide advice. Should I go home to Pest like the prodigal son to resume life as a senior partner, or should I start a new life and become a labourer elsewhere? Since I've learnt the family business and could become a skilled worker. Don't leave me to my own devices – I'm so very alone as it is. What shall I do?"

Ervin fished out an enormous peasant's watch from the depths of his habit.

"For now, go to sleep. It's nearly midnight, and I have to go to church. Go to sleep – I'll lead you to your lodging. And I'll think about your situation during matins. Perhaps it'll become clear... such things have happened before. I might have something to tell you in the morning. Now go to sleep. Come."

He led Mihály to the hospice. This half-lit hall, into which centuries of pilgrims had dreamt their sufferings, desires and hopes for some miraculous cure, suited the deep agitation that had taken hold of

Mihály. Most of the berths were empty, but two or three pilgrims were asleep in the far reaches of the hall.

"Lie down, Mihály, and sleep well. A restful good night to you," said Ervin.

He made the cross over Mihály and hurried away.

Mihály sat on the edge of his hard bed for a long while after, his hands folded in his lap. He wasn't sleepy, and he was very sad. "Is there any help for me? Can my path yet lead somewhere?"

He knelt and prayed, for the first time in many years.

Then he lay down. He had great difficulty falling asleep on the hard bed in unaccustomed surroundings. The pilgrims squirmed restlessly on their beds, sighing and groaning in their dreams. One called to Saints Joseph, Catherine and Agatha for help. Dawn was already nearing by the time Mihály fell asleep.

He awoke that morning with the sweet sensation of having dreamt of Éva. He no longer remembered his dream, but his entire body felt that silky euphoria that only dreams can offer, and waking love only very, very exceptionally. This soft sensation felt odd, paradoxical and sickly sweet on the hard, ascetic bed.

He rose, washed himself – at the cost of no little self-denial – in a not very modern washroom, and stepped out into the courtyard. It was a brilliant, chilly, windy morning; the bells were just ringing for Mass; friars and laypeople, the cloister's servants and pilgrims, hurried from all directions to the church. Mihály also entered and listened devoutly to the rite's timeless Latin words. A ceremonial and joyful feeling suffused him. Ervin would surely tell him what to do. Maybe he'd need to do penance. Yes, he'd become a simple workman, earning his bread with his hands... He felt something begin within him, and now the song soared for him; the fresh, deep-voiced spring bells rang for him, for his soul.

The Mass concluded, and he went out into the courtyard. Ervin approached, smiling.

"How did you sleep?" he asked.

"Well, very well. I feel entirely different from last night, and I don't even know why."

He looked at Ervin full of expectation, and then, met with silence, he asked:

"Have you thought about what I should do?"

"Yes, Mihály," said Ervin quietly. "I think you have to go to Rome."

"To Rome?" asked Mihály with deep astonishment. "Why? How did that occur to you?"

"Last night, during the chorus... I can't explain it to you – you're not familiar with this type of meditation... I know that you must go to Rome."

"But why, Ervin, why?"

"So many pilgrims, fugitives and refugees have already gone to Rome over the centuries, and so much has happened there... as a matter of fact, everything always happened there. That's why they say that all roads lead to Rome. Go to Rome, Mihály, and then you'll see. I can't say anything more right now."

"But what should I do in Rome?"

"It makes no difference what you do. Maybe you should visit the four great basilicas of Christianity. Go out to the catacombs. Whatever you like. It's impossible to be bored in Rome. And most importantly, don't do anything at all. Surrender to happenstance. Give yourself over to it completely: don't have a schedule... Will you do it?"

"Yes, Ervin, if you say so."

"In that case, get going right away. Your face isn't as harried as it was yesterday. Use this lucky day to set out. Go. God be with you."

Not waiting for a reply, he embraced Mihály, pressed his right and left cheeks to Mihály's face in priestly fashion and hurried away. Mihály stood there for a bit in wonderment, then collected his pilgrim's pack and headed down the mountain.

6

WHEN SHE RECEIVED THE TELEGRAM that Mihály had sent via the little Fascist, Erzsi didn't stay in Rome any longer. She didn't want to go home, because she didn't know how to explain the story of her marriage in Pest. Pulled by certain lines of geographical attraction, she too travelled to Paris, the way people used to do when, utterly devoid of hope, they wanted to begin a new life.

In Paris, she looked up her childhood friend, Sári Tolnai. Sári was known for her masculine nature and extraordinary practicality, even as a youngster. She never married, not having the time for it; there always just happened to be a burning need for her at the firm, company or newspaper for which she was working. She conducted her love life at the pace of a business traveller. In time, when she reached the point of disgust with everything, she emigrated to Paris to begin a new life, in which she continued to do just what she'd done in Pest, except now at French firms, companies and newspapers. When Erzsi arrived in Paris, she just happened to be a secretary at a large film studio. She was the token ugly woman in the house, the cliff face that the erotic atmosphere surrounding the film craft could never climb, someone whose sobriety and impartiality one could always trust, someone who worked much more and earned much less than the others. Meanwhile, she'd gone grey, and with her short hair she had a face as noble as a military bishop's, atop her fragile, girlish body. Everyone turned to stare at her, and she was very proud of that.

"What will you live on?" she asked, after Erzsi had hurriedly sketched the story of her marriage, assisted by a few interjections imported from Pest. "What'll you live on? Do you still have all that money?"

"Well, you know, my financial situation is quite complicated. When we divorced, Zoltán returned my dowry and my paternal inheritance (which, by the way, is much, much less than people think), and I put most of it in Mihály's firm, and the remainder, as a contingency plan, in the bank. So I'd have enough to live on, but it's really hard to get my hands on it. There's no honourable way to transfer my bank deposit over here. So I have to rely on what my ex-father-in-law sends me. Which is also no simple matter. When it comes to letting go of money, my ex-father-in-law tends to be a very, very difficult man. And we have no agreement in place about it."

"Hmm. You have to extract your money from the firm. That's the very first thing."

"Yes, but to do that, I'd have to get an official divorce from Mihály."

"Well, naturally, you've got to get a divorce from Mihály."

"It's not that natural."

"After what went on? You must be joking!"

"Yes. But Mihály isn't like other men. That's exactly why I married him."

"And that worked out *so* well. I don't like people who aren't like other people. Other people are revolting enough. So imagine people who aren't like them."

"Fine, Sári, let's leave it at that. Besides which, I'm not going to do Mihály the favour of just getting a divorce like that."

"But why the devil don't you go home to Pest, when your money is there?"

"I don't want to go home until these things have been settled. What will I tell people back home? Imagine the things my cousin Juliska would say!"

"Rest assured: she'll talk no matter what."

"But here, at least, I can't hear it. And then… no, I can't go home, because of Zoltán too."

"Because of your first husband?"

"Because of him. He'd be waiting for me at the train station, bouquet in hand."

"You don't say. So he's not angry at you for dropping him so unceremoniously?"

"Of course he isn't angry. He thinks I was completely justified and is waiting with humility, in case I should ever return to him. And I'm sure that, in his remorse, he's broken off relations with his typists and is living a life of celibacy. If I were to return home, he wouldn't stop hanging round my neck. And that's unendurable. I can tolerate everything except goodness and being forgiven. Especially on Zoltán's part."

"You know what? In this one instance, you're right. I don't like it when men are good and forgiving."

Erzsi took a room where Sári lived, in that modern, flavourless, odourless hotel behind the Jardin des Plantes, from which one could see the great cedar of Lebanon as it extended its pillowy, broad branches with exotic, Eastern dignity into the unruly Parisian spring. The cedar did no good for Erzsi. Its foreignness always made her think about a different, magnificent life, foreign to her, whose arrival she awaited in vain.

At first she had a separate room, and then they moved in together, because it was less expensive. They dined together, up in their room, eating food they'd brought in themselves, despite the hotel's prohibition. It turned out that Sári was just as expert at preparing supper as she was at everything else. Erzsi had to take luncheon alone, because Sári ate in town – a sandwich and coffee, while standing – and then returned immediately to her office. At first, Erzsi sampled various types of better restaurants, but then she realized that the better restaurants overcharge foreigners, so she began to frequent small *crèmeries** instead, where "you can get the same things, only much cheaper." At first she always drank an espresso after luncheon, because she adored the fine Parisian espressos, but then she fathomed that this was no life essential either, and renounced it except once a week, every Monday, when she went to the Maison de Café on the Grand Boulevard to drink a cup of their famed espresso.

The day after her arrival, she bought herself a gorgeous reticule at a fashionable store near La Madeleine, but this was her sole luxury purchase. She discovered that the same things offered to foreigners at such dear prices in the more glamorous neighbourhoods could be had for much less in the side streets, in simple shops or in the bazaar districts, on the Rue de Rivoli or the Rue de Rennes. At first, she indeed purchased a great many things, because they were so much less expensive than elsewhere. But finally she realized that not shopping at all was even less expensive, and from then on she derived particular pleasure from things that she would have liked to buy, but didn't. And then she discovered a hotel two streets over that, while not as modern as the one in which they were presently living, still had hot and cold running water and, after all, was just as liveable as the other, except that it was much cheaper – by a third. She convinced Sári, and they relocated.

Slowly, thriftiness became her major occupation. It occurred to her that she had always had a strong inclination to thrift. As a child, she ordinarily set aside the chocolate bonbons she received as gifts, until they got mouldy; she also hid her pretty clothes, and her maids sometimes found them in the most astonishing places, having become soiled and unwearable: a silk scarf, a pair of fine stockings, an expensive pair of gloves. Life later prevented Erzsi from carrying out her passion for thrift. As a young girl she had to keep up appearances at her father's side and, indeed, to be improvident in order to increase her father's credit. And as Zoltán's wife she could not even dream of being thrifty. Whenever she declined an expensive pair of shoes, the next day Zoltán would surprise his wife with three even more expensive pairs. Zoltán was a "man of grand gestures", a patron of the arts and of female artists, and he insisted unconditionally on inundating his wife with everything, in part to ease his conscience – and all the while, Erzsi's main passion, thrift, remained unfulfilled.

Now, in Paris, that repressed passion erupted with elemental force. The French atmosphere contributed to this, the French lifestyle, which evokes the desire for thrift in even the flightiest souls; as did more mysterious factors: her frustration in love, the failure of her marriage, the pointlessness of her life – all this somehow sought compensation in her thrift. When she then went so far as to renounce her daily bath, because the hotel charged too much for it, Sári could not let it go any further without speaking up:

"Tell me, why the hell are you economizing so much? I can give you money, in exchange for a promissory note, of course, for form's sake..."

"Thank you – you're very kind – but I have money: I received three thousand francs from Mihály's father just yesterday."

"You hear that? Three thousand francs – that's an enormous sum. I don't like it when a woman economizes that much. Then something's not right. It's just the same as when a woman spends the whole day cleaning the house, hunting for dead motes of dust, or when a woman washes her hands all day and takes a separate hand towel with her to wipe her hands with when she goes visiting. Female madness has a thousand forms. Tell me please – I've only just thought of it – what do you do all day while I'm at the office?"

It turned out that Erzsi wasn't very capable of accounting for her time. All she knew was that she was being thrifty. She didn't go here and didn't go there, and didn't do this and didn't do that, all in order not to spend any money. But what she did instead was hazy, half-dreamlike...

"Madness!" Sári shouted. "I always imagined that you had someone and were spending the time with him, and now it turns out that all you do all day is to stare into space and daydream like half-mad women, but those who are on the straight and narrow. And meanwhile, of course, you're putting on weight, no matter how little you eat – of course you're gaining weight: you ought to be ashamed of yourself. All right, this is going to change. You have to get out among people, and something's got to interest you. Devil take it, if only I had the time for something in this stinking world…"

"Say, tonight we're going on a spree," she said radiantly, a day or two later. "There's a Hungarian gentleman who wants to conduct some very shady business with the studio, and he's trying to seduce me very hard because he knows how much *le patron** listens to me. Now he's invited me to supper: he says he wants to introduce me to his money man, in whose name he's negotiating. I told him that *moche** money men don't interest me – I have enough business with beastly characters in the office. He says he's not *moche* at all, he's a lovely man, a Persian. Well, I said, fine, then I'll go, but I'm taking a girlfriend with me. To which he said that's wonderful: he'd just been thinking about how to arrange it so that I would not be the only woman in the group.

"My dear little Sári, you know I can't go: what an idea! I'm not in the mood at all, and I don't have anything to wear. All I have are lousy things from Pest."

"Have no fear, you're very elegant in those things. Go on, compared to these pencil-necked Parisian women, it's really no contest… and the Hungarian will no doubt be delighted that you're a compatriot."

"It's out of the question for me to go. What is this Hungarian gent's name?"

"János Szepetneki – at least, that's what he claims."

"János Szepetneki… wait, I know him!… Say, he's a pickpocket!"

"Pickpocket? Could be. Although I pegged him as a burglar. You know, everyone in the movies begins that way. But that aside, he's a very charming man. So are you coming or not?"

"Yes, I'll come..."

The small *auberge* where they went to dine belonged to the sort that is decorated in country French style, with checked curtains and checked tablecloths, few tables, serving expensive and superb cuisine. When she had been to Paris with Zoltán, Erzsi had often eaten at such places, and better ones, but now, surfacing from the depths of her thrift, she was overcome as the restaurant's intimate atmosphere, redolent of wealth, hit her. But her emotion lasted only an instant, because the greater sensation was already hurrying towards them: János Szepetneki. He kissed Erzsi, whom he didn't recognize, on the hand, very courteously and in fine gentry manner; he complimented Sári on her excellent taste in friends, and then led the ladies to the table where his friend was already awaiting them.

"Monsieur Lutphali Suratgar," he introduced him. From behind an aquiline nose, the beams from a mercilessly intense pair of eyes drilled into Erzsi's. Erzsi shuddered. Sári too was visibly shaken. Their first sensation was of sitting at table with a tiger that was only tamed on the surface.

Erzsi didn't know which of them she feared more: Szepetncki the pickpocket, who spoke Parisian too well and who chose from the menu with such a perfect mixture of expertise and *nonchalance* as only a dangerous con man could (it occurred to Erzsi how much even Zoltán feared the waiters at the more distinguished Parisian restaurants, and how his fear made him such a bumpkin in dealing with them) – or, on the other hand, the Persian who sat there without a word, on his face a friendly European smile as ready-made and inappropriate as a pre-tied necktie. But after the hors d'oeuvre and the first glass of wine, the Persian's tongue loosened, and from then on he led the conversation, in an odd, chesty and staccato French.

He completely captivated his audience with his words. Some kind of romantic exaltation gushed from this man, something medieval, some rawer and truer humanity as yet untainted by mechanization. This man did not yet live in pengős and francs but in the currency of roses, cliffs and eagles. But nevertheless, the feeling persisted that they were seated at a table with a superficially tamed tiger. It was his eyes that elicited this sensation.

It turned out that back home in Persia he owned rose gardens and iron mines and, most important, poppy plantations, and his main occupation was the manufacture of opium. He had an extremely low opinion of the League of Nations, which had banned international trade of opium and thus caused him great material harm. He was forced to support a band of robbers on the Turkestan border in order to smuggle opium to China.

"But in that case, my good sir, you are the enemy of mankind," said Sári. "You're propagating the white poison. You're ruining the lives of hundreds of thousands of poor Chinese. And yet you wonder that every honourable person should unite against you."

"*Ma chère*," said the Persian with surprising vehemence, "do not speak whereof you do not understand. The stupid humanitarian chorus of the European newspapers has misled you. How could opium harm the 'poor' Chinese? Do you think they have the money for opium? They're happy if they have enough for rice. In China, only the very wealthy smoke opium, because it's expensive, and it's the prerogative of the privileged, like all the other good things on this earth. It's exactly the same as if I were to fret that the labourers of Paris drink too much champagne. And if they don't prohibit the wealthy Parisians from drinking champagne, then by what right do they prohibit the Chinese?"

"The analogy is flawed. Opium is much more destructive than champagne."

"This too is a European sort of idea. It's true that once a European begins to smoke opium, there's no stopping him. Because Europeans lack a sense of proportion in all things: in gluttony, in construction and in spilling blood alike. But we can retain a proper sense of scale. Or does it appear to you that I've been harmed by opium? For in fact I smoke it regularly; I even eat it."

He puffed out his immense chest, then displayed his muscled arms in a gesture slightly reminiscent of the circus, and then he wanted to lift his leg; but Sári waved him to stop: "Hold on. Leave something for the next time."

"If you please... Europeans lack proportion in their alcohol consumption too, but what a disgusting sensation it is to have too much wine in your stomach and to feel that, sooner or later, you're going to be sick. The influence of wine increases continually, and then one suddenly collapses. It can't provide the consistent, lasting intoxication that opium can, and which is the sole happiness on this earth... and in any case, what do you Europeans know? You have to understand the circumstances first, before interfering in a region's business."

"That's why we want to make this enlightening propaganda film with you," said Szepetneki, turning towards Sári.

"What's that? A propaganda film in favour of smoking opium?" asked Erzsi, who had been sympathetic to the Persian's standpoint before, but was shocked now.

"Not in favour of opium-smoking, but in favour of the free movement of opium and, in general, in favour of human liberty. We intend this film to be a great outcry for individualism and against tyranny in every form."

"What would its plot be?" asked Erzsi.

"At the beginning, you'll be able to see," Szepetneki replied, "a simple, good-hearted, conservative Persian opium farmer in his peaceful family circle. He can only give his daughter, the protagonist, in marriage to the young man she loves in a manner fitting his status if he succeeds in placing his opium crop on the market. At this, the intriguer, who is also in love with the girl but is a scoundrel and communist capable of anything, reports the father to the authorities, and at night, in a surprise raid, they commandeer his entire opium output. This'll be very exciting, with automobiles and sirens. But later the girl's innocence and spiritual nobility will move the grim colonel, and he'll return all the confiscated opium, which then will travel to China gaily, in wagons tinkling with bells. That's the main outline of the plot..."

Erzsi didn't know whether Szepetneki was joking or not. The Persian listened to him seriously – indeed, with a sort of naive pride. Maybe he had come up with the story.

After supper, they repaired to an elegant dance establishment. Here, various acquaintances joined them and they sat around a large table, conversing every which way, in so far as the general racket allowed. Erzsi wound up far from the Persian. János Szepetneki asked her for the pleasure, and they began to dance.

"How do you like the Persian?" Szepetneki asked as they danced. "He's a most interesting man, isn't he? A complete romantic."

"You know, an old and mad English poet's lines keep running through my mind when I look at him," said Erzsi, in a sudden flare-up of her old intellectual ego. "'Tiger, tiger burning bright, in the forests of the night...'"

Szepetneki looked at her in wonder, and Erzsi felt ashamed.

"A tiger," said Szepetneki, "but a monstrously difficult traveller. As a matter of fact, he's as naive as he is uncertain and cautious in business matters. Not even the motion picture people can swindle him. Yet he doesn't want to make the film for business reasons, but for its propaganda value, and I think mainly in order to fashion a harem for himself out of the female extras. So when did you leave Italy?"

"So you recognized me?" asked Erzsi.

"Of course. Not now. Days ago, on the street, when you were walking with Mademoiselle Sári. You should know that I have an eagle eye. And I arranged this evening in order to speak with you… But tell me, where did you leave my outstanding friend, Mihály?"

"Your outstanding friend is most likely still in Italy. We don't correspond."

"Sensational. You separated on your honeymoon?"

Erzsi nodded.

"Tremendous. That's the ticket. That's Mihály's style. The old boy hasn't changed a bit. He always abandoned everything in his worldly life. He has no patience for anything at all. For example, he was the best centre half not only in our high school but, I dare say, in all the high schools in the country. And then one fine day…"

"How do you know that he left me, and not the other way round?"

"Oh, pardon me. I didn't even ask. Well, of course. You left him there. And I understand. Such a man is unbearable. I can imagine what suffering it must be to live at the side of such a poker face… who's never angry, who's…"

"Yes. He left me there."

"Aha, I see. I thought so at once, by the way. Back then already, in Ravenna. You know, now I'm speaking in all seriousness. Mihály is not cut out to be a husband. He… how should I put it… he's a seeker… He's been seeking something his entire life, something that's different. Something about which this Persian, I believe, knows much more than we do. Maybe Mihály should smoke opium. Yes, I'm absolutely certain: that's what he should do. Honestly, I confess I never did understand that man."

And he waved his hand dismissively.

But Erzsi sensed that this offhand dismissal was merely a pose and that Szepetneki was terribly curious about what had happened between her and Mihály. He never left Erzsi's side for the rest of the evening.

They sat down beside each other; Szepetneki let no one else approach Erzsi. By this point, an older distinguished Frenchman was attending to Sári, while the Persian sat, his eyes gleaming, between two movie actress types.

"Interesting," thought Erzsi, "how different everything is from up close – and how indifferent." When she had first visited Paris, she had still been full of those preconceptions she'd picked up as a schoolgirl. She believed that Paris was a perverse and sinful world city, and the two innocent artists' and emigrants' cafés facing each other in Montparnasse, the Dôme and the Rotonde, looked to her eyes like the two incandescent jaws of the maw of hell. And now that she was sitting here, likely between people who were indeed perverse and sinful, everything seemed so ordinary.

But she didn't have much time to philosophize, because she was listening attentively to Szepetneki. She hoped to learn something crucially important about Mihály from him. Szepetneki happily spoke of their years together; but of course, in his representation everything became distorted and seemed at odds with Mihály's version. Only Tamás remained magnificent; he had departed early, before having to make compromises. According to Szepetneki, Tamás was so refined that he couldn't sleep if something moved three rooms away, and a penetrating odour could drive him mad. His only problem was that he was in love with his sister. They had relations, and when Éva became pregnant, his guilty conscience drove Tamás to kill himself. Besides, everyone was in love with Éva. Ervin became a monk because he was hopelessly in love with Éva. Mihály too was hopelessly in love with Éva. He followed her around like a lapdog. It was comical. And Éva exploited him. She took all his money. And stole his gold watch. Because it was Éva, of course, who stole it, and not him, but they didn't want to mention this to Mihály out of *délicatesse*. But Éva didn't love any of them. Only him, János Szepetneki.

"And what's become of Éva since? Have you seen her since then?"

"Me? Of course! We've remained on very good terms since then. Éva's made a big career for herself, not entirely without my assistance. She has become a very important woman."

"How do you mean?"

"Well, in *that* way. She always attracted the most distinguished possible benefactors. Princes of the press, kings of oil, even actual heirs to thrones, not to mention the great writers and painters whom she required more for propaganda purposes."

"And what is she up to now?"

"Now she's in Italy. She travels to Italy whenever she can: it's her passion. And she collects antiquities, like her father."

"Why didn't you tell Mihály that Éva was in Italy? And how did you wind up in Ravenna, anyhow?"

"Me? I was passing through Pest and heard that Mihály had married and gone to Venice on his honeymoon. I couldn't resist the temptation to see the old boy and his wife on this occasion, and that's why I returned to Paris via Venice. And from Venice I made a jaunt to Ravenna when I learnt that you were there."

"And why didn't you mention Éva?"

"I thought about it. Only for him to go and look for her?"

"He wouldn't have gone looking for her, given that he was on his honeymoon with his wife."

"Don't be angry, but I don't believe that would have prevented him."

"Really! For twenty years it hadn't occurred to him to look for her."

"Because he didn't know where she was, and, besides which, Mihály is much too passive for that. But once he finds out…"

"And why would it upset you if Mihály found Éva Ulpius? Jealous, are you? Still in love with Éva?"

"Me? Nonsense. I never was. Éva was in love with me. But I didn't want to create problems in Mihály's marriage."

"You're just an angelic good boy, eh?"

"No. It's just that you instantly struck me as extremely sympathetic."

"Splendid. In Ravenna, you said exactly the opposite. And you succeeded in offending me quite a bit."

"Oh, well, I only said that because I was wondering if Mihály would slap me across the face. But Mihály never slaps anyone's face. That's his problem. A slap releases so much... but to return to the subject: you made a great impression on me from the first instant."

"Wonderful. So now I should feel honoured, right? Tell me, couldn't you woo me with a bit more wit?"

"I can't woo with wit. That's for impotent men. If I find a woman attractive, all I think about is making her aware of it. Then she'll either react or not. But usually they do."

"I'm not 'usual'."

But she was aware of the fact that János Szepetneki did indeed find her attractive, that he desired her body: hungrily, like an adolescent, lacking all male wisdom, simply, repulsively. And this felt so good to her that the blood circulating under her skin sped up all over her body, as if she had been drinking. She wasn't used to this raw instinctiveness. Men, in general, used to approach her with romance and fine words. And furthermore, when they first met, Szepetneki had deeply offended her feminine vanity. The collapse of her marriage might have begun then, and Erzsi had been carrying Szepetneki's painful words inside her ever since. And now here was the antidote, the reparation. She behaved more flirtatiously towards Szepetneki than she ever knew she could: in order for her finally to reject him all the more coldly, in revenge for Ravenna.

But the reason she reacted to Szepetneki's advances was, above all, because she sensed with her feminine instinct that they were being directed at her primarily because she was Mihály's woman. She knew what a strange relationship Szepetneki had with Mihály: that he constantly sought to prove, using every means at hand, that he was the more exceptional of the two, and that this is why he now wanted to seduce Mihály's wife. Erzsi bathed in Szepetneki's desire with a sickly and widow-like yearning for consolation and felt that now, with this desire and its awakening, she would truly become Mihály's woman: now she would step inside the magic circle, the old, Ulpius circle that constituted Mihály's sole reality.

"Let's change the subject," she said, but under the table, their knees were rubbing hard against one another. "What is it exactly that you do here in Paris?"

"I facilitate major business deals. Only extremely large deals," said Szepetneki, beginning to stroke Erzsi's thigh under the table. "I have excellent connections to the Third Reich. One could say that, in certain respects, I'm the Third Reich's trade representative here. And as a side business, I want to cement this deal between Lutphali and the Martini-Alvaert film studio, because I need the cash. But I say, why are we talking so much? Let's dance."

They partied until three in the morning, and then the Persian pushed the two film actresses with whom he'd been amusing himself into his automobile, invited everyone else to his villa in Auteuil on Sunday afternoon and bade farewell. The others also headed home. The French gentleman accompanied Sári home, and Szepetneki, Erzsi.

"I'm coming up to your place," Szepetneki announced at the gate.

"You're mad. Besides which, I share a room with Sári."

"The devil take it. Then come to my place."

"It's clear, Szepetneki, that you left Pest a long time ago. Otherwise I couldn't comprehend how you could so badly misunderstand what sort of woman I am. Now you've spoilt everything."

And she left him standing there, without so much as a goodbye, but most triumphantly.

"Say, what were you doing, flirting with that Szepetneki?" said Sári when they were both in bed. "Just be careful."

"It's over already. Imagine, he wanted me to go up to his place."

"And so? You're behaving as if you still lived in Pest. Kiddo, don't forget that Pest is Europe's most moral city. They don't conceive of these things the same way here."

"But Sári, on the first night... Well, a woman simply has to have enough dignity to..."

"Of course. But then she shouldn't be on speaking terms with men... that's the only way a woman can preserve her honour here. The way I do it. But tell me, why bother preserving your honour; tell me, I say, why? You think I wouldn't have gone with that Persian happily, if he'd asked? But, well, did he ask? He had it in mind. What a gorgeous man! By the way, you did well not to get involved with that Szepetneki. He's quite handsome, I'm not denying it, and very masculine – well, I mean it in a certain sense... well, in other words, the way I said it – but you know he's a con man. By the end he'll have taken your money. Be very careful, kid. One time, they stole five hundred francs from me in a similar situation. All right, cheerio."

"A con man," thought Erzsi to herself as she lay sleepless. "That's exactly what he is." Her whole life, Erzsi had been a model little girl: the love of her nannies and *Fräulein*s, the pride of her father, the best student in class – she was even sent to academic competitions. Her entire life had flowed in orderly and protected fashion, in strict adherence to the hallowed charter of the good bourgeois life. When the time came, she married a wealthy man, dressed elegantly, ran an upper-class household, made appearances and was the ideal housewife. She always wore the same hats as the other ladies who belonged to her social class, summered where it was proper; she was a conformist – as Mihály would put it – in all respects. But then she began to get bored; the boredom intensified to the point of cardiac neurosis; and then she chose Mihály for herself, because she sensed that Mihály was not entirely a conformist: there was something in Mihály that was utterly alien to the limits of bourgeois life. She thought that, by Mihály's side, she too could break through the walls, out onto the flood plain, overgrown with wild thickets, which spread to unknown distances out there. But Mihály sought to conform precisely through her; he'd used her as his instrument to become a proper bourgeois and only stole out to the flood plain on his own – until he got bored with conformism and fled back into the thickets alone. "What about János Szepetneki, who indeed doesn't want to conform, who conducts raids past the walls as a sort of profession, who's much hardier and healthier than Mihály... I wonder... Tiger, tiger burning bright, in the forests of the night..."

The Sunday afternoon in Auteuil was perfectly agreeable and boring; no film types were in attendance, the whole thing had a *mondain** and distinguished character, and the French haute bourgeoisie turned out in force; but this world didn't interest Erzsi, being still more conformist and still more tigerless than the one in Pest. She could only breathe deeply when, on the way home from Auteuil, János Szepetneki took her to supper, and then they went dancing. János was devilish: he plied her with drinks, he swaggered, he orated, he wept and, from time to time, he was very manly – but as a matter of fact, all this was hardly necessary. János overacted his part yet again, because even if he hadn't said a single word, Erzsi would likely have spent the night at his place, following the inner logic of things and her search for yellow tigers.

Part Three

ROME

Go thou to Rome – at once the Paradise,
The Grave, the City, and the Wilderness.
PERCY BYSSHE SHELLEY

1

MIHÁLY HAD ALREADY BEEN IN ROME for days, and still nothing at all had happened to him. No romantic leaflet fluttered down from heaven to set him on his course, the way he'd been secretly hoping since Ervin's words. The only thing that happened to him was Rome itself, in a manner of speaking.

All the other Italian cities shrank into insignificance next to Rome. Compared to it, Venice – where he'd been with Erzsi, officially – wasn't enough, nor was Siena – where he'd been with Millicent, fortuitously. For Rome stood alone and was, he felt, the result of guidance from a higher power. Everything he saw in Rome stood under the sign of fatefulness. He had encountered this feeling before: the sense, during a predawn stroll or an unusual late-summer afternoon, that everything is suffused with a rare, inexpressible significance; but here, the feeling never left him for so much as an instant. Streets and houses had awakened far-reaching presentiments before, but never to the extent that Rome's streets, palaces, ruins and gardens did. Meandering among the immense walls of the Teatro Marcello, or gazing at the way little baroque churches sprout among the antique columns in the Forum, or looking down at the star-shaped Regina Cœli prison from one of the hills, or wandering the alleys in the ghetto, or crossing peculiar courtyards from Santa Maria sopra Minerva to the Pantheon, through whose huge oculus, big as a millwheel, the dark blue summer evening's sky looks down – these are what filled his days. And at night, falling into bed tired, dead tired, in the ugly little stone-floored hotel room near the train station, where he'd taken frightened refuge the first night and which he hadn't had the energy to exchange for a different residence since.

He was shaken from his reveries by Tivadar's letter, which Ellesley had forwarded from Foligno.

Dear Mischi, wrote Tivadar, *the news of your illness has filled us with great anxiety. In your customary vague manner, you forgot to write what exactly was the matter, though you can imagine that we'd dearly like to know: please do rectify this mistake now, after the event. Have you recovered completely yet? Your mother is most fretful. Don't take it ill if I can only send you the funds so late, but you well know how many difficulties these foreign-currency transfers entail. I hope the delay hasn't caused any discomfort. You write that I should send lots of money; you expressed yourself a bit vaguely: "a lot of money" is always relative. It could be that you'll find the transferred sum to be too little, since it's in fact hardly more than the amount you said you owe. But for us, even this much is a lot, given the present state of business – about which the less said, the better – and the large investments that we've made recently and which will be amortized only in several years' time. But in any event, the money will be enough for you to pay your hotel bill and come home. Luckily, you already have a return train ticket. Because I don't even have to tell you that no other solution is possible. You can imagine that our firm, given its current circumstances, cannot support the burden of financing the expensive foreign sojourn – the completely unfounded and incomprehensible foreign sojourn – of one of its members any longer.*

All the less, because you can imagine that in consequence of the given situation, your wife has also approached us with needs – furthermore, completely legitimate needs – and it is naturally our principal responsibility to fulfil these needs. Your wife is presently residing in Paris and, for the time being, is satisfied by our supporting her living expenses there; the final settlement will only take place on the occasion of her return home. I don't need to explain that this final settlement may put the factory into an extraordinarily uncomfortable situation. You know very well that we invested all the cash your wife brought to the firm into machinery, advertising and supporting the firm's diversification, so liquidating the assets would not only cause difficulties but shake the firm to its foundations, so to speak. I believe that another man would have taken this into account as well, before abandoning his wife on their honeymoon. Not to mention that your actions, independent of all economic considerations, are unspeakable and absolutely ungentlemanly *in and of themselves, especially with respect to such an unimpeachable, proper gentlewoman as your wife.*

Well, that's the situation. Your father cannot bring himself to write to you. You can imagine how much these events have upset and broken him, and how uneasy he's made by the prospect that, sooner or later, he'll have to repay your wife. All this has worn him out so much that we'd like to send him on summer holiday, so he can relax; we considered Gastein first of all, but he won't even hear of it, given the extra expense such a holiday would incur.

Thus, dear Mischi, as soon as you're received my letter, be so kind as to pack up and come home, the sooner, the better.

We all send our loving greetings.

Tivadar had undoubtedly written this letter with great delight: he was glad that he, the happy-go-lucky bon vivant of the family, was for once in the situation of being able to preach morals to the solid and serious Mihály. Just the mere fact of such a superior tone on the part of his least congenial brother made Mihály lose his temper. That alone made him unable to conceive of returning home as anything other than an imposition, a horrible and repulsive coercion.

It seemed, however, that there was indeed no other solution in the offing. If he repaid his debt to Millicent, he'd have no money to remain in Rome any longer. And what Tivadar had written about their father made him deeply uneasy. He knew that Tivadar wasn't exaggerating: his father was prone to depression, and the whole affair, in which so many material, social and emotional unpleasantnesses combined so messily, was itself highly suited to disturbing his father's emotional peace. If nothing else, there was the fact that his favourite son had behaved so impossibly. He must return home indeed, at least to set this right, to explain to his father the extent to which he could not have acted in any other way – in Erzsi's interest as well as his own. He must show that he was no fugitive and take responsibility for his deed, as befitting a *gentleman*.

And once back he must take his place at work again. Today, everything is work: the reward for the youth just setting out, for his studies, is work; equally, the penance and punishment for those who fail at something is work. If he returned home and worked diligently, sooner or later his father would forgive him.

But when he thought about the details of "work" – his desk, the people he had to deal with and, above all, the things that would fill his life outside work: games of bridge, the Danube, ladies of good breeding – he became bitter to the point of tears.

"How did the ghost of Achilles put it?" he mused. "'Better to be a cotter in my father's house, than a prince among the dead...'* It's just the opposite for me: I'd rather be a cotter here, among the dead, than a prince back home in my father's house. If only I had a clearer notion of what a cotter is..."

Here, among the dead... For by this time, he was already going out beyond the city walls, behind the Pyramid of Cestius, to the small Protestant cemetery. Here rested his colleagues, the northern dead, who'd been drawn here by unnameable nostalgias, and with whom death had caught up here. This lovely graveyard with its shady trees always tempted northern souls with the illusion that extinction would be sweeter here. At the end of one of Goethe's *Roman Elegies* stands, as a memento: "*Cestius' Mal vorbei, leise zum Orcus hinab.*"* In a beautiful letter, Shelley wrote that he'd like to rest here, and indeed, here he lies, or at least his heart, and above it, the inscription: *Cor cordium.**

Mihály was just about to leave when he noticed an isolated, small group of graves in a corner of the graveyard. He went over and read the inscriptions on the simple Empire-style tombstones. One of them said merely, in English: *Here lies One Whose Name was writ in Water.* On the neighbouring grave was a longer text, explaining that there lay Severn the painter, best friend and faithful deathbed nurse of John Keats, the great English poet, who did not allow his name to be carved on the adjacent tombstone beneath which he rests.

Mihály's eyes filled with tears. For here lays Keats, the greatest poet since the world was the world... no matter how senseless it was to be so moved, seeing that his body had been resting there for a very long time already, and his poems preserved his soul more faithfully than any funerary inscription. But how magnificent, how English, how amiably compromising and innocently hypocritical was the manner in which they honoured his final request and yet unequivocally gave notice of the fact that it was Keats resting beneath the stone.

When he looked up, some unusual people were standing next to him. A gloriously lovely and indubitably English woman, a *nurse* in uniform and two very pretty English children, a little boy and girl. They just stood motionlessly, staring perplexedly at the grave, each other and Mihály. Mihály remained in place and waited, expecting them surely to say something eventually, but they said nothing. After a while, an elegant gentleman arrived with a face just as expressionless as the others'. He resembled the woman strongly; they could have been twins, or at least siblings. He stopped in front of the grave and the woman pointed at the inscription. The Englishman nodded and, very serious and perplexed, regarded alternately the grave, the family and Mihály; and he too said not a word. Mihály moved away a bit, thinking that perhaps they felt embarrassed in front of him, but they just kept on standing there, nodding occasionally and looking at each other in their perplexity; the two children's faces were just as perplexed and expressionlessly beautiful as the adults'.

As he turned around and now stared at them with undisguised astonishment, Mihály suddenly felt that they weren't even humans but eerie puppets, automata at a loss here above the poet's grave, inexplicable beings – had they been less beautiful, they might have been less dumbfounding, but their beauty was as inhuman as an advertisement's; and an inexpressible terror took hold of Mihály.

Then the English family headed off, slowly and nodding all the while, and Mihály came to his senses. It was when his sober consciousness recalled the past few minutes that he became truly frightened.

"What's wrong with me? What shameful nervous condition, reminiscent of my darkest adolescence, have I fallen into again? Obviously there's nothing unusual about these people other than that they're bashful and extremely stupid English who found themselves face to face with the fact that this is Keats's grave, here, and they didn't know what to do about it, perhaps because they didn't know who Keats was; or maybe they did, but they couldn't figure out what the proper thing is for well-bred English to do over Keats's grave, and this is why they were ashamed of themselves in front of each other and in front of me. One can't imagine a less significant and more everyday scene, yet the entire inexpressible horror of the world bore down upon my heart. Yes: horror is not at its strongest in the context of nocturnal things and fear, but when it stares at us in full sunlight out of some everyday thing: a window display, an unfamiliar face, from between the branches of a tree…"

He stuffed his hands in his pockets and hurried back the way he'd come.

He decided to return home the next day. He couldn't go the same day, because he'd received Tivadar's letter around noon and had to wait until morning both to cash the cheque Tivadar had sent and to send Millicent the money he owed. He was spending his last evening in Rome; he wandered the streets much more passively than he had before, and he found everything yet more insignificant.

He bade farewell to Rome. There were no specific, individual buildings that endeared themselves to him: it was rather the entirety of Roman life that constituted his greatest city experience. He wandered without a set goal, in despair, with the feeling that the city was still hiding thousands upon thousands of details that he'd never see, and once again he felt that the important things were elsewhere, not wherever he happened to be; nor had he received the mysterious sign; his life's path also led nowhere, and now his nostalgia would remain eternally tormenting and unfulfilled, until he himself should pass away – *Cestius' Mal vorbei, leise zum Orcus hinab...*

Darkness fell, Mihály walked on with his head down, and by now he was hardly looking at the streets until, in a dark alley, he bumped into someone, who said: *Sorry*. Mihály jerked his head up at the English word and saw the same young Englishman before him who had so dumbfounded him at Keats's grave. There must have been something in Mihály's expression when he looked at the Englishman, because he doffed his hat, mumbled something and hurried away. Mihály turned and stared after him.

Only for a moment or two; then he hurried after him, striding decisively, without thinking about why he was doing it. In his childhood, under the influence of detective novels, one of his favourite amusements was to start suddenly following strangers, and he'd track them, taking care that they not notice him, sometimes for hours on end. Even back then, he didn't follow just anyone. The subject had to be full of significance in some cabbalistic sense, the way this young Englishman was: for it was no mere happenstance that he'd encountered him twice in one day, and on such a significant day in this big city, and that both encounters should have elicited such baseless astonishment in him. There was something hidden beneath all this, and he had to get to the bottom of it.

With the excitement of a detective, he tailed the Englishman down the narrow streets and out onto the Corso Umberto. He had retained his childhood skill and could still follow him as unnoticed as a shadow. The Englishman paced up and down the Corso for a while, then took a seat on a café terrace. Mihály also sat down, drank a vermouth and watched the Englishman with anticipation. He knew that something had to happen. It seemed that even the man wasn't as calm and expressionless as at Keats's tomb. There might yet be some life beating under his regular features and frighteningly clear skin. Of course, his restlessness left only as much of a trace on his perfect English surface as when a bird's wing brushes the surface of a lake, but he was still visibly uneasy. Mihály knew that the Englishman was awaiting someone, and the anxiety of expectation transferred to him and was amplified, like sound in a megaphone.

The Englishman began glancing at his watch, and Mihály could scarcely stay in his seat; he squirmed, ordered another vermouth and then a maraschino: he needn't be thrifty any more, since he was going home the next day anyway.

Finally, an elegant automobile stopped in front of the café, its door opened and a woman looked out from within. At this instant the Englishman sprang up and into the car, which smoothly and noiselessly headed off with them.

This took just a moment, and the woman barely appeared in the door's opening, but – more by intuition than with his eyes – Mihály recognized Éva Ulpius inside. Mihály also leapt up and saw Éva's gaze brush across him for an instant – and furthermore, it seemed as if some very thin smile might have appeared on Éva's face, but all this flashed by, and Éva disappeared into the automobile and into the night.

Mihály paid and staggered out of the café. The signs hadn't deceived him; this was why he had to come to Rome: because Éva was here. And by now, he also knew that she was the source and veritable harbour of his nostalgia: Éva, Éva...

He also knew that he wasn't going home. Not even if he had to wear a sack and wait for fifty years – now that at last there was a place on the earth where he had a reason to be, a meaningful place. He'd sensed this significance, subconsciously, for days in Rome's streets, buildings, ruins and churches: everywhere. One couldn't say that this significance "filled him with happy anticipation" – happiness is incompatible with Rome and its millennia in any case – and what he expected from the future was not the sort of thing that typically awakens happy anticipation. He awaited his fate: the meaningful destiny appropriate to Rome.

He wrote at once to Tivadar, stating that his health precluded long-distance travel. He wouldn't send the money to Millicent. Millicent was so well off that the amount wouldn't affect her well-being; and if she had waited all this time, she could wait a little while longer. And Tivadar was responsible for the delay: why hadn't he sent more money?

That night, in the anxiety and elation of expectation, he drank himself under the table on his own, and when he awoke late at night to his heart pounding, he felt once again that sense of being doomed, which had been the main accompaniment to his youthful love for Éva. He knew very well – much more clearly now than the day before – that he ought to go home for a thousand and one reasons; and when he nevertheless remained in Rome because of Éva – considering how uncertain he was ever to see her again – he was risking a great deal, possibly sinning irreparably against his family and his bourgeois status; and he faced very uncertain days ahead. But not for a minute did it occur to him that he might act any differently. This also was part of the play, this risk and this sense of doom. Not tomorrow and not the day after, but one day they would meet, and until then he'd live, live anew, not the way he had over the past years. *Incipit vita nova.**

2

HE READ THE ITALIAN NEWSPAPERS from cover to cover every day, with highly mixed feelings. He enjoyed the paradoxical notion that they wrote the Italian papers in Italian, in this grandly flowing, magnificent language; yet when broken into items of daily news, the language seemed as if it were operating ranks of sewing machines. But he found the papers' content deeply depressing. Italian papers are constantly, ecstatically joyful, as if it weren't even people who were writing them but triumphant saints just descended from one of Fra Angelico's paintings to celebrate the perfect political system. There was always cause for rejoicing: an institution had just turned eleven on one occasion, and on another, a roadway had just turned twelve. At such events, someone would give a major speech and the people would cheer passionately, at least according to the press reports.

Like every foreigner, Mihály also wondered whether the people indeed celebrated everything as enthusiastically – whether they were as untiringly, constantly, uninterruptedly happy – as the papers claimed. Naturally, he understood perfectly well that a foreigner could only measure the temperature and sincerity of Italian happiness with difficulty, especially if he didn't talk to anyone and made no connection of any kind with Italian life. But to the extent that someone as distracted and distant as Mihály could judge, he felt that the Italian people were indeed indefatigably happy and enthusiastic, ever since it had come into fashion. But he also knew how little – and what foolishness – it takes for people to be happy, either as individuals or as a mass.

But he didn't occupy himself too much with this issue. His instincts told him that, in Italy, the identity of those who wielded power – and the principles in the name of which they ruled the people – didn't matter at all. Politics only touched on the surface; the people – the vast, vegetative Italian people – bore the changing times on their backs with amazing passivity, and they didn't acknowledge having anything to do with their magnificent history. He suspected that even Republican and Imperial Rome, with its gigantic gestures, with its heroism and its scandals, had merely been superficial manly histrionics: all that ancient Roman posturing was the private affair of a few actors of genius, and beneath it all, the Italians calmly ate their pasta, sang of love and conceived their innumerable progeny.

One day, a familiar name in *Popolo d'Italia** struck his eye: "La Conferenza Waldheim". He read the article, from which it turned out that Rodolfo Waldheim, the world-renowned Hungarian classical philologist and historian of religion, had given a lecture at the Accademia Reale, under the title *Aspetti della morte nelle religioni antiche.** The fiery Italian journalist praised the lecture for shining an entirely new light not only on concepts of death in ancient religions but on the nature of death in general, and that by the same token it constituted an important document of Italian-Hungarian friendship. He reported that the audience had enthusiastically applauded the professor, whose youth had also made a surprising and pleasant impression.

Mihály determined that this Waldheim could be none other than Rudi Waldheim, and a very pleasant sort of feeling took hold of him, for he'd felt great affection for Rudi at one time. They had attended university together. Although neither of them was very sociable – Mihály, because he looked down on strangers who hadn't been habitués of the Ulpius house, and Waldheim, because he felt that compared to himself everyone was ignorant, shallow and cheap – a sort of friendship nevertheless developed between them, thanks to history of religion. The friendship wasn't very solid. Waldheim knew a tremendous amount even back then; he read every article on the topic in every language, and he expounded it willingly and splendidly to the eagerly attentive Mihály; but then he discovered that Mihály's interest in history of religion was not too deep: he sensed the dilettante in him and withdrew in suspicion. For Mihály's part, it was precisely Waldheim's enormous erudition that dismayed him: he figured that if a beginning historian of religion already knew that much, then think how much a bearded, practising historian of religion must know – and he lost his courage about the whole enterprise. In any event, he abandoned his university studies not much later. Waldheim, on the other hand, went to Germany to perfect himself at the feet of the field's great masters, and in this way they lost touch with each other completely. As the years passed, newspapers kept Mihály informed about the progress of Waldheim's rapidly advancing scholarly career, and when Waldheim became a university professor, Mihály came very close to writing him a congratulatory letter, but then didn't write, after all. He no longer met him in person.

Now, upon reading his name, Waldheim's quite peculiar amiability, which he'd entirely forgotten in the meantime, came to mind: the fox terrier-like liveliness of his head, shaved bald, round and shiny; his amazing loquaciousness, because Waldheim would expound constantly, loudly, in perfectly formed long sentences and, for the most part, interestingly, so one might suppose that he continued doing so even in his sleep; his indefatigable vitality; his constant appetite for women, with which he bustled around even those female colleagues who were not always very attractive; and mainly his distinguishing quality, which he called – after Goethe but a bit inappropriately – "being engrossed": the fact that scholarship, both its individual components and the abstract whole, the concept of Spirit, kept him in a constant white-hot glow, so that he was never indifferent but always feverishly engaged in something – whether adoring some great and, if possible, ancient manifestation of the Spirit or loathing some "shallow" or "cheap" or "inferior" stupidity – and always put in a trance by that word – Spirit – which, it seems, meant something to him.

The memory of Waldheim's vitality was unexpectedly refreshing. The force of the urge that now suddenly seized him to meet Waldheim, even briefly, instantly made him realize the utter isolation in which he'd been living for weeks already. Isolation, of course, was an unavoidable part of awaiting his fate, which was his only occupation in Rome and which he couldn't share with anyone. But it was only now that he noticed how deeply he'd begun to sink into this patient and dreamy expectancy and presentiment of doom that drew him, like seaweed, down towards weird, wondrous deep-water creatures; suddenly he thrust his head up out of the water and drew a breath.

He must meet Waldheim, and one possible practical solution suddenly dawned on him. The article reporting on Waldheim's lecture also made passing mention of a reception given in the Palazzo Falconieri, the seat of the Collegium Hungaricum. Mihály recalled that a Collegium Hungaricum existed in Rome, where young artists and scholars lived on scholarships; they'd certainly know Waldheim's address there, if indeed he was not a resident himself.

It wasn't hard to find out the address of the Palazzo Falconieri: it stands on the Via Giulia, not far from the Teatro Marcello, in the neighbourhood where he preferred to wander. Now too he cut through the ghetto's alleys and soon stood there in front of the lovely old palazzo.

The porter acknowledged Mihály's enquiry sympathetically and informed him that the professor was indeed in lodgings here in the Collegium, but that he was still asleep at this time of day. Surprised, Mihály looked at his watch: it was already half-past ten.

"Yes," said the porter, "the professor sleeps until noon every day, and it's forbidden to wake him – and in any case it's not really possible, because he sleeps very soundly indeed."

"Well, then, perhaps I'll return after luncheon," said Mihály.

"Unfortunately, after lunch the professor goes back to bed to sleep, and we're not allowed to disturb him then either."

"And when is he awake?"

"All night," said the porter reverently.

"Then it will be best if I leave my calling card here with my address, and the professor will contact me if he wishes to meet."

When he went home that day, towards evening, a telegram was already awaiting him, in which Waldheim asked him to come visit him for supper. Mihály boarded a tram right away and rumbled down to the Palazzo Falconieri. He loved the C, that fantastic electric line that carried him there from the train station, circumnavigating half the city, passing through forests here and there, stopping in front of the Colosseum, sidling past the Palatine's ruins, leaping along the Tiber's bank: the cavalcade of millennia marched past both sides of the tracks, and the whole journey only took a quarter of an hour.

"Come in," shouted Waldheim when Mihály knocked, but the door he wanted to open got stuck somehow. "Wait, just a moment…" shouted Waldheim from inside, and then after a time the door opened.

"It was slightly blocked," said Waldheim, pointing at the piles of books and manuscripts on the floor. "Don't worry, just come in."

Coming in was not so simple, because the entire floor of the room was piled with all sorts of objects. Between the books and manuscripts were Waldheim's underwear, his garishly bright summer clothes, surprisingly many pairs of shoes, swimming attire and other sports accessories, newspapers, cans of food, boxes of chocolates, letters, reproductions and photos of women.

Mihály looked around, a bit nonplussed.

"You see, I don't like it when they tidy up while I'm here," Waldheim explained. "The cleaning women make such a mess that I can't find a thing. Please, do sit down. Wait, just a moment…"

He swept a few books off one of the book piles, upon which the pile turned out to be a chair, and Mihály sat down warily. Disorder always discomfited him, and this disorder, furthermore, somehow radiated an aura that commanded respect for the sanctity of scholarship.

Waldheim also sat down and immediately began to explain why he was so disordered. His disorder had more than one abstract, intellectual cause, but heredity also played a role.

"My father – I'm sure I've talked about him before – was a painter, perhaps you even remember his name. He too would not allow anyone to touch the objects piled up in his studio. Gradually he became the only person who knew how to get about the studio: only he knew the location of those islands onto which one could step without falling into something. But later, these islands too were buried in the irresistible flood of objects. At such times, my father would lock up the studio, rent another one and begin a new life. When he died, we found out that he had five studios, every one of them stuffed full."

Then he related his life story, beginning from the last time he'd seen Mihály: his university career, his worldwide renown as a philologist, about which he could boast as endearingly and naively as a little boy. He "just happened to have at hand" newspaper articles in various languages that reported on one or another of his lectures in a most courteous tone, among them the one Mihály had seen in *Popolo d'Italia*. And then letters were produced, from a succession of notable foreign scholars and writers who were his friends, as well as his invitation to Doorn, to the annual summer conference of the German ex-Kaiser's archaeological team.* From somewhere, he even magically produced a silver chalice with the ex-Kaiser's monogram.

"Look, I got this from him, following which the entire group drank Hungarian wine, a Tokaji, in my honour."

Then he showed photographs, a great mass of them, flicking through rapidly: in some he could be seen in the company of gentlemen of most scholarly mien, and in others he could be seen in the company of less scholarly-seeming ladies.

"Yours truly in pyjamas," he explained. "Yours truly completely naked… the lady is covering her face in shame…"

And then in one photo, Waldheim appeared in the company of a very ugly woman and a little boy.

"Who are they, this ugly woman and this little boy?" Mihály asked adroitly.

"Oh yes, this is my wife and son," said Waldheim, and laughed heartily. "My family!"

"You have one of those too?" asked Mihály in astonishment. "Where do you keep them?"

For Waldheim's room, his manner, his entire personal presence made such an impression of the inveterate and incorrigible university student, the Stud. Phil. who could never grow up, that Mihály could not imagine adding a wife and child to it.

"Oh, I've been married for centuries," said Waldheim. "This is a very old photograph. Since then, my son has become much larger and my wife much uglier. I acquired her back in Heidelberg, in my third year of studies. She's called Kätzchen – isn't that great? And she's forty-six. But we don't trouble each other very much: they live in Germany, at my dear father-in-law's, and they despise me. Not only for my morals but, more recently, also because I'm not German."

"But you must be German, at least by descent."

"Fine, fine, but you know this sort of *Auslandsdeutsche*, this sort from Pozsony,* an outpost in the Danube basin so remote it doesn't count as equal in rank. That's what my son says, at least, and he's deeply ashamed of me in front of his colleagues. So what can I do? Nothing. But please, eat. Oh, I haven't set out dinner yet? Wait, just a moment… The tea has come to the boil already. But you don't need to drink tea. You can have red wine too."

From somewhere among the mysteries of the floor, he extracted a large package; removing many items and manuscripts from the desktop and placing them on the floor, he set the package down and opened it. Great quantities of cured Italian ham and salami and bread were revealed.

"You see, I only eat cold meats, and nothing else," said Waldheim. "But to make it less boring for you, I took care to provide some variety too, wait, just a moment..."

After a lengthy search, he produced a banana, and the smile with which he extended it to Mihály said: "Have you ever seen such a thoughtful host?"

Mihály was utterly enchanted by this student-like negligence and lack of pretension.

"Here is a man who has achieved the impossible," he thought to himself enviously, while Waldheim stuffed himself with the cured ham and continued to expound. "Here is a man who succeeded in ossifying himself in the stage of life that most suited him. For it's a fact that every man has a stage of life suited uniquely to himself. Some remain children their whole lives long, and some are awkward, anomalous, not finding their place their whole lives long until they suddenly become wise and lovely old ladies or old men: they have found their true home in their old age. What's miraculous about Waldheim is that he managed to remain a university student in his soul without it forcing him to give up his place in the world, his success and intellectual life. He set out on a career in which his spiritual backwardness, it seems, isn't noticeable – on the contrary, it's even advantageous – and he only acknowledges as much of reality as is compatible with his obsessions. That's the ticket! If only I could have arranged things this way too..."

Shortly after dinner, Waldheim looked at his watch and said in agitation: "Good Heavens, I have very urgent business with a woman, here in the neighbourhood. Please, if you have nothing better to do, it would be most kind of you to accompany me and wait for me. It really won't take long. And afterwards we can sit down in some dive and continue our fascinating dialogue." ("He surely hasn't even noticed that I haven't spoken a word," thought Mihály.)

"I'll be delighted to accompany you," he said.

"I love women awfully much," said Waldheim on the way. "Maybe even to excess. You know, in my youth I didn't connect with as many women as I ought, or as I'd like to have had, partly because of the stupidity of youth, and partly because my strict upbringing forbade it. My mother raised me; she was a *Pfarrer*'s daughter, a true imperial German *Pfarrer*.* I spent time with them once during my childhood, and I asked the old gentleman – I no longer know why – who Mozart was. "*Der war ein Scheunepurzler*," he said, which means, more or less, that he entertained the public with somersaults in a barn – the old man lumped all artists into this category. So in other words, nowadays I feel that I'll never be able to make up for what I missed in the way of women before the age of twenty-five."

He disappeared into a dark gateway. Bemused but in a good mood, Mihály strolled back and forth. After a while, he heard an odd, high-spirited cough; he looked up, and Waldheim was sticking his shiny round head out a window. "Ahem. I'm on my way already."

"A very likable woman," he said when he'd come down. "Her breasts sag a bit, but that's all right: one must get used to that too. I chanced to meet her in the Forum and seduced her by explaining that the Black Stone* may have a phallic meaning. You, of course, have no idea how effective the history of religion is in seducing women. They eat history of religion out of my hand. On the other hand, I'm afraid that one can also seduce women with differential calculus or double-entry bookkeeping, as long as one explains it with sufficient passion. They pay no attention to the words anyhow. And if they do pay attention, then they don't understand them. Yet they can deceive you on occasion. Sometimes they behave quite as if they were men. That's all right. I love them. And they love me too: that's the main thing. Ah, we'll go in here."

Mihály made an involuntary grimace when he saw the tavern that Waldheim wanted to enter.

"I'm not saying it's pretty, but it's so cheap," said Waldheim. "But I see that you're still such a fastidious little boy, like you were at university. I don't mind: just this once let's go to some better place, to make you happy."

Again that smile appeared, acknowledging his own generosity: that he was willing to pay for his own drinks in a more expensive place just for Mihály's sake.

They entered a tavern just a shade better than the previous one. Waldheim talked for a while longer, and then he seemed to tire a bit. He brooded, staring ahead, for a few moments, and then, suddenly astonished, he turned to Mihály: "So what have you been doing all this while?"

Mihály broke into a smile. "I learnt the trade and worked in my father's firm."

"You worked? That's all? And in the past tense? So what about now?"

"I'm not doing anything now. I fled from home, I'm idling here and I'm considering what I should do."

"What you should do? Well, can you even ask? Take up history of religion. Believe me, it's the most relevant discipline today."

"But why do you think I should occupy myself with scholarship at all? How could I get involved in scholarship?"

"Because everybody who isn't stupid must engage in scholarship for the salvation of his own soul. It's the sole occupation worthy of man. I'm not saying, perhaps the visual arts and music, too... But to engage in anything else, for instance working at a commercial firm, for a man who isn't a complete idiot... I'll tell you what it is: an affectation!"

"An affectation? How so?"

"Look, if you please: I recall how you set out to become a proper historian of religion. I'm not saying... well, you weren't a particularly quick-witted boy, but one can compensate for a lot with diligence, and people much less talented than even you have become outstanding scholars, indeed... And then, I don't know exactly, but I can imagine what might have gone on inside your bourgeois soul: you realized that a scholarly career doesn't ensure material well-being, that you have no interest in the boring routine of a high-school teacher's work and this and that: in other words, you'd have to set out on a practical career, taking account of your economic requirements. The practical life is a myth, a bluff discovered for their own reassurance by those incapable of engaging in intellectual matters. But you have more brains than to fall for that. Your behaviour was just an affectation. And now is the most important time for you to discard that pose and return where you belong: the scholarly life."

"And what should I live on?"

"My God, that's not a problem. You can see that I too live on something."

"Yes: a university professor's salary."

"True. But I'd survive even without it. One needn't be a spendthrift. I'll teach you how to live on salami and tea. It's very healthy. You people don't know how to be thrifty: that's the problem."

"But Rudi, I have other problems too. I'm not sure that engagement in scholarship would satisfy me as much as it does you... I'm not passionate enough about it... I can't believe in the importance of these things as much..."

"What are you talking about?"

"Well, for instance, the history of religion's findings. I don't know, sometimes I think that it's almost irrelevant why it was precisely a wolf that raised Romulus and Remus..."

"How the hell could it be irrelevant? You've gone utterly mad. No, you're just putting on an affectation again. But we've talked enough now. Now I'm going home, and I'm going to work."

"Now? It's already past midnight!"

"Yes, this is when I can work: nothing bothers me this time of night, and somehow not even thoughts of women distract me now. I work from now until four in the morning, and then I go running for an hour."

"You do what?"

"I go running. I can't fall asleep without it. I go down to the bank of Tiber and run up and down there. The policemen already know me and don't bother me. Just like back home. All right, let's go. Along the way, I'll tell you what I'm working on now. It's utterly sensational. You still remember that Sophron* fragment that turned up not too long ago..."

By the time he reached the end of his exposition, they'd arrived in front of the Falconieri palace.

"But to return to what you ought to do," Waldheim said suddenly. "It's only difficult at the start. You know what, tomorrow I'll get up somewhat earlier, for your sake. Come meet me here, let's say at half-past eleven. I'll take you to the Villa Giulia. I'll wager that you haven't been to the Etruscan Museum yet, right? Well, if you're not seized by the urge to pick up the thread there, then you're indeed a lost man. And, in that case, off you go to your father's factory. Well, God be with you."

And he hurried into the dark palace.

3

THE NEXT DAY, THEY INDEED WENT OFF to the Villa Giulia. They looked at the graves, the sarcophagi on whose lids the old dead Etruscans lived gaily, eating, drinking and embracing their wives, proclaiming the Etruscan philosophy, which, however, they never wrote down, because the Etruscans were so wise that they never developed a literature in the course of their cultural lives, although it could be read unmistakably from the statues' faces: only the moment counts, and a beautiful moment never comes to an end.

Waldheim showed him broad drinking bowls; the ancient Italians drank their wines from them, as the inscription said: *Foied vino pipafo, cra carefo.**

"I drink wine today, tomorrow there shall be none," Waldheim translated. "Well, tell me, can it be formulated more concisely and truly? This sentence, in its archaic magnificence, is as definitive, as immovable as the fortress walls of polygonal stones, the cyclopean structures. *Foied vino pipafo, cra carefo.*"

Statue groups stood in one cabinet: dreaming men led by women, dreaming women led – or ravished – by satyrs.

Surprised, Mihály asked, "What are these?"

"This is death," said Waldheim, and his voice suddenly sharpened, as always when a serious scholarly issue became the subject. "This is death, or perhaps dying, rather. Because they're not the same thing. These women luring the men away, these satyrs making off with the women are death demons. But did you notice? Male demons seize the women and female demons the men. These Etruscans knew perfectly well that dying is an erotic act."

Something shivered right through Mihály. Could it be that someone else knew this too, not just Tamás Ulpius and himself? Could it be that this underlying sense of life was, for the Etruscans, at some time a self-evident spiritual reality that could be depicted, and that Waldheim's genius for religious-historical intuition could fathom this reality just as well as so many other mysteries and horrors of the ancients' faith?

The issue brought him into such a state of confusion that he didn't say a word, neither in the museum nor on the tram on the way back; but that evening, when he looked Waldheim up and the red wine emboldened him, he asked him after all, taking care not to let his voice tremble: "Tell me, please, how did you mean it, when you said that dying is an erotic act?"

"I mean everything the way I say it: I'm no symbolist poet. To die is an erotic act, or if you prefer, a sexual pleasure. At least, it was for the people of ancient cultures: for the Etruscans, for the Homeric Greeks, for the Celts."

"I don't understand," Mihály pretended. "I always thought that the Greeks feared death horribly; after all, the afterlife was no consolation to the Homeric Greeks, if I recall Rohde's* book properly. And the Etruscans, who lived for the moment, trembled even more in fear of death."

"That's all true. Those peoples apparently feared death much more than even we do. Civilization grants us such a splendid spiritual apparatus that for the great majority of our lives, we can forget that one day we shall die; eventually, we'll push death aside from our awareness just as much as we've already pushed the existence of God aside. This is civilization at work. But for archaic man, nothing was more present than death and the dead: the dead man himself, whose mysterious further existence, fate and desire for vengeance constantly preoccupied him. They feared death and the dead horribly, save that everything was even more ambivalent in their souls than in our own:

the great contradictions were still much closer together. The fear of death and the longing for death were immediate neighbours in their souls, and fear was often longing, and longing often fear."

"My God, the death wish is no archaic matter but an eternally human one," said Mihály, defending himself from his own thoughts. "There have always been and always will be the exhausted and the world-weary who seek redemption in death."

"Don't talk nonsense, and don't pretend you don't understand me. I'm not talking about the exhausted and the sick, or about the death wish of the suicidal, but about those who long for death in the fullness of life – indeed, precisely because their lives are so full: as for the greatest ecstasy, what is often referred to as mortal passion. Either you understand it or you don't – it can't be explained – but it was self-evident to the ancients. That's why I say that dying is an erotic act: because they longed for it and, in the final analysis, all desire is erotic – or rather, we call erotic anything that contains the god Eros: that is to say, desire. A man always longs for some woman, said our friends the Etruscans: therefore death and dying is a woman. It's a woman for the man; for the woman a man, a rapacious satyr. That's what those statues that you saw this morning are saying. But I could show you other things, too; the images of death hetaerae* in different archaic reliefs. Death is a strumpet who lures young men away. They portray her with a huge vagina. And this vagina clearly also means more than that. That's where we came from and that's where we're headed, these people said. We were born thanks to an erotic act and out of a woman, and we die thanks to an erotic act and through a woman, through the death hetaera, who is the Mother's great opposite and culmination... when we die, we are reborn... understand? By the way, this is what I said the other day in my lecture at the Accademia Reale, under the title *Aspetti della morte*; it was a great success in the Italian papers. I happen to have it with me, wait just a moment..."

Shuddering, Mihály looked around at the merry chaos of Waldheim's room. It reminded him, to some extent, of the old room in the Ulpius house. He sought some sort of sign, something that would corroborate it in a completely concrete form... Tamás's proximity, Tamás, whose thoughts Waldheim was propounding here with scholarly clarity and objectivity in this summer night. Now Waldheim's voice was cuttingly sharp and whistling, as always when his explanations rubbed up against "the essence". Mihály quickly downed a glass of wine and stepped to the window to draw a breath; something had weighed him down very heavily.

"The death wish is one of the most important myth-generating forces," Waldheim continued to explain, now more excitedly and for his own benefit. "When we read the *Odyssey* properly, well, the whole thing doesn't even deal with anything else. There are the death hetaerae, Circe and Calypso, who lure the traveller into their caverns on the happy isle of the dead and don't want to let them go on; entire empires of the dead, the lotus-eaters, the land of the Phaeacians; and who knows whether Ithaca itself isn't also a nation of the dead?... Far to the west: the dead always sail following the sun into the west... and Odysseus's nostalgia for and return to Ithaca might mean the nostalgia for nonexistence and a return birth... It's possible that Penelope means 'duck' and was originally a soul bird, but I can't prove it for the time being. You see, this is the sort of topic one ought to take up with unconditional urgency: you too... You could work out a part of it to become proficient in the methods of religious scholarship. For instance, it would be most interesting if you were to write something about Penelope as a soul duck."

Mihály politely turned the commission down: at the moment, this did not much interest him. "Why is it that only the ancient Greeks sensed the presence of death so intensely?" he asked.

"Because the nature of civilization everywhere – including among the Greeks – is to distract people's attention from the reality of death and counterbalance the death wish at the same time as it also diminishes the raw desire for life. Christian civilization did the same thing. And yet the peoples that Christianity had to tame brought even greater death cults with themselves than the Greeks did. As a matter of fact, the Greeks were not a particularly death-obsessed people; it's just that they could express everything better than others. The truly death-obsessed peoples were the northern ones, the Germanic tribes in the deep midnight of their forests and the Celts, the Celts most of all. Celtic legends are full of isles of the dead; the later Christian scribes, in their characteristic fashion, remade these islands into isles of the blessed, and the stupid folklore researchers generally fell for it. But tell me, please, is it really the isle of the blessed that sends its emissary, the fairy, to Prince Bran in the guise of an irresistible compulsion?* Or when the man returning from bliss suddenly turns to dust and ashes the moment he leaves the blessed isle, tell me, please, what do you think, why are those people on the island – the other isle – laughing? From happiness? The hell they are: they're laughing because they're dead, and their laughter is the horrid death grin visible on Indian masks and Peruvian mummies. But this, alas, is not my field, the Celts. But you could study them. You should learn Gaelic and Cymric, quickly and without fail – after all, you don't have anything else to do. And you should go to Dublin."

"Fine," said Mihály, "but keep going, I beg you: you can't believe how fascinating it is. How did humanity stop longing for the isles of the dead? Or do they still long for them, perhaps? In other words, how does the story end?"

"I can only respond with a small Spenglerism* of my own manufacture. One of the first consequences of the northern races taking their place in the Christian alliance of peoples, in European civilization, if you recall, was that for two centuries there was no other topic of discussion than death: during the tenth and eleventh centuries, the centuries of the Cluniac monastic reform.* The danger threatening

Christianity in the early Roman era was that it could become the darkest of death religions, something like that of the Mexican Indians. But then its original Mediterranean and humanist character broke through in the end. What happened? The Mediterraneans succeeded in sublimating and rationalizing the death wish – or, in plain Hungarian, they diluted the death wish into a longing for the afterlife: they refashioned the horrid sex appeal of the death sirens into the beckoning, angelically musical message of the heavenly chorus. Now the believer could long freely for a beautiful death; he wasn't longing for the pagan, erotic joys of dying, but for the civilized and honourable joys of heaven. For its part, the raw, ancient pagan death wish went into exile, into the subliminal layers below faith, among the elements of superstition, witchcraft and Satanism. The stronger civilization becomes, the more deeply the love of death is buried in the subconscious.

"Consider this: in civilized society, death, taken in its entirety, has ended up among the taboo concepts. It's not proper to speak of it; people write euphemisms for it, as if it were some obscenity, and the dead, the corpse, becomes the deceased, the departed, the late, just the same as they paraphrase the acts of digestion. And whereof one does not speak, thereof it is also improper to think.* This is civilization's defence against the terrible danger that consists of the fact that in man the instinct for life is opposed by an instinct in the opposite direction, an instinct that is most cunning, calling him towards annihilation with a sweet and powerful allure. This instinct is all the more dangerous to the civilized soul because civilized man's appetite for raw vitality is already diminished. This is why he must suppress the other longing with fire and sword. But this suppression doesn't always succeed. The other longing breaks out in decadent eras and inundates all the territories of the spirit to a surprising degree. Sometimes entire classes knowingly dig their own graves, like the French aristocrats before the Revolution, and I'm afraid that the most contemporary example today is provided by the transdanubian Hungarians...*

"I'm not sure you understand me perfectly. In general, people used to misunderstand me spectacularly when I'd speak on this subject. But I can perform a test: do you know this feeling? Someone's walking on a slippery sidewalk and slips; one of his legs slips out from under him, and he begins to fall backwards. For my part, at the instant when I'm losing my balance, I'm seized by a sudden joy. Of course, it only lasts an instant, and then I automatically snatch my leg back, regain my balance and happily note that I haven't fallen. But for a moment! For a moment I suddenly freed myself from the terrible laws of equilibrium and began to fly into some annihilating freedom... Are you familiar with this sensation?"

"I know the feeling much better than you can imagine," Mihály said quietly.

Waldheim suddenly gazed at him with astonishment. "My word, how odd you sounded when you said that, old chap! And how pale you are! What's happened to you? Come out on the terrace."

Once on the terrace, Mihály instantly recovered.

"The devil take you," said Waldheim. "What is this? Are you too warm, or are you a hysteric? I warn you, if you commit suicide under the influence of my words, I'll deny that I ever knew you. Everything I say is always of a strictly theoretical nature. I detest the sort of people who draw practical conclusions from scholarly truths, who 'transfer the lessons to life', like the engineers who fabricate bedbug insecticides from the audacious theorems of chemistry. It's the opposite of what Goethe said: all life is grey, and the golden tree of theory is green.* And especially when it's a matter of theories that are still green, like this one. So, I hope I've restored your spiritual equilibrium. And really... you shouldn't live a spiritual life at all. I think that's your problem. The intelligent man has no spiritual life. And tomorrow, come with me to the Archaeological Institute of America's garden party. You have to amuse yourself a bit. So. Go home now, and I'll get back to work."

4

THE ARCHAEOLOGICAL INSTITUTE of America occupies a beautiful villa in the middle of a large garden on the Gianicolo Hill. Its annual garden party is a major event for the Anglo-Saxon community in Rome; its organizers are not only American archaeologists, but primarily American painters and sculptors living in Rome, and its participants are all those with any connection to them. An extraordinarily diverse, and thus extraordinarily interesting group used to gather here.

But Mihály experienced little of the company's diversity and interest. He was again in a psychological state in which things reached him as if through a veil or fog: the summer night's uniquely fragrant happiness, mixed with the dance music, the drinks and the women with whom he chatted – about what, he himself did not know. His Pierrot costume and mask abstracted him completely: it wasn't even he himself who was present, but somebody else, a sleepy mask.

The hours passed in a pleasant daze; it was already very late, and now he again found himself standing on the lawn at the top of the little hill, under the umbrella pine, and again he heard those strange, inexplicable voices that had disquieted him again and again during the night.

The voices sounded from behind a very high wall, and as the night progressed, the wall grew higher, reaching the sky. The voices came from behind the wall, now louder and now dying away, sometimes with the intensity of shouting into one's ear and sometimes just like the distant moaning of mourners on the shore of some distant lake or sea, under an ashen sky... Then they fell silent, remaining quiet for a long time, and Mihály began to forget about them and feel just like a man at a garden party; and he let Waldheim, who was wonderfully in his element, introduce him to a new lady, when the voices spoke up yet again.

The mood had just begun to develop most pleasantly: everyone was falling under the influence of that subtler and stronger inebriation resulting not from alcohol but from the night itself. One crosses the threshold of sleep; one's accustomed bedtime has passed by irretrievably; by now it's all the same: one no longer has a guilty conscience and freely gives oneself over to the night. Waldheim sang excerpts from *La Belle Hélène*,* Mihály was occupied with a Polish lady, and everything was most pleasant, when he heard that singing again. Excusing himself, he went up to the top of the hill and stood there alone, his heart pounding a bit, and listened intently, as if everything depended on his solving this mystery.

Now he could hear it clearly: beyond the trees were several voices, probably men, singing some wailing tune resembling nothing else, in which certain discernible but incomprehensible words recurred rhythmically. There was a deep and tragic pain in this song, but something not human, just short of human, something reminiscent of the howling of animals in a drawn-out night, some sort of pain left over from the age of trees, the age of the umbrella pines. Mihály sat down under the pine and closed his eyes. No, these weren't men, after all, who were singing over there, but women, and he already saw them before him, a strange company that reminded him of the Naconxipan, the inhabitants of that fantasy land painted by the mad Gulácsy,* in deep, intoxicatingly purple dresses – and then he thought that this might be how gods used to be mourned – Attis, Adonis*... and Tamás, Tamás who died unmourned at the beginning of time, and now lay on a bier over there, behind the wall, the dawn of the next day glimmering on his face.

When he opened his eyes, a woman was standing above him, leaning her shoulder against the pine, in a classicizing costume – just as Goethe and his ilk had imagined the Greeks – and wearing a mask. Mihály straightened himself up out of politeness, and asked the lady in English: "Would you happen to know who those men or women are, who are singing over there?"

"Of course," replied the lady. "There's a Syrian cloister next door, whose monks chant psalms every other hour. Eerie, isn't it?"

"Yes," said Mihály.

They were silent for a while. Finally the woman spoke up: "I must give you a message. On behalf of an old, old acquaintance of yours."

Mihály stood up at once. "Éva Ulpius?"

"Yes, the message is from Éva Ulpius. She says not to seek her, since you won't find her anyhow. It's too late. You should have come and found her, she says, in the house in London, when she was hiding behind the tapestry. But then you shouted Tamás's name, she says. And now it's too late."

"Is there any way I could speak to Éva?"

"No way at all."

Now the singers' lament beyond the wall welled up again, louder than before, as if they were crying against the dawn, or mourning the waning night with what had by now become a choked, broken yelling, tearing at themselves murderously. The woman shuddered. "Look, the dome of St Peter's," she said.

The dome swam there above the city, white and very cold, like indomitable eternity itself. The woman hurried down the hill.

Mihály felt boundless fatigue, as if he had been hitherto clutching his life convulsively in both hands and was now about to let it slip away from him.

Then he suddenly gathered himself together and hurried off after the woman, who had already disappeared.

There was a great scrum of people down below: most of the guests were bidding farewell, but Waldheim was reading from, and expounding upon, the *Symposium*.* Mihály rushed to and fro in the throng, then hurried out the garden gate: perhaps he would find the woman among those who were getting in their vehicles there.

He arrived just at the right moment. The woman got into a beautiful, old-fashioned, open carriage, in which another female figure was already seated, and the coach headed off quickly. Mihály instantly recognized the other woman. It was Éva.

5

THE NEGOTIATIONS BETWEEN THE BANKS were long drawn out. The matter could, in fact, have been dealt with very simply, if only intelligent men had been sitting around the table – but this tends not to happen in life. The lawyers dazzled each other with their ability to slide down the steepest sentences without falling over; the big money men spoke little, keeping their mouths shut suspiciously, and their silence said, more clearly than any words could: "I'm not giving you any money."

"There'll be no deal here, as usual," Zoltán Pataki, Erzsi's first husband, thought with resignation.

He became more and more anxious and impatient. Lately he had noticed more than once that he couldn't pay attention during negotiations, and he'd become still more anxious and impatient ever since.

An automobile horn's long blast now sounded under the window. In bygone days, Erzsi had often waited down below in the car when negotiations dragged on too long.

"Erzsi... don't think of her now; it still hurts too much, but time will cure you. Let's move on, let's move on. Emptily, like the limousine after we disembarked – but let's just go."

He made a gesture of resignation with his hand, drew his mouth into an odd expression and felt very, very tired. Lately these four actions, connected to one another and following each other automatically, returned like nervous tics: Erzsi came to mind, he made a resigned gesture, pulled his mouth to one side and felt very tired, as many as thirty times a day. Should he go to the doctor because of this fatigue? Nonsense: "we'll get over it, old boy, we'll get over it."

Now he pricked up his ears. They were saying that someone ought to go to Paris to negotiate with a certain financial organization. A different gentleman said that it was totally unnecessary, since it could be dealt with by post.

"Erzsi's in Paris now… Mihály in Italy… Erzsi hasn't written so much as a word, whereas she must be feeling so frightfully lonely. Does she have enough money? Maybe she has to take the metro, poor thing; if she leaves before nine and returns after two, she can get a much cheaper return ticket; poor thing, that must be what she's doing. But maybe she isn't alone, after all. It's hard for a woman to remain alone in Paris, and Erzsi's so good-looking…"

It wasn't a gesture of resignation that followed this thought, but rather, the blood rushing to his head, and the phrase "Death, death, there's no other solution…"

Meanwhile, the conviction grew among the assembled that they ought to send someone after all. Pataki asked to speak. Throwing all his effort into it, he argued that it was absolutely necessary to continue the negotiation with the French counterparts in person. When he began to speak, he wasn't entirely clear what the issue was, but as he spoke, it dawned on him, and he crafted a series of irrefutable arguments. And indeed, he convinced the gathering. Then the great fatigue took hold of him again.

"Of course someone must go to Paris. But I can't go. Nor can I leave the bank here, at this time; and in any case, why would I go? Erzsi hasn't invited me. And for me to chase after her, to run the very likely risk of rejection, that really can't be… Ultimately, a man also needs his self-respect."

He finished speaking abruptly. Convinced, the meeting decided to send a young director, son-in-law of one of the big money men, who spoke French splendidly. "This will be good schooling for him," the older financiers thought to themselves paternalistically.

After the meeting followed the day's most difficult stretch: the evening. Pataki once read that the most important difference between a married man and a bachelor is that the married man always knows with whom he'll be eating supper that evening. Indeed, this had been the biggest problem in Pataki's life ever since Erzsi had left him. With whom should he dine? He never liked men and was unfamiliar with the notion of friendship. Women? This was the oddest thing. While he had been Erzsi's husband, he had needed women in great number, and always new ones; he found every woman attractive: one because she was so skinny, another because she was so plump, a third because she was precisely the golden mean. He spent every free moment with women, and often moments that were not free as well. There was his *maîtresse de titre*,* connected in some inscrutable way with the theatre and costing him enormous sums of money, but who by the same token provided publicity for the bank, and then, from time to time, there were genteel loves, the wife of one colleague or another, but most often the girls in the typing pool, sometimes supplemented by a maidservant here or there for variety's sake: an awful collection. Erzsi had a legitimate grievance, and in his more optimistic moments Pataki thought that this was why Erzsi had left him. In his pessimistic moments, he saw clearly that Erzsi had left him for other reasons, for deficiencies that he could not make good, and this knowledge was dreadfully humiliating. When Erzsi went away, as a chivalrous final indemnification he dismissed his *maîtresse de titre* – or rather, immediately handed her over to an older colleague who had long campaigned for the honour; he "reorganized" his secretaries, placing one of the bank's ugliest employees by his side, and lived a life of abstinence.

"We should have had a child," he thought, suddenly feeling that he'd have loved his child, Erzsi's child, immensely, had there been one. Swiftly making his mind up, he telephoned one of his nieces who had two adorable children and went there for supper. He purchased a tremendous quantity of sweets along the way. The two adorable little children would probably never learn to what they owed this opportunity to upset their stomachs for three days running.

After supper, he took a seat in a coffeehouse, read the newspapers and dithered over whether to go to his club for a bit of cards, but he couldn't bring himself to do it. He went home.

The house without Erzsi was still unspeakably depressing. "It's truly high time I did something with Erzsi's furniture. Erzsi's room can't just stay like this, as if she were coming home at any moment, whereas... I ought to have it taken up into the attic or put into storage. I'll furnish it as a sort of club room, with huge armchairs."

Once again he made a gesture of resignation, pulled his mouth to one side and felt very tired. He definitely could not stand it in his home. He ought to move out. He should live in a hotel, like an artist. And change hotels often too. Or maybe in a sanatorium. Pataki adored sanatoriums, with their white calm and medical security. Yes, I'll go up to Sváb Hill. My nerves could really use it. One more wife who leaves me and I'll go mad.

He lay down and then got up again, sensing that he wouldn't be able to sleep, anyhow. He got dressed, but no idea for a destination came to mind, so instead he took some Sevenal* (although he knew perfectly well that it would be of no help at all) and got undressed again.

As soon as he was in bed, the alternatives again presented themselves to him in all their torturousness. Erzsi in Paris: either she's alone, terribly alone – perhaps not even eating properly, going to who knows what awful little *prix-fixe* places – or she's not alone at all. This latter thought was unbearable. He'd already got accustomed to Mihály somehow. Oddly, he was unable to take Mihály seriously, despite the fact that he had seduced Erzsi away from him. Mihály didn't count. Mihály wasn't a man. In the depths of his consciousness, he was convinced that one day it would still be revealed, somehow, that he really wasn't... Erzsi and Mihály might have had relations; they lived as a couple; yet they still didn't belong together as man and wife. It was impossible to imagine that about Mihály. But now, in Paris... the unknown man... the unknown man was a hundred times more tormenting that any known seducer. No, this could not be endured.

He had to go to Paris. He had to see what Erzsi was doing. What if she was starving? But what about his self-esteem? Erzsi wouldn't give a damn, she didn't need him, she wouldn't want to see him...

"Well, then? Isn't it enough that I want to see her? The rest will become clear."

Self-respect! How long have you been so self-respecting, Mister Pataki? If you had always been so dignified in your business life too, then, I ask you, where would you be now? You'd have a flourishing spice shop in Szabadka,* like your dear Papa. Why should you insist on self-respect precisely with regard to Erzsi? Let a man stand on dignity where he takes a risk. Facing the president or, let's say, the state secretary, Krychlovác.* (Well, no, that would be yet another exaggeration.) But to be self-respecting with regard to a woman? That's not even chivalrous, not even gentlemanly. It's laughable.

The next day was one of furious activity. He convinced the bank and all the interested parties that the young son-in-law was not the ideal person; a more experienced man was needed, after all, to negotiate with the French gentlemen.

The interested parties gradually came to the realization that Pataki himself was the appropriately experienced man.

"But do you speak French, Mr Director?"

"Not very much, but nevertheless, they won't take me for a ride; and besides, those with whom we've done business surely know German as well as you or I. Have you ever seen a financier who doesn't speak German? *Deutsch ist ä Weltsprache.*"*

The next morning, he was already on his way.

He took care of the trip's business aspects in half an hour; the Frenchman with whom he had to negotiate, named Loew, indeed spoke German and, in addition, was an intelligent man. The matter was also resolved quickly because Pataki, in contrast to those who were inexpert and uninformed, didn't take economic and financial matters seriously; he treated them the way doctors deal with the sick. He knew that things in this arena were just like in other fields: the talentless often reaped more success than the talented, the people who didn't know what they were doing often worked out better than the experts; a bunch of pseudo-financiers occupied the top spots and directed the world economy, while the true financiers spent their time theorizing in the Schwartzer or the Markó. Here too the quest goes on for legendary and baseless fictions, just as in scholarly fields, where they seek the non-existent and even undesirable Truth. The difference here is that they seek the Wealth that, even in terms of scale, is pointless; for its sake they lose the wealth that actually does have a point. And in the final analysis, this whole pursuit is just as unserious as everything else on earth.

He was proud that he understood this, and that Mihály, for example, didn't. Mihály was an intellectual, and for just this reason, he still believed in money while at the same time he doubted everything else. For instance, Mihály would say things such as: "Psychology as it stands today is an utterly unreliable, primitive science..." or: "Humanism? We preach against war in vain: it just bides its time and then comes..." By contrast, Váraljai Hemp and Flax, now that was serious: you couldn't say anything against it; that was a matter of money, and you couldn't joke about money. Pataki laughed to himself. Váraljai Hemp and Flax, my God... if Mihály and his colleagues only knew... Even lyric poetry is a more serious concern.

"And now we can calmly deal with the second item on our little programme." Mihály's family had given Pataki Erzsi's Parisian address. For Pataki, as he did with everyone, maintained good relations with

Mihály's family too (after all, they weren't really responsible for anything that had happened), and he even brought a present for Erzsi from Mihály's sister. He was pleased to ascertain that Erzsi was no longer living on the left bank, the suspiciously bohemian and émigré Parisian Buda, but on the respectable right bank, near the Étoile.

It was twelve o'clock. He had a café waiter call Erzsi's hotel, since he didn't trust his French enough to wrestle with the difficulties of the Parisian telephone exchange. Madame was not at home. Pataki went on reconnaissance.

He entered the small hotel and asked for a room. As he spoke French poorly, it was easy to play the stupid foreigner. He used hand gestures to indicate that he found the room they showed him to be too dear, and left. But meanwhile he had determined that it was a proper, genteel little hotel: apparently some English also lived there, although he could also sense a hint of shadiness, especially in the chambermaids' faces: there must surely also be rooms here that old Frenchmen rent as a *pied-à-terre*, paying for the full month but only using them for two hours a week. Why did Erzsi move here from the opposite bank? Does she want to live more elegantly, or does she have a more elegant lover?

At four in the afternoon he telephoned again. This time, Madame was at home.

"Hello, Erzsi? Zoltán speaking."

"Oh, Zoltán..."

Pataki thought he heard Erzsi's pounding heart stifling her voice. Was that a good sign?

"How are you, Erzsi? Is everything all right?"

"Yes, Zoltán."

"I'm here in Paris, you know – there were all sorts of complications with Váraljai Hemp and Flax and I had to come out. I've got loads of running around to do – I've nearly walked my feet off the past three days. I'm so bored of this city already..."

"Yes, Zoltán."

"And I thought that, as long as I'm already here, and now that I have a bit of time today to take a breath, I'd enquire as to how you are."

"Yes... most kind of you."

"Are you well?"

"I'm fine."

"Tell me... hello... could I see you?"

"What for?" asked Erzsi from a vast distance.

Pataki staggered a bit and leant against the wall. But he continued gaily: "What do you mean, what for? Why shouldn't I see you, if I'm already here in Paris, right?"

"I suppose."

"Can I come up to see you?"

"Yes, Zoltán. No, don't come up. Let's meet somewhere."

"Splendid. I know a most charming tea room here. Do you know where Smith, the English bookshop, is on Rue de Rivoli?"

"More or less."

"Well then, it has an English tea room on the upper floor. You enter through the bookshop. Come over, and I'll be waiting for you there."

"Good."

He chose that place because, as far as Erzsi was concerned, he found everything French to be suspect. He imagined that to Erzsi, Paris and Frenchness represented everything he lacked and couldn't offer her. In French cafés (which he detested in any case, because the waiters didn't respect him enough and didn't bring water along with the coffee), all of France would support Erzsi in her struggle against him, and Erzsi would gain the upper hand. He selected the English tea room's cool and neutral extraterritoriality in the interest of *fair play*.

Erzsi indeed showed up, they ordered and Pataki strove to behave as if nothing at all had transpired between them, neither marriage nor divorce. Two intelligent people from Pest, a woman and a man, meeting in Paris. He regaled her with the latest juicy gossip about their common acquaintances in Pest. Erzsi listened to him attentively.

All the while, Pataki was thinking: "This is Erzsi here. She hasn't changed significantly – of course, not that much time has passed since she was my wife. She's wearing one or two Parisian items; they're chic, but my sense is that they're not of the highest quality. Erzsi seems a little broken. There's a very slightly veiled quality to her voice that pains my heart. My poor dear! That cad, Mihály! So is this what she wanted? It seems that she hasn't got over it yet… or could new disappointments have befallen her in Paris? The unknown man… O my God, my God, here I am talking about Péter Bodrogi's sister-in-law, and meanwhile I just want to die.

"This is Erzsi here. Life-sized. Here in front of my eyes is the woman I cannot live without. Why, oh why? Why is she the only desirable woman for me, when now, for instance, I don't desire her in the least? There were many much 'better women' among the others, for example Gizi, not even to mention Mária… I'd feel a rush of blood the moment I caught sight of them. And, more to the point, there were much younger ones too. Erzsi isn't even all that young any more… Why is it that, nevertheless, here and now, with cool reason and in the absence of any passionate fog, I'd pay half my net worth if only she'd go to bed with me?"

Erzsi rarely looked at Zoltán, but she smiled as she listened to the gossip and thought: "How much he knows about everyone! One is so at home with him. Mihály didn't know anything about anyone. He was incapable of remembering who was whose in-law or girlfriend. I don't understand why I was afraid and why I became so upset. Does the cliché 'the abandoned husband' really exist in the flesh? After all, I should have known perfectly well that Zoltán could never wind up in a situation that was even the least bit tragic. Something's always smiling in his eyes. He recoils from anything magnificent. If his fate were to bear him to a martyr's death, then he'd surely be telling one more joke or piece of gossip at the stake, to take the tragic edge off the situation. Yet he must have suffered a lot: he's gone more grey than he was before. But at the same time, he's shoved the suffering aside somehow. And from time to time, he's felt splendid. One can't feel sorry for him."

"Well? And what's up with you?" Zoltán asked suddenly.

"With me? What should there be? You obviously know why I came to Paris..."

"Yes, I know the story in its outlines, but I don't know why everything happened the way it did. Won't you tell me?"

"No, Zoltán. Don't be angry. I can't imagine why I would talk to you about what happened between Mihály and me. I didn't tell Mihály anything about you either. It's only natural."

"This is Erzsi here," thought Zoltán. "Refined and thoroughly well brought up. No catastrophe can make her indiscreet. She is self-control on two legs. And the way she's looking at me, with such cold and judgemental politeness! She's retained her ability to make me feel like a spice-shop assistant merely by looking at me. But I won't let myself be scared off so easily."

"Still, perhaps you can at least tell me what your plans are," he said.

"For the time being, I have no plans at all. I'll stay here in Paris."

"Do you feel good here?"

"Pretty good."

"Have you filed for divorce yet?"

"No."

"Why not?"

"So many questions, Zoltán! I haven't filed for it because the time hasn't yet come."

"So you think that he might... don't be angry... that he might still return to you?"

"I don't know. It's possible. I don't even know if I'd like it if he returned. Maybe I'd refuse to speak with him. Since we didn't suit each other. But... Mihály's not like other people; first, I'd like to know what his intentions are. What do I know? It's possible that he'll wake up one fine day and look around, wondering where I am. And then, in despair, he'll realize that he left me by accident there on the train. And he'll search the length of Italy for me."

"Do you really think so?"

Erzsi bowed her head. "You're right. I don't really believe that."

"Why was I so honest?" the question bit into her. "Why did I reveal myself this way, as to no one else? It seems that something has remained between Zoltán and me after all: some intimacy that can't be terminated. You can't undo four years of marriage. There's not another person on earth to whom I'd talk about Mihály."

"My time has not yet come," thought Zoltán. "She still loves that oaf. Fortunately, Mihály will spoil everything in due course."

"What have you heard about Mihály?" Pataki asked.

"Nothing. I'm just guessing that he's in Italy. There's a good friend of his here, whom I also know, a fellow by the name of Szepetneki. He says that he's on the trail and will soon discover where Mihály is and what he's up to."

"How will he do that?"

"I don't know. Szepetneki is a most unusual man."

"Really?" Zoltán snatched his head up and looked hard at Erzsi. She stubbornly returned his gaze.

"Really. He's a most unusual man. The most unusual I've ever seen. And then there's also a Persian here..."

Pataki lowered his head and downed a big gulp of tea. Which of the two? Or both? "My God, my God, it would be best to die..."

They didn't sit together for long after that. Erzsi had things to do, and she didn't say what.

"Where are you staying?" she asked distractedly.

"At the Édouard VII," said Zoltán.

"Well, goodbye, Zoltán. It really felt very good to see you, as a matter of fact. And... live in peace, and don't think of me," she said softly, with a sad smile.

That day, Pataki took a little Parisian woman home with him. "After all, when in Paris..." he thought, and he was unspeakably revolted by the smelly little stranger who lay breathing heavily in the bed next to him.

In the morning, after the woman left and Pataki arose to begin shaving, there was a knock at the door.

"*Entrez!*"

A tall man, over-elegantly attired and sharp-featured, stepped in. "I'm looking for Mr Pataki, the director, on a very important matter, of great importance to him."

"That is me. With whom do I have the pleasure?"

"My name is János Szepetneki."

Part Four

THE GATES OF HELL

V. *A porta inferi* R. *erue,*
Domine, animam eius.
OFFICIUM DEFUNCTORUM*

1

NIGHT WAS FALLING. Slowly and dragging his feet slightly, Mihály crossed the Tiber.

He'd already been living on the Gianicolo for a long time, in a very shabby little room that Waldheim had found, run by a very shabby old lady who usually also cooked luncheon for him, *pastasciutta*,* which Mihály would round off with a little cheese, and sometimes an orange. All its shabbiness aside, the room was much more like a proper room than a hotel room: the furniture in it was all old – real furniture, large and nobly proportioned, not the sort of pseudo-furniture usually found in hotel rooms. Mihály would have liked his room, had the conditions for washing and performing bodily functions not filled him, over and over again, with the tormenting sensation of having gone down in the world. And he complained about it to Waldheim, who in turn ridiculed him and presented long and not very appetizing discourses on his experiences in Albania and Greece.

This is how poverty introduced itself to him. Now he really had to weigh every centesimo before spending it. He gave up espresso and smoked cigarettes so bad that he could barely finish them, so constantly did they irritate his throat; and it occurred to him with increasing frequency that soon even this money would run out. Waldheim constantly reassured him that he'd find him a position: there were so many crazy old American ladies running around here that one of them would certainly take him on as a secretary or tutor for her grandchildren, or perhaps as a doorman, which is an extraordinarily comfortable job – but for the time being, those American women lived only in Waldheim's imagination. Besides, Mihály trembled at the thought of any occupation, since after all, he could just as well find one in Pest.

He already had two occupations, and these two were entirely enough for him. One was that, as per Waldheim's instructions, he "read up" on the study of Etruscan matters, went to libraries and museums and listened every night to the conversations between Waldheim and his scholarly friends. Not even for a moment did he feel the any of Waldheim's great passion for the topic, but he compulsively stuck to its systematic study because it slightly softened the suffocating bourgeois self-reproach he felt, despite everything, on account of his idle life. Even though Mihály had never liked to work, he'd nevertheless toiled strenuously during his bourgeois years, because he very much liked the knowledge of having been productive during the day. And studying distracted his attention for a while, for a few hours, from his other and more important occupation, which was waiting to meet Éva.

He couldn't reconcile himself to never seeing her again. On the day following that memorable night, he kept walking in the city in a stupor, not knowing what he wanted himself; but later he saw clearly that he could only will one thing – to the extent that one could even use the word "will" here. The Scholastics* had taught that there are levels of existence and only the Perfect exists completely and truly. The time he spent searching for Éva was much more existent, much more true in its reality, than the months and years without Éva; whether it was good or bad, no matter how dreadful the anguish and sense of doom that came with it, he knew that this was life, and without Éva there was no other reality than thinking of Éva and waiting for her.

He was tired; he felt himself utterly doomed, and he dragged his feet as if he were limping. When he reached the bank of the Tiber, he became aware of the sensation that someone was following him. But he suppressed the feeling, convinced that it was just a fleeting delusion.

As he wandered through the alleyways of the Trastevere quarter, however, this inner sensation grew continually stronger. A powerful wind kicked up and the alleys were much less crowded than usual. "If someone's following me, then I'll surely see him," he thought, and turned around from time to time. But several people were walking behind him. "It's possible that someone's following me, and it's also possible that no one is."

As he made his way upward on the narrow streets, this feeling that he was being followed gradually became so oppressive that he didn't bear left onto the way up the hill, but rambled on through the Trastevere alleys, thinking that at an opportune location he'd await the person tracking him. He stopped in front of a small tavern.

"If he wants to attack me," he thought (because such a possibility is easy to imagine in the Trastevere quarter), "here is where I can count on help: someone will have to come out of the tavern if I shout. But in any event I'll wait and see."

He stopped in front of the small tavern and waited. Several people came that way, those who were coming behind him in the alley, but nobody at all paid him any attention; everyone went along on his own path. He was just beginning to think of going when a man approached in the semi-darkness, and Mihály instantly knew that this was the one. His heart pounding, he saw the man heading straight for him.

When the figure drew near, he recognized János Szepetneki. In the entire episode, the most extraordinary aspect – perhaps the only extraordinary aspect – was that he wasn't even particularly surprised.

"Hello," he said quietly.

"Hello, Mihály," said Szepetneki loudly and heartily. "It's good that you finally waited for me. And I was planning to bring you to precisely this tavern. Well, do come in."

They entered the small tavern, whose most characteristic feature, apart from its smell, was its darkness. Mihály could tolerate the odour; oddly, Italian odours didn't bother his otherwise finicky nose. Here there was something staggering, something romantic, even in the stink. But he didn't care for the darkness. Szepetneki was already shouting for a lamp. A languid and gorgeous Italian girl, with large earrings, flashing eyes and astonishing slenderness, brought the lamp. Szepetneki, it seems, was already an old acquaintance of hers, because he gave the girl an affectionate slap on the rump, at which she smiled with large white teeth and launched into a story, in the Trastevere dialect, of which Mihály understood practically not a single word; but János, with his talent for languages (as usual with con men), provided expert commentary. The girl brought wine, sat down at their table and talked. János listened to her with pleasure, forgetting about Mihály entirely. At most, he occasionally offered an opinion in Hungarian, such as: "Damn fine woman, eh? They know what they're doing, these Italians!"

Or: "Do you notice how her eyes flash, eh? Who can do it like that in Pest?"

Or: "She says that they've locked up every one of her boyfriends so far, and that means they're certainly going to lock me up too... she even has a brain, eh?"

Mihály nervously downed one glass of wine after the other. He knew János Szepetneki and knew that he'd take his sweet time getting around to saying what he had to say. Szepetneki needed the appropriate romantic context for everything. Hence this pantomime with the Italian girl; one simply had to wait for it to run its course. It was possible that he'd set up a band of burglars in Trastevere and that this girl and this tavern were also part of it, at least as set decoration. But he also knew that Szepetneki hadn't come here to manage a band of burglars but wanted something from him, and what this might be caused him infinite disquiet.

"Leave that woman in peace and tell me why you followed me and what you want from me. I have neither the time nor inclination to participate in your comedies."

"Why?" asked Szepetneki with an innocent expression. "Does this woman not please you, perhaps? Or this tavern? I thought we could enjoy ourselves for a bit, since it's been so long since we've been together..."

And he began to busy himself with the girl again.

Mihály stood up and prepared to leave.

"No, Mihály, for God's sake don't go yet, since I came to Rome specifically to speak with you. Just stay for one more minute." With that, he turned to the girl. "You be quiet now for a bit."

"How did you know that I'm in Rome?" asked Mihály.

"Oh, I've always known everything about you, my dear Mihály. For years now. But until now nothing about you was worth knowing. You're just beginning to become interesting. That's why we're meeting more frequently now."

"Fine. And now be so kind as to tell me what you want from me."

"I must confer with you."

"Confer, on top of everything? And about what?"

"You'll laugh. About business affairs."

Mihály's face darkened. "Have you been speaking with my father? Or my brothers?"

"No. Not for the time being. For the moment, I have nothing to do with them, only with you. But tell me truly, isn't this girl magnificent? Look what fine hands she has – it's just a shame they're so filthy."

And once more he turned to the girl and began to babble in Italian.

Mihály leapt up and hurried out. He headed uphill. Szepetneki ran after him and soon caught up. Mihály didn't turn around but just let Szepetneki speak to him from behind his back, over his left shoulder, like the Tempter.

János, panting a bit from the climb, spoke rapidly and softly. "Mihály, listen here. As it happens, I've become acquainted with a certain gentleman by the name of Zoltán Pataki, who it turns out is your wife's husband. But that's nothing. It also turns out that this Pataki still adores Her Ladyship to death, whether you believe it or not. He wants to have her back. He's clinging to the hope that, now that you've tossed the lady aside, she may yet recover her wits and return to him. Which would be, beyond a doubt, the best solution for all three of you. You're not saying a word? Fine. You don't yet understand where the opportunity lies, and what I have to do with it. But you know that I've long since outgrown all tact. In my field... In any case, listen here. Her Ladyship, your wife, not only doesn't want to get a divorce from you, but secretly still has faith that the two of you will at some point become happy and peaceable spouses, and that Heaven might even bless your wedlock with children. She knows that you're different, but she has no idea what it means when someone's different. She thinks a great deal about you, to an irritating extent, and at times when she shouldn't. But nonetheless, don't feel sorry for her. She's actually doing quite well; I just don't want to gossip. She's doing quite well, even without you..."

"What do you want?" shouted Mihály, coming to a halt.

"Nothing. It's about a small business matter. Mr Pataki thinks that if you were to take a definitive step, your wife would see that she can no longer expect anything from you, and that this matter is closed."

"What sort of definitive step are you talking about?"

"For example, if you were to initiate divorce proceedings against her."

"How the devil can I do that? Since I'm the one who left her. And besides, even if she had left me, I wouldn't do it. That's the woman's responsibility as the aggrieved party."

"Well, yes. Naturally. But if the woman doesn't want to do it, then you have to. That, at least, is Mr Pataki's position."

"I have nothing to do with Pataki's position, and I no longer have anything to do with the whole thing. You two go talk to Erzsi. I'll agree to anything she wants."

"Look, Mihály, but this is precisely where business opportunity lies: be a bit reasonable. Mr Pataki isn't asking you to file for divorce for nothing. He's willing to make a significant material sacrifice. He's filthy rich, and he can't live without Erzsi. He has even authorized me to disburse a small advance – a rather agreeable small sum – to you right here, right now."

"Rubbish. On what basis could I file for divorce against Erzsi – since I abandoned her? If the court calls on her to restore our common household, she'll even return to me, and then what will I do?"

"Really, Mihály, don't worry about that. You submit the divorce papers, and we'll take care of the rest."

"But on what basis?"

"Adultery."

"You've gone insane!"

"Of course not. Just leave it to me. I'll be able to prove she committed adultery as pure as the driven snow. I have a large clientele in this field."

By this point they were standing in front of Mihály's house. Mihály could hardly wait to be upstairs. "God bless you, János Szepetneki. This time I'm not offering you my hand. What you have said is beyond contempt. I hope not to see you for a very long time."

He hurried up to his room.

2

"I don't know what it's all about, but I'm convinced that your fretting is completely unfounded," said Waldheim with great animation. "You are still your honourable grey father's meek son; you're still a petit bourgeois. If they want to give you money through whatever channel, you must accept it: every eminence in the history of religion agrees on this point. But you still haven't learnt that money... simply does not matter. It doesn't matter in the grand scheme of things. Money always has to exist, and even when you don't concern yourself with it, there is still always some of it around. How much and for how long and where from: completely irrelevant, the way that everything connected with money is irrelevant. Money cannot buy anything important: and what money *can* buy may be life necessities, but they are unimportant.

"Nothing that is truly worth living for costs money. It doesn't cost so much as a penny of yours that your intellect can apprehend the thousandfold magnificence of things, of scholarship. It doesn't cost so much as a penny of yours that you are in Italy, that the Italian sky spreads above you, that you can walk Italian streets and sit in the shade of Italian trees, and that the sun sets above you in Italian. It doesn't cost so much as a penny of yours when a woman finds you attractive and gives herself to you. It doesn't cost so much as a penny of yours that you're occasionally happy. The only things that cost money are the secondary things that are peripheral to your happiness, the stupid and boring stage props. It costs no money that you're in Italy, but it costs money for you to get there and for you to sleep under a roof there. It doesn't cost money for a woman to be your lover, except for the fact that meanwhile she has to eat and drink, and she has to dress up in order to then get undressed. But philistines have lived so long by providing each other insignificant things that cost money that they've already forgotten the things that don't cost money, and they attach importance to the expensive things. This is the greatest insanity. No, Mihály, one mustn't take notice of money. One must accept it like the air one breathes, not asking where it came from, if it has no odour.

"And now go to the devil. I have to finish my Oxford lecture today. Have I shown you the letter of invitation to Oxford? Wait, just a moment... Wonderful, isn't it, the things they write about me? Of course, if you just read it like this, it doesn't say so very much, but when you consider that the English like to *understate* – to say less than they think – then you'll understand what it means when they describe my work as *meritorious*..."

Mihály set off, bemused. He headed south along the Tiber, out of the city, in the direction of the great, dead *maremme*.* A strange hill stands at the city's edge, the Monte Testaccio, and he ascended it. They call this hill the pottery mountain, because the entire mound was formed of pottery shards. Here, in Roman times, was the wine market. They transported wines from Spain here, in ceramic amphorae. Then they broke them apart, having poured the wine into barrels, and they swept the shards together until they grew into this mountain.

Dreamily, Mihály picked up a few ruddy pottery fragments and pocketed them. "Historic relics," he thought. "Genuine imperial pottery. There can be no doubt of their authenticity, which cannot be said of every relic."

On the mountain, little Roman boys, the late progeny of the Quirites,* were playing at war, heaving bits of pottery at each other, shards two thousand years old, without any sense of awe whatsoever.

"This is Italy," he thought. "They're heaving history at each other because two millennia are as natural to them as the smell of manure in a village."

Twilight was deepening when he stood there in front of the small tavern in the Trastevere quarter where he'd met János Szepetneki the night before. Following the local custom, he slapped his worn hat onto his head and stepped into the smoky establishment. He couldn't see a thing, but he heard Szepetneki's voice right away. Once again, Szepetneki was occupying himself with the girl.

"I'm not disturbing you, am I?" asked Mihály, laughing.

"The hell you are. Have a seat. I've been waiting for you most impatiently."

Mihály was taken aback and overcome by shame. "Excuse me... but I just came in for a glass of wine; I was wandering this way, and I had a feeling that you'd be here."

"My dear Mihály, don't even mention it. Let's consider the matter closed, and I'm delighted that it happened this way, in my name and that of every interested party. And now, listen here. This little witch, Vannina, reads palms splendidly. She told me who I am and what I am, and she painted a portrait of me that, while not overly flattering, is on the mark. She's the first woman who hasn't been taken in by me, and she doesn't believe that I'm a crook. Yet she's predicting a bad end for me. A long and uneasy old age... Now have her predict your future. I'm curious what she'll say about you."

They brought a lamp, and the girl lost herself in examination of Mihály's palm. "O *signore*, you're a lucky man," she said. "You'll find money in an unexpected place."

"Well, what do you say to that?!"

"Somewhere abroad, a lady is thinking a lot about *signore*. A balding man is also thinking a lot about *signore*, but his thoughts aren't entirely good ones. This line means much war. *Signore* can lie with women without concern: he won't have children."

"What do you mean?"

"Not that you can't make children, just that you won't have any. The father line is missing. Don't eat oysters in summertime. You'll participate in a baptism fairly soon. An older man is arriving from beyond the mountains. The dead visit you often…"

Mihály suddenly withdrew his hand and asked for wine. He examined the girl more closely. He now found her large-breasted slimness much more beautiful than he had the previous night, and she was also much more frightening, more witch-like. Her eyes sparkled in a very Italian way, and she constantly displayed the whites of her eyes, and again that northern thought ran through Mihály's head: that this whole nation was insane, which was precisely what made it magnificent.

The girl grabbed Mihály's hand and continued to read, now very gravely. "You will soon receive very bad news. Beware of women. All your troubles are because of women. Oh!… *Signore* has a very good soul, but he doesn't belong in this world. Oh, *Dio mio*, poor *signore…*"

With that, she drew Mihály to herself and kissed him hard, with tears in her eyes, out of pity. János broke out laughing. "Bravo!" he cried, and Mihály was flustered.

"Come here again, *signore*," said Vannina. "Yes, again and often, you'll enjoy yourself here. You'll come again, won't you? Will you come?"

"Yes, of course. Since you ask so nicely…"

"You'll really come by? Do you know what? My cousin will be having a baby soon. She always longed for her baby to have a foreign godfather – that would be such an honour. Wouldn't you like to be the *bambino*'s godfather?"

"Why yes, gladly."

"Promise me."

"I promise."

János was a tactful scoundrel. He hadn't mentioned the "business matters" during the entire time. Only when it grew late and Mihály was slowly preparing to return home did he send the girl away and say: "Please, Mihály, Mr Pataki requests that you write to him about this business in your own hand, in detail, making it completely clear that you authorize him to submit the divorce papers against your wife in your name, and that you understand that he will pay you twenty thousand dollars in two instalments. You should know that, for some reason, Pataki doesn't trust me a hundred per cent, and I can't say I'm surprised. He wants to be in touch with you directly. Until such time, I'll now give you an advance of five thousand lire."

He counted the money out onto the table and Mihály, embarrassed, stuffed it into his pocket. "So," he thought, "this is how they throw the dice, this is how they cross the Rubicon, so lightly that they don't even notice that they're doing it."

"Also, write to Pataki," said Szepetneki, "to tell him that you've received the money he sent from me, but you don't have to specify the amount – it really doesn't need to read like a receipt or a business letter, as I'm sure you'll understand that it wouldn't be elegant."

Mihály understood. Right away, he made a mental calculation of how much Szepetneki might have skimmed off the advance money. Perhaps as much as fifty per cent, but definitely no more. That was not a problem: let him earn something.

"Well then, God be with you," said János. "With this I've concluded my business and I'll leave first thing tomorrow. But I'll spend the rest of the night with Vannina. I tell you, she's a fantastic woman. Drop by and see her often, once I'm no longer here."

3

IT GOT WARMER AND WARMER. Mihály lay naked on the bed, but he couldn't sleep. Ever since he'd accepted Pataki's money and written that letter, he felt out of place.

He got up, washed and set out to wander about in the summer night. Soon he reached the Acqua Paola and delighted in the classical waterfall that performed its craft with timeless calm, disdain and dignity in the moonlight. He thought about the little Hungarian sculptor whom he'd met through Waldheim at the Collegium Hungaricum. The sculptor had reached Rome on foot from Dresden, entering on the Via Flaminia, the road, as Mihály had learnt in his high-school days, on which the northern foreign conquerors had always marched into the city. Then he'd come up here on his first night, to the Gianicolo. He'd waited until they'd chased everyone out of the park and locked the gate. Then he'd climbed over the wall and slept there in a bush, above Rome, the City at his feet. He'd risen at dawn, undressed and bathed in the basin of the Acqua Paola, in the classical waters.

That is how a conqueror enters Rome. Perhaps the little sculptor would never amount to anything; his fate might be perennial hunger and who knows what else. Yet he was a conqueror, nevertheless, but for his missing army, but for "good fortune and none other".* His life's course, nevertheless, was an upwards-leading path, even if he should perish on the ascent. Mihály's path lead downwards, even if he should survive, even if he should survive everything and attain a calm, boring old age. We bear our life's path within ourselves, and the eternal stars of our fate burn within us.

Mihály rambled over the Gianicolo, on the banks of the Tiber, and in the alleyways of Trastevere for a long time. It was late at night, but the sort of Italian summer night when there is someone awake everywhere, hammering away or singing light-heartedly – this nation doesn't know the sleepiness and the time consecrated to torpor of the northern races – and one stumbles from time to time across little children who, entirely out of nowhere, play marbles on the street from three to four in the morning, or a barber who suddenly opens his shop and shaves a few good-humoured bridegrooms at four thirty.

On the Tiber, tugboats were slowly floating towards Ostia with classical solemnity. They weren't even boats, but pictures from a high-school Latin textbook illustrating the word *Navis, navis*.* On one boat a man was playing the guitar, a woman was washing hosiery and a small dog was barking; and behind that boat sailed another: the ghost ship, the Tiber Island that had been built out long ago in the shape of a vessel, because they didn't trust it to stay where it was, and which, sure enough, would occasionally set out on nocturnal excursions towards the sea, carrying the hospital and its dying on its back.

The moon was anchored to the far bank, above the immense and oppressive ruins of the Teatro Marcello, and out of the next-door synagogue – so it seemed to Mihály – a throng of long-bearded, ancient Jews marched out, winding sheets around their necks, to the bank of the Tiber, and, wailing faintly, scattered their sins into the river. Three aeroplanes circled in the air, caressing one another's sides with their headlights from time to time, and then flew off in the direction of the Castelli Romani, as if to rest on the rocky crags, as is proper for great birds.

Then an enormous lorry arrived, rumbling deafeningly. "Here is the dawn," thought Mihály. Figures clad in dark grey leapt out of the vehicle with frightening alacrity and rushed into an archway that opened before them. Then a cowbell sounded and a shepherd boy sang to urge a wondrous, Virgilian cow on its way.

Now a tavern door opened and two labourers stepped up to him, asking him to order them some red wine and tell them his life story. Mihály ordered the wine, and helped consume it too, and in fact even ordered some cheese to accompany it, but he didn't relate his life story because of the language barrier – even though he felt great friendship towards these men who'd surely sensed his loneliness and taken him to their hearts, and who were saying things that seemed so funny that it was a shame he didn't understand them. But then, without any transition, he began to fear them, so he paid and ran off.

He was in the Trastevere quarter again. In its menacing little alleyways, his soul was again filled with images of violent death, as so often in his adolescence when they "played" in the Ulpius house. What folly it had been to mingle with those labourers! They could have killed him; they could have dumped him in the Danube, the Tiber, for his thirty florins. And to meander in the devilish Trastevere quarter at this time of night, where in every yawning gateway they could strike him dead three times before he'd opened his mouth. What madness… and what madness that something in his soul drew and tempted him towards crimes and death!

At this point, he was standing in front of the house where Vannina lived. The house was dark, a small Italian house with a flat roof, decorated with tiles and arched window openings. Who might live in it? What deeds might be lurking in the darkness of such a house? What horrors might happen to him if he should enter? What if Vannina… yes, it surely wasn't without cause that Vannina had been inviting him so insistently the other day. She also could have known that he'd received a lot of money from János. Every one of her fiancés had been imprisoned… yes, Vannina would do it… And if he only knew for sure, he'd enter.

He stood before the house for a long time, submerged in his sick fantasies. Then he was suddenly overcome by a leaden fatigue and, yet again, by the nostalgia that accompanied him from station to station on his Italian journeys. But his fatigue told him that his final station was already near.

4

THE NEXT DAY, MIHÁLY RECEIVED a letter. The handwriting was familiar, very familiar, but he didn't know whose it was, and he felt ashamed that he did not remember. Erzsi had written the letter. She informed him that she'd arrived in Rome, because she must, without fail, speak to Mihály about a most important issue concerning him. She wrote that he should know her well enough to realize that it was not just a case of female flightiness; indeed, her pride would not have allowed her to seek contact with Mihály, had she not wanted to defend his interests in connection with a very painful issue: she thought that she still owed Mihály that much. That is why she begged him to come see her in her hotel, that afternoon.

Mihály was at a loss. He feared a meeting with Erzsi a great deal; his conscience was particularly guilty now, and besides, he could not imagine what Erzsi might want from him. But then he was overcome by the feeling that he'd already hurt Erzsi so much in the past, he couldn't hurt her yet again by refusing to meet her. He took the new hat that he'd purchased with the money he had received from Pataki and hurried to the hotel where Erzsi was lodging.

He had a message sent to Erzsi, who came down soon enough and greeted Mihály without a smile. His first impression was that he could not expect much good from this encounter. Erzsi arched her eyebrows high, as she always did when she was cross, and she didn't lower them. She was beautiful, tall and elegant in every respect, but an angel with a flaming sword... They walked beside each other in silence, after which they laconically concluded their enquiries as to each other's travels and health.

"Where shall we go?" asked Mihály.

"It's all the same to me. It's warm. Let's sit down in a confectionery."

The ice cream and *aranciata** brought temporary relief. They came to the point shortly.

"Mihály," said Erzsi with restrained ire, "I always knew that you were helpless and had no idea about anything at all that goes on in the world, but I thought that even your stupidity had its limits."

"You're off to a fine start," said Mihály. But secretly, he was a bit glad that Erzsi only considered him an idiot and not a rotter.

Indeed, she was right. "How could you have written this?" asked Erzsi, setting the letter on the table – the one he'd written to Pataki at Szepetneki's request.

Mihály blushed and, in his shame, he felt such fatigue that he couldn't even speak.

"Well, speak up!" Erzsi, the angel with the flaming sword, shouted at him.

"What can I say, Erzsi?" said Mihály, dragging the words out of his mouth. "You're intelligent, and you already know why I wrote it. I need the money; I don't want to go home to Pest for a thousand reasons... and this was the only means to obtain money."

"You're insane."

"That could be. But don't explain to me how immoral it is. What a cad I am. I know that anyhow. If the only reason you came to Rome, in this heat, was to tell me—"

"The hell you're a cad," said Erzsi in high dudgeon. "If only you were that, at least. You're merely stupid."

She fell silent. "As a matter of fact, I really oughtn't to speak in such a tone," she thought. "Since I'm no longer his wife..."

After a while, Mihály spoke up. "Tell me, Erzsi, how did this letter get to you?"

"What do you mean, how? Really, do you still not understand the whole thing? They entrapped you: János Szepetneki and that despicable Zoltán. All he wanted was for you to put your lack of character in writing. He immediately sent me the letter, but only after making a notarized photographic copy of it, which he keeps in his possession."

"Zoltán? Zoltán does things like having items notarized, such incredibly shady things that would never even occur to me, such fantastical dirty tricks?... I don't understand."

"Well, of course you don't understand," said Erzsi more gently. "You're not a cad, just foolish. And, unfortunately, Zoltán sees it all too clearly."

"But after all, he'd written me such a kindly letter..."

"Yes: Zoltán is kindly, but he's smart. You are not kindly, but, on the other hand, you're foolish."

"But then why is he doing all this?"

"Why? Because he wants me to return to him. He wants to show me what a boy you are. He doesn't consider that I already know that; I've known it longer than he, and I also know what baseness lurks behind his kindliness and tender fidelity. Since if all that was at issue were to win me back, then the entire business turned out the opposite of what he wanted, and that's why it's not such a good thing to be smart. But that's not the only thing at issue."

"Go ahead."

"Listen here." The previous irritation in Erzsi's expression gave way to terror. "Zoltán wants to exterminate you, Mihály; he wants to wipe you off the face of the earth."

"Really now! He's not a big enough boy for that, after all. How do you imagine he'd do it?"

"Look, Mihály, I don't know exactly, because I'm not as cunning as Zoltán, so I'm just guessing. First of all, he'll do everything to make your position with respect to your family impossible. Which, at least temporarily, won't be difficult, because you can imagine the face your father will make, or has already made, on seeing this letter."

"My father? You really can't imagine that he'll show him?"

"On the contrary, I'm sure of it."

Now it was Mihály who became terrified. A shivering and adolescent terror seized him, the ancient fear of the father, of losing paternal goodwill. He set down the glass of *aranciata* and buried his face in his hands. Erzsi understood his motives, he knew that. But he couldn't explain them to his father. He would lose his honour in his father's eyes, once and for all.

"And then he'll get to work all over Pest," Erzsi continued. "He'll spread such reports about you that you won't be able to walk the length of a street. Even though I know, my God, that the disgrace you intended to commit is not so unusual: countless men who've sold out their wives in some form go running about Pest, and they enjoy general respect, especially if they earn a lot and God's blessing accompanies their further business – but Zoltán will take care that the weekly press and the other leaders of public opinion present the affair so that you'll be unable to walk the length of the street. You'll have to stay abroad, which you won't mind so much, but your family will be hardly able to support you, if at all, because Zoltán will surely do everything in his power to ruin your father's firm."

"Erzsi!"

"Yes. For instance, he'll find a way to force me to withdraw my money from the firm; and if news of this affair gets out, I'll have to do it: your father himself will demand it – and this in itself will be a terrible blow."

They remained silent for a long time.

"If only I could at least know," said Mihály finally, "why he hates me so much. Since he used to be so understanding and forgiving that it didn't even seem natural any more."

"That's exactly why he hates you so much now. You have no idea how much resentment lurked behind his kindliness even back then, and what despair and hatred was built into precisely this forgiveness.

To be sure, he himself believed that he'd forgiven you, until the opportunity arrived for him to take revenge. And then, like a wild beast raised on milk, who's suddenly fed meat..."

"I always knew him to be such a soft, slimy fellow."

"So did I; and I confess that I'm much more impressed by him now that he's taken on such Shylockian proportions. It turns out that he's a real man after all..."

Again, they stayed silent for a long time.

"Say," Mihály spoke up, "you must have some plan for what I must do, or what we must do, since you've come to Rome for that reason."

"First of all, I wanted to warn you. Zoltán thinks that you'll stroll just as unsuspectingly into the subsequent traps as you did into this one. For example, he wants to offer you a splendid position to lure you home to Pest. So you can be there, on location, when the scandal breaks out. But you mustn't go home now, at all cost. And next, I wanted to warn you about a... friend of yours. You know who."

"János Szepetneki?"

"Yes."

"How did you get mixed up with him in Paris?"

"We met in society."

"Did you meet often?"

"Yes. Fairly often. Zoltán also became acquainted with him through me."

"And what do you think of János? He's unique, isn't he?"

"Yes, truly unique."

But she said this with such reluctance that a suspicion ran through Mihály's mind. Could it really be? How odd that would be... But his keen sense of discretion instantly took over and suppressed his curiosity: if it was at all possible for this to be true, then he must refrain from speaking any more about János Szepetneki.

"Thank you, Erzsi, for warning me; you're very good to me and I know just how undeserving I am. And I can't believe that, in time, you would also turn against me as savagely as Zoltán Pataki."

"I wouldn't think so," said Erzsi with utmost seriousness. "I feel no desire for revenge against you at all. And as a matter of fact, there's no reason why I should."

"I can see that you want to say more. Is there anything else I need to do?"

"I have to warn you about one more thing, but it's most awkward, because you might misunderstand my reasons for saying it. You might even suppose that I am speaking out of jealousy."

"Jealousy? I'm not that conceited. I know that I've lost any right for you to be jealous of me."

Inside, he knew very well that Erzsi didn't feel indifferent towards him, even now. Otherwise she wouldn't have come to Rome. But he felt bound by chivalry to ignore the fact that Erzsi was still attracted to him. In any case, his comfort also demanded it.

"Perhaps we should leave my feelings to one side," said Erzsi with irritation. "They have nothing to do with the matter. So… how should I put it… look, Mihály, I know whom you're in Rome for. János told me. The person in question wrote to him that you've seen each other."

Mihály bowed his head. He sensed that his love for Éva hurt Erzsi immeasurably, but what should he say? How could he change something that was true and irremediable?

"Yes, Erzsi. If you know, fine. You also know the whole back story. In Ravenna I told you everything there is to know about me. Everything is as it had to be. If only it weren't so hard on you…"

"Please, drop the subject. I didn't utter so much as a word about it being hard on me. That's truly not the issue. But tell me… do you know who this woman has become? What sort of life she's lived until now?"

"I don't know. I've never even tried to find out."

"Mihály, I've always marvelled at your detachment, but you're beginning to surpass even yourself. I've never heard of such a thing:

someone is in love with a woman, and who or what she is doesn't interest him…"

"Because the only thing that interests me is who she was back then, in the Ulpius house."

"Maybe you are also unaware that she's won't be staying here much longer? That she's succeeded in ensnaring a young Englishman who's taking her with him to India. They're leaving any day."

"That's not true."

"But it *is* true. Look at this."

She took another letter out of her reticule. It was in Éva's handwriting. The letter was addressed to János; Éva curtly informed him of the upcoming journey to India, and of the fact that she never even intends to return to Europe. "You didn't know this either, did you?" asked Erzsi.

"You win," said Mihály. He stood up, paid and left. He even left his hat behind.

Outside, he staggered wildly and in a daze for a time, pressing his hand to his heart. Only much later did he notice that Erzsi was walking there alongside him, and had brought his hat.

By now, Erzsi was completely transformed: humble, frightened, her eyes brimming with tears. The sight of this tall, dignified lady in this girlish attitude was almost moving, as she walked by his side without a word, his hat in her hand. Mihály broke into a smile and took the hat.

"Thank you," he said, and kissed Erzsi's hand. Shyly, Erzsi caressed Mihály's face.

"Well, if you have no more letters in your reticule, then perhaps we should go have dinner," said Mihály, sighing.

They spoke little during dinner, but what they said was intimate and tender. Erzsi was full of consolatory good intentions; his pain, and the large quantity of wine consumed in that pain, softened Mihály. He considered how much Erzsi still loved him, and what happiness it would be if he were also to love Erzsi and be liberated from the past and its dead. But he knew that was impossible.

"Erzsi, in the depths of my heart I'm so blameless, where the two of us are concerned," he said. "True, that's easy for me to say. But you see, for so many years I did everything to conform, and when I thought that at last everything was in order and I'd finally made my peace with the world, then I married you to reward myself. And that's when all the demons assailed me: my entire youth and all the nostalgia and all the rebellion. There's no medicine for nostalgia. Perhaps I should never have allowed myself to come to Italy. They built this land out of the nostalgia of kings and poets. Italy is paradise on earth, but only the way Dante saw it: the earthly paradise is only a stopping point on the peak of Mount Purgatory, only an airfield of the afterlife, where souls take off for the distant heavenly spheres, when Beatrice removes her veil and the soul 'feels the great power of ancient desire...'"

"Oh, Mihály, the world doesn't allow a man to give himself over to nostalgia."

"It doesn't. The world doesn't tolerate any deviation from the norm, any escape and defiance, and sooner or later, it releases the Zoltáns against you."

"And what do you want to do?"

"That I don't know. What are your plans, Erzsi?"

"I'm returning to Paris. We've discussed everything now. I think it's time for me to go home. I'm leaving early tomorrow morning."

Mihály paid and walked Erzsi home. "I so much would like to know that it will turn out well for you," he said along the way. "Say something encouraging."

"It's not as bad for me as you think," said Erzsi, and now her smile was candidly proud and self-satisfied. "My life is very full even now, and who knows what wonderful things still await me. I've found myself, a little, in Paris, as well as what I'm seeking in the world. The only thing I regret is that you're not part of my life."

They stood there in front of Erzsi's hotel. By way of farewell, Mihály took one more good look at Erzsi. Yes, she had changed a lot. For better or worse, who knows? She was not as refined a presence as before; there was something broken inside her, something weather-beaten inside that was also expressed in her clothing and her expression, and in the fact that she made herself up too much in the Parisian style. Erzsi had become somewhat more common, and the presence of a male stranger somehow lingered around her, a mysterious stranger worth envying. Or maybe the presence of János, his enemy... This new aspect to a long-known woman was inexpressibly alluring and disquieting.

"What will you do now, Mihály?"

"I have no idea. I'm in no mood to go home, for a thousand and one reasons, and I also have no desire to be alone."

For a moment, they looked at each other with that conspiratorial gaze that they had developed in the year spent together, and without another word they hurried up to Erzsi's room.

The passion that had bound them together so laceratingly when Erzsi had still been Zoltán's wife now flared up in both of them. Back then too, both had tried to resist the desire alive within them, but the desire was too strong and resistance only made it more savage. Now too they came together despite strong resistance; the grievances that had arisen between them and that seemed irremediable divided them dreadfully; but that just intensified the passion that now threw them into each other's arms. Mihály discovered Erzsi's body anew – with fantastic elation at this recognition – as the body he now desired more than any other woman's: Erzsi's tenderness, Erzsi's wildness, Erzsi's entire nocturnal being, which in no way resembled the Erzsi revealed in daylight, words and deeds; the passionate, loving – expertly loving – Erzsi. For her part, Erzsi loved the extent to which she could divest Mihály of the lethargic indifference with which he lived out the greater part of his days.

Afterwards, released and happy, they gazed at each other, exhausted and satisfied, with wondering eyes. Only now did the realization of what had happened dawn on them. Erzsi broke out in laughter. "You wouldn't have believed it this morning, eh?"

"Not I. And you?"

"Me neither. Or rather, I have no idea. I came with the attitude that I really wouldn't mind if it happened."

"Erzsi! You're the world's best."

And Mihály indeed thought so. He was deeply moved by the womanly warmth streaming from Erzsi towards him; he was grateful and childishly happy.

"Yes, Mihály, I must always be good to you. I feel I must never hurt you."

"Tell me... shouldn't we give our marriage another chance?"

Erzsi grew serious. Of course she had been expecting the question; her erotic vanity also desired it, after what had transpired... But could it really be a viable option?... She looked at Mihály, undecided, scrutinizing him for a long time.

"We've got to give it another try," said Mihály. "Our bodies understand each other so well. And in general, they are usually right. Nature's imperative, don't you think?... What we spoilt with our souls our bodies can still repair. We need to give our relationship another chance."

"Why did you leave me if... if this is how it is?"

"Nostalgia, Erzsi. But now it's as if I've been freed from some spell. True, I was content to be a slave and a condemned man. But now I feel myself so sound and strong. I'm dead certain that I should remain with you. But of course I'm being selfish. The question is whether it would be better for you."

"I don't know, Mihály. I love you much more than you do me, and I'm afraid that you'll cause me much suffering. And... I don't know how you feel about that other woman."

"About Éva? Well, do you think I've spoken with her? I've just longed for her. A spiritual sickness. I'll recover from it."

"Recover first, and then we'll talk."

"Good. You'll see that we'll talk about it soon. Sleep well, darling."

But Mihály awoke during the course of the night. He stretched his hand out for Éva, and only when he'd grasped the hand lying on the coverlet did he realize that it belonged to Erzsi, and he let it go with a very guilty conscience. Then he thought, sourly, sadly, tiredly, that Éva was entirely different after all. An intense desire drove him to Erzsi from time to time, but then that desire would be consummated, leaving behind nothing more than the sober and boring cognizance of the facts. Erzsi was desirable and good and intelligent and all, but what she lacked was mystery.

*Consummatum est.** Erzsi was his last connection to the world of people. Now the only thing that existed was she who didn't: Éva, Éva… and once Éva was gone, only extinction would remain.

Erzsi, for her part, awoke in the predawn hours and thought: "Mihály hasn't changed, but I have. Before, Mihály represented the great adventure, rebellion, the stranger, the mysterious. By now I've learnt that Mihály just passively allows outside forces to seize him. He's no tiger. Or at least, there are much more exceptional men than he: János Szepetneki. And men whom I don't yet know. The fact that now Mihály longs to return to me is precisely because he's seeking petit-bourgeois order and security in me: in other words, everything from which I fled to be with him. No, it makes no sense. I've cured myself of Mihály."

She rose, washed up and began to dress. Mihály also awoke and was, somehow, instantly clear about the situation; he too got dressed; they had breakfast with barely a word spoken between them; Mihály accompanied Erzsi to the train and waved as she departed. They both knew that their mutual affair had now come to an end.

5

DREADFUL DAYS FOLLOWED Erzsi's departure. Waldheim also set off to Oxford not long after, and Mihály remained utterly alone. He was in no mood for anything at all; he didn't even budge from home, lying on the bed all day, fully clothed.

The dose of reality contained in Erzsi's news was absorbed into his system like a poison. He thought a great deal and with accumulating anxiety about his father, whom his behaviour and the threat of financial ruin had surely cast into an awful psychological state. He saw the old gentleman before him, sitting despondently at the head of the table during the family dinner, twisting his moustache or rubbing his knees in his distress, trying to behave as if nothing at all were the matter, and depressing the others still more with his strained attempts at good humour; he saw the others not responding to his jests, everyone slowly falling silent and eating on the double to escape the torment of the family gathering as soon as possible.

And whenever he succeeded in forgetting his father, Éva came to mind. The knowledge that Éva was going to unattainably distant lands, perhaps for ever, was most horrific of all. For the fact that Éva didn't even want to hear from him was terrible enough – but life remained unendurable as long as he knew that she was living in the same city, and they could encounter each other by accident, or at least he could see her from a distance... but if she left for India, then nothing, nothing at all would remain for Mihály.

One afternoon, a letter arrived from Foligno: Ellesley had written it.

Dear Mike,

I have some very sad news I must impart to you. Pater Severinus, the monk from Gubbio, fell critically ill. That is, he had already been ill with lung disease for some time, and now he arrived at the stage when he could no longer remain in the monastery and was brought here to hospital. I had occasion to speak with him during the hours when neither his illness nor his religious devotions occupied him, and I obtained a few glimpses into his phenomenal spiritual world. I believe that in earlier centuries this man would have been honoured as a saint. Pater Severinus spoke of you often, and in tones of deepest friendship; from him I learnt – how astonishing the paths of Providence – that the two of you had been good friends in childhood and still loved each other very much. He asked me to inform you when the inevitable happened. Now I am fulfilling his request, for Pater Severinus died in the night, just before dawn today. He was fully conscious until the last minute and was in prayer with his fellow monks, who were sitting by the bedside when his time came to pass away.

Dear Mike, if you believed in eternal life as unconditionally as I do, you would receive this news with relief, because I trust that your friend is now in the place where his fragile earthly existence receives its worthy fulfilment: the infinite.

Do not forget me entirely, and write on occasion to your faithful

Ellesley

PS: Millicent Ingram received the money in good order; she finds your begging for pardon silly between friends; she sends hearty greetings and thinks of you with affection; at the same time, I should mention that she has become my bride.

It was a terribly warm day. Later that afternoon, Mihály wandered the Borghese gardens in a daze, went to bed early, fell asleep from exhaustion and then awoke again.

In his half-sleep, he saw a rugged, wild landscape before him, a familiar landscape. Still not quite awake, he pondered where he might have seen this narrow valley, these windswept trees and this stylized-seeming ruin; perhaps he'd seen it from the train on that gorgeous stretch between Bologna and Florence, perhaps during his wanderings above Spoleto, or perhaps in a painting by Salvator Rosa* in a museum somewhere. The landscape had an ominous, foreboding cast, and the small figure in it was also foreboding: a traveller who crossed the landscape leaning on his staff, the moonlight shining above his head. He knew that the traveller had been crossing lands, each more desolate than the last, for a very long time, under windswept trees and stylized ruins, imperilled by storms and wolves; perhaps no one else even exists who would wander in such a night and so alone.

The bell rang. Mihály turned on the light and looked at his watch. It was already past midnight. Who could this be? Probably no one had rung after all. He turned over.

The bell rang again. Anxiously, he rose, threw some clothes on and went out. Éva stood in the doorway.

Mihály was so flustered he even forgot to greet her.

That's how it is: you long for someone maniacally, with a sense of foreboding, at the edge of hell and death, seeking her, chasing her, all in vain, and your life withers away in nostalgia. Ever since he'd been in Rome, he'd awaited this moment constantly; this was what he'd prepared for, and gradually he grew to believe he'd never speak with Éva again. And after all this, she suddenly appears, and then he draws his cheap pyjamas tight across his chest, ashamed that he's unkempt and unshaven, infinitely ashamed of his lodging, and wishes fervently that the person for whom he'd been longing so indescribably weren't there.

Bu Éva didn't care about all that. Without notice and without a greeting, she rushed into Mihály's room, sank into an armchair and stared stiffly into space in front of her.

Mihály shuffled after her.

Éva hadn't changed a bit. Love eternally preserves one moment: the moment it was born; and the person one loves never ages, remaining for ever sixteen in the lover's eyes, and the same breeze that blew back then, at that fateful moment, continues to ruffle her unkempt hair and light summer dress throughout a lifetime.

Mihály was so nonplussed that the only thing he could ask, was: "How did you know my address?"

Éva waved him off irritably. "I telephoned your brother in Pest. Mihály, Ervin has died."

"I know," said Mihály.

"How do you know?" asked Éva.

"Ellesley wrote to me – the little doctor with whom, so I know, you also met once in Gubbio, in the house in which the door of the dead was open."

"Yes, I remember."

"He tended Ervin in his final hours, in the Foligno hospital. Here's his letter."

Éva read the letter and fell deep into thought.

"Remember his big, grey overcoat," she then said, "and how he'd always turn its collar up, as he paced with his head bowed?..."

"And how his head always preceded his body, somehow, and the rest of him trailed after his head, like those big snakes that cast their heads forward, and their bodies slither after them... And how much he smoked! No matter how many cigarettes I set in front of him, they'd all be consumed."

"And how sweet he was, when he was in a good mood, or when he was drinking..."

Pater Severinus had vanished, and in the dead man in Foligno it was only Ervin who had died, the unusual boy and dear friend and most beautiful memory of youth.

"I knew that he was very ill," said Mihály. "I even tried to convince him to undertake a cure. Do you think I should have tried harder to convince him? Maybe I should have stayed there in Gubbio and not left until something had happened for his health."

"I think that our care, tenderness and worry would not have even reached as high as Pater Severinus. Illness wasn't the same for him as for others: not a blow, but perhaps a gift. What do we know about it? And how easy it was for him to die."

"Yes indeed, given that he dealt with the matters of death so routinely; in the last few years, I don't think he even occupied himself with anything else."

"It's possible, nevertheless, that it was terrible for him to die. There are very few people who die their own death like... like Tamás."

The warm orange-yellow glow of the lampshade fell on Éva's face, and now her face was yet more like the face she wore in the Ulpius house, when... when they played, and Tamás and Mihály would die for her or be killed by her. What sorts of fantasies or memories might be playing within her now? Mihály pressed his hands over his pained and pounding heart, and a thousand things ran through his mind: the memory of the sick pleasures of their old stage plays and the Etruscan statues in the Villa Giulia, Waldheim's explanations, the Other Longing and the death hetaerae.

"Éva, you killed Tamás," he said.

Éva shuddered, her facial expression changed completely and she pressed her hands to her forehead. "That's not true! Not true! How could you think such a thing?"

"Éva, you killed Tamás."

"No, Mihály, I swear I didn't. It wasn't I who killed him... you can't think of it that way. Tamás committed suicide. I told Ervin, and Ervin, as a priest, gave me absolution."

"Tell me too."

"Yes, I'll tell you. Listen to me. I'll tell you how Tamás died."

Éva's hand was ice-cold in Mihály's, and tremors also ran through Mihály; his heart became terribly heavy. They descended irresistibly into the quarries, through corridors, mines and subterranean salt lakes, and now they entered the cavern where, at the innermost centre of things and the night, the secret and the horror dwelled.

"You remember, of course, how it was. My suitor, and how insistent my father was, and that I asked to be allowed to go on travel for a few days with Tamás before marrying."

"I remember."

"We went to Hallstatt. Tamás picked this place. When I arrived there, I understood everything. I can't even express it to you... an ancient, black town beside a dead, black lake. There are mountain towns in Italy too, but that was much darker, much more horrible, the sort of place where the only possible thing to do is to die. Along the way, Tamás had already said that he'd be dying soon. You remember, of course, his office job... and he couldn't reconcile himself to the fact that he'd have to tear himself away from me... and besides, you recall how he was always longing for death, and you also know that he didn't want to die an accidental death, but a conscientiously prepared one...

"I know that anyone else would have appealed to his conscience, or sent telegrams right and left, asking for help from his friends and the police and the emergency services, and I don't know where that custom comes from. At first I too had the feeling that I should do something, that I should shout for help. I didn't, and in despair, I took heed of the steps Tamás was taking. But then, all of a sudden it dawned on me that Tamás was right. How I came to realize it, I can't say... but you remember how close we always were to each other, and how much I knew what was going on inside him – and now I knew that he was beyond help. If not now, some other time soon, and if I weren't there, then he'd die alone, and that would be dreadful for both of us.

"Tamás noticed that I was resigning myself to it, and he let me know on which day it was going to happen. That day we still went rowing on the dead lake, but by afternoon it was raining, and we returned to our room. It had never before been as autumnal on this earth, Mihály.

"Tamás wrote his farewell letter, using meaningless platitudes, giving no rationale whatsoever. Then he asked me to prepare the poison and give it to him...

"And why did I agree to this?... And why did I do it... you see, this is something that perhaps only you can understand – you, who used to play with us back in the day.

"I haven't felt the slightest pang of conscience since then. Tamás wanted to die, I couldn't have prevented it in any event and I didn't even want to, because I knew it was better for him this way. I did the right thing in fulfilling his final request, and I've never regretted it. Maybe if I hadn't been there, if I hadn't handed him the poison, he might not have had enough courage; he might have spent hours struggling with himself, and finally he might have drunk it anyway, and he might have proceeded into death awkwardly, ashamed of his cowardice. But this way, he killed himself bravely, without hesitation, because he was performing: he acted it out that I was killing him; he played the theatrical scene that we'd rehearsed so often back home.

"Then he lay down calmly, and I sat down on the edge of the bed. When the deadly drowsiness approached, he drew me to himself and kissed me. And he kept kissing me until his arm slid off me. These weren't brotherly kisses, Mihály, it's true. By that point, we weren't siblings, but someone who kept living and someone else who was dying... by that point, he was free, I think."

They were silent for a very long time.

"Éva, why did you send the message that I shouldn't seek you out?" Mihály finally asked. "Why don't you want to meet me?"

"Oh, but don't you understand, Mihály, don't you sense that this is impossible?... When the two of us are together, we're not a just a couple... Tamás can be present at any moment. And now, Ervin too... I can't be together with you, Mihály, no."

She stood up.

"Sit down for just another minute," said Mihály, with the softness of someone speaking in the throes of deepest emotion. "Is it true that you're going to India?" he asked. "For a long time?"

Éva nodded.

Mihály wrung his hands. "You're really going away, and I'll never see you again?"

"Really. What will happen to you?"

"Only one thing: to die my own death. Like... like Tamás."

They fell silent.

"You really think so, seriously?" Éva asked finally.

"I can't be more serious. There's no point in my staying in Rome. And there's even less point in going home. There is no longer a point in anything."

"Can't anyone help you?" asked Éva, without any conviction at all.

"No. Come to think of it, there is one way, after all. You could do something for me, Éva."

"Well?"

"I don't dare say it, it's so hard."

"Say it."

"Éva... be at my side when I die... like you were with Tamás, Éva."

Éva lost herself in thought.

"Will you do it? Will you do it? Éva, this is all I ask of you, and after that, nothing, as long as the world lasts."

"Fine."

"You promise?"

"I promise."

6

Erzsi arrived back in Paris. She telephoned János, who came to take her to dinner that very evening. Erzsi found him distracted, and not particularly happy to see her. Her suspicion grew when János said: "We're dining with the Persian tonight."

"Why? The first night I'm back!"

"True, but I can't help it. He insisted, and you know I must stay in his good graces."

During dinner, János kept largely silent, and Erzsi and the Persian carried the conversation.

The Persian spoke about his homeland. There, love was a romantic and difficult craft; there, the youthful lover still had to climb over a stone wall three metres high, had to hide in the garden of the beloved lady's father to await the moment when the beloved lady strolled by with her chaperone. At such times they could exchange a word or two in secret, but the youth would be risking his life.

"And is that a good thing?" asked Erzsi.

"Yes, very good," replied the Persian, "very good. A man values something much more highly when he's had to wait for it, battle for it and suffer for it. I often think that Europeans don't even know what love is. And true enough, they really don't know, technically speaking."

His eyes glowed, his gestures were exaggerated yet distinguished: untamed, real gestures.

"I'm most happy that you've returned, Madame," he said suddenly. "I was beginning to fear that you'd remain in Italy. And that would have been a shame… I'd have regretted it deeply."

In a grateful gesture, Erzsi put her hand for an instant on the Persian's. It contracted under hers and became like a claw. Erzsi took fright and withdrew her hand.

"I very much would like to ask you for something," said the Persian. "Accept a small gift from me. A token of my happiness at your return."

He produced a very finely wrought gold *tabatière*.*

"As a matter of fact, it's an opium case," he said. "But it can also hold cigarettes."

"I don't know on what basis I can accept it," said Erzsi, flustered.

"On no basis at all. On the basis that I'm enjoying myself. On the basis that I'm not European, but come from a place where people give gifts freely and good-heartedly, and are grateful when they're accepted. Accept it because I am Lutphali Suratgar, and who knows when you'll ever see such a bird again in your life."

Erzsi looked enquiringly at János. She found the *tabatière* most attractive and would have liked to accept it. János signalled his approval with his eyes.

"Well then, I'll accept it," said Erzsi, "and I thank you very much. I wouldn't accept it from anyone else but you. Because who knows when I'll ever see such a bird again in my life."

The Persian paid for all three dinners. This made Erzsi a bit nervous. Indeed, it seemed as if János were procuring her for the Persian, as if he were her impresario, to put it delicately, and he were discreetly withdrawing into the background... But she drove the thought away. Undoubtedly, János was out of money again, and that's why he was letting the Persian pay. Or the Persian was insisting on it, with his oriental magnificence. Besides which, in Paris, only one person in the party ever paid.

That night, János fell asleep quickly, and Erzsi had time to think.

"The affair with János is starting to come to an end, that's for sure, and I'm not even sorry. I've already learnt everything of interest about him. I was always rather scared of him, that he'd stab me some time, or steal my money, but it seems my fear was unfounded, and I'm a little disappointed. What will happen next? Maybe the Persian? I seem to please him."

She thought for a long time about what the Persian might be like, very close up. Oh yes, he was certainly a real tiger, tiger burning bright in the forests of the night. "How his eyes burn… He could be frightening. Yes, he could be frightening. I should give him a try him sometime. Love still has so many unknown territories, secrets, wonders, paradises…"

Two days later, the Persian invited them on an automobile excursion to Paris-Plage. They bathed in the sea, dined and headed for home in the dark.

The journey took a long time, and the Persian, who was driving, became more and more hesitant.

"Say, did we see this lake on the way here?" he asked János.

János looked, bemused, into the darkness. "You might have. I didn't."

They stopped and studied the map.

"The devil knows where we are. I don't see any sign of a lake here."

"I said right away that the driver shouldn't drink so much," Szepetneki said irritably.

They went on, uncertain. Neither human nor vehicle in the entire region.

"This car isn't in good order," said János. "Do you notice how it's spluttering every so often?"

"Yes, as a matter of fact, it is spluttering."

As they went on, the spluttering became more conspicuous.

"Do you understand the mechanics?" asked the Persian. "Because I know nothing about them. As far as I'm concerned, a car engine is still a devilish wonder."

"Stop, and I'll see what the problem is."

János got out, lifted the bonnet and began his examination. "The fan belt is badly damaged. How can you go driving around everywhere with a belt like that? You ought to have your car looked at from time to time."

All of a sudden he swore loudly and uncouthly. "*Sacrebleu, ventrebleu*, the belt just broke! Well, we fixed *that* just fine."

"*You* fixed it."

"I fixed it. We certainly aren't moving on from here until we find another belt. You might as well get out."

They got out. Meanwhile the rain began to fall, and Erzsi buttoned her rubber raincoat.

The Persian was furious and impatient. "The devil take it, now what'll we do? Here we are, standing in the middle of the main road – in fact, I have a strong suspicion that this isn't even a main road."

"I see a house over there," said János. "Let's try our luck there."

"What do you mean – this late at night? Everyone's already asleep in the French countryside at this hour, and whoever's still awake won't speak to suspicious foreigners."

"But the lights are on over there," said Erzsi, pointing at the house.

"Let's give it a try," said János.

They locked the car and set out in the direction of the house. It was surrounded by a wall at the bottom of the hill, but the gate was open. They went up to the house.

The house had an aristocratic exterior; in the dark, it seemed like a miniature castle, with a strongly projecting canopy and noble French lines.

They knocked at the door. An old peasant woman stuck her head out the door's small window. János explained their predicament.

"I'll go inform His Lordship and Her Ladyship."

Shortly, a middle-aged Frenchman in country attire came and looked them over thoroughly, while János explained their situation again. His face gradually cleared, and he became quite amicable.

"Welcome to our abode, my ladies and gentlemen. Do come inside, and then we'll discuss the matter."

He led them into an old-fashioned room, reminiscent of hunting lodges, where a woman sat by the table over her needlework. Obviously his wife. The man briefly related the situation to her and bade the guests be seated.

"Your misfortune is our good fortune," said the woman. "You have no idea how boring these country evenings are. But, well, one can't abandon the estate at this time of year, isn't that right?"

Erzsi felt ill at ease somehow. The whole castle wasn't authentic – or rather it was too authentic, like the stage set for a naturalist play. These two people either sat here by the lamp eternally, wordlessly, waiting – or they had just came into being the moment the party had arrived. She had a tingling sensation that something wasn't quite right.

It turned out that the nearest village where they might find a garage was three kilometres away, but the hospitable couple had nobody they could send out, because their male staff were sleeping out in the grange.

"Spend the night here," the woman suggested. "We have beds for all three of you."

But János and the Persian insisted that they had to be back in Paris that night.

"I'm expected," said the Persian, indicating with a discreet smile that there was a woman involved.

"There's nothing else for it," said János. "One of us has to go to the village on foot. Three kilometres is really not far. Naturally, I'll go, since I broke the belt."

"Of course not," said the Persian, "I'll go, because you are my guests, and I must take care of you."

"Let's draw lots," suggested János.

The lots decided that János would go.

"I'll be right back," said János, and he hurried off.

Their host served wine, his own vintage. They sat round the table, drinking and conversing quietly, from time to time listening to the rain pattering on the window panes.

Erzsi's sense of unreality grew and grew. She no longer knew what the host and hostess were talking about. Apparently they were laying out the monotonous regularity of their village life, as monotonously and hypnotically as the rain. Or perhaps it was the rain's pattering that was so hypnotic, or the fact that she no longer belonged together with anyone at all in the world and was sitting here in the middle of nowhere in a French castle whose very name she didn't know and where she'd ended up for no reason at all, because she could just as well be sitting in the middle of some other nowhere in a different castle – and equally without reason.

Then she sensed that this wasn't what was lulling her, but the Persian's gaze that periodically caressed her from one end to the other. With a tender, warm, touched gaze, entirely differently from the way that cold blue European eyes looked. There was animal warmth and reassurance in the Persian's gaze. Assuaging. "Yes, this man loves women... but not just that way... he doesn't love them because he's a man, but because they are women: dear and needing love. That's it: he loves them the way a true dog-lover loves dogs. And this may be the very best that a woman can receive."

Half-asleep, she caught herself with her hand under the table, holding and caressing the Persian's hand.

The Persian didn't betray himself by so much as a tenth of a movement. He conversed politely with the hosts. Nevertheless, Erzsi felt the entire man becoming inflamed, so volcanically that she even expected flames to erupt from him. And the Persian just waited, perhaps not even thinking of any plan in particular, so late at night...

"Does he think that I'm an unapproachable Persian lady? My God, we should go outside for a stroll... but it's raining."

All of a sudden, someone knocked. The peasant woman led in a youngster, soaked to the skin; the hosts knew him. The fellow recounted that János had reached the neighbouring village but had found no suitable belt there; he had, however, sprained his ankle and thought it best to spend the night there, at the home of the local doctor, who was a very nice man. He asked that they pick him up once they'd managed to repair the car.

They received the news with astonishment, and then decided that, if this is how things stood, it would be best to go to bed, since it was long past midnight. Their hostess led them upstairs. After establishing, with the greatest tact, that Erzsi and the Persian were not together, she showed each of them to a separate room and excused herself. Erzsi also bade farewell to the Persian and entered her room, where the old peasant woman prepared the bed and wished her a good night.

It was as if everything had been prepared in advance. By that point, Erzsi no longer doubted that it had all been set up. János had surely planned this little piece of theatre that they now acted out in his honour. The car breaking down, the little castle along the way, János's accident – and now for the final act, with a *happy end*.

She looked around her room. She locked the door carefully, and then broke into a smile: the room had another door, and that one had no lock. Cautiously, she opened that door: a dark room lay before it. But there was a door on the dark room's opposite wall, and below it glowed a strip of light. She stole silently over to it; someone was pacing in the next room. She remembered the arrangement of the rooms from when they'd walked the length of the corridor and determined that it was the Persian's room behind the door. The Persian would certainly not lock his door. He'd stroll comfortably over to her room. And that was only natural too: after they had sat so intimately downstairs, beneath the lamp. She returned to her room.

In the mirror, she saw how deeply she'd been blushing. János had sold her to the Persian, and the Persian had purchased her like a calf;

he'd given her the *tabatière* (which, as Sári would establish, was much, much more valuable than one would have thought at first glance) as an advance – János had surely received cash. Deep humiliation and fury inundated her. She could have loved the Persian so much… but for him to treat her this way, as a piece of merchandise! Oh how stupid men are! He's gone and spoilt everything.

"Why is it that everyone puts me up for sale? Mihály sold me to Zoltán – he even confirmed the bargain in his letter – and now János is selling me to the Persian and, God knows, in time the Persian will sell me to some Greek or Armenian; and to top it all off I'm constantly being sold by the sorts of men whom I don't at all conceive of as my owners." She racked her brains: what was it about her that made men sell her? Or, maybe, could the fault be not in herself, but in the men she'd been with, in Mihály and János, and in the fact that both of them loved Éva, a woman who was for sale, herself, and they couldn't imagine it any other way?

Another couple of minutes, and the Persian would enter and want to consummate the deal in the most natural way in the world. Disgraceful! She must do something. Should she go down to the hostess and make a big scene, asking for protection? That would be ridiculous, given that the hosts had been paid off by the Persian. (Who could they be? They performed their roles very well; maybe they were actors, since, after all, the Persian was a film producer now.) She paced up and down, at a loss.

What if she was mistaken? What if the Persian hadn't the faintest intention of entering?

This was when she realized that if the Persian didn't enter it would be just as insulting as if he did.

If he were to enter… maybe it wouldn't really be so offensive and humiliating. The Persian knew very well that Erzsi found him attractive. Erzsi herself had hinted that he might come in. He wouldn't be approaching her like a slave woman in his harem, but like a woman who loved him, and whom he loved in turn, after having conscientiously cleared the obstacles out of the way. So had they sold her? Yes, they'd sold her. But the fact of the matter was that the men had been paying impressive sums for her, which wasn't humiliating at all; on the contrary, it was very flattering, since one only pays money for things one finds valuable... Suddenly, she began to undress.

She stopped in front of the mirror and looked over her shoulders and arms with satisfaction for a moment, as parts of that whole "for which men pay impressive sums". By this point, she found the thought decidedly amusing. "Well, is it worth it? If it's worth it to them..."

Earlier, downstairs under the lamp, she'd desired the Persian's amorous embraces intensely. Not out of pure arousal: it was mostly curiosity, a longing for the exotic. But at the time, she hadn't thought it could actually become a reality. Now, however, she'd soon feel in her entire body the volcanic glow she imagined the Persian to contain. How strange and frightening, such preparation and expectation!

She was so overcome with excitement that her teeth were chattering. This would be the greatest night of her life. The goal, the fulfilment towards which every path had led. Now, now at last, she'd leave behind every petit-bourgeois convention, everything that was still Pest within herself, and somewhere in the depths of France, in an antique castle, she'd give herself up to a man who'd purchased her; she'd give herself over to an exotic wild beast, utterly losing her gentlewomanly character, like an oriental courtesan in the Bible or the Arabian Nights. This image of desire had always been lurking at the bottom of her fantasies, even back when she had cheated on Zoltán with Mihály... and her instinct had chosen well, because her path with Mihály had – behold! – led here.

And now here was this man, who might be the ultimate. The true tiger. The exotic. The man of passion. A few minutes, and she'd find out. She shivered. Was it cold? No: she was scared.

Quickly, she donned her blouse again. She stopped at the door leading to the corridor and pressed her hand to her heart, with that simple-minded and sincere gesture that she'd seen so many times in the movies.

The secret appeared in her imagination, bodiless and headless, terrifying. The oriental secret, the secret of men, the secret of love; who knows with what sort of alarming, tormenting, mauling motions and deeds this alien – tenfold alien – man was approaching her; who knows whether she might not be annihilated, like dying women in the arms of the gods long ago. Who knows what sort of mysterious monstrosities…

Then her well-bred, gentlewomanly, model-pupil nature reclaimed its power: her thrift, everything from which she had ever fled. No, no, she didn't dare… Fear made her strong and resourceful. Within moments, she dragged all the furniture to the lockless door; she even grasped the heavy bed and, weeping, swallowing her tears, dragged it, too, to the door. Then she fell on it in exhaustion.

Just in time. The Persian's soft footfalls could be heard in the next room. The Persian stopped in front of the door. He listened for a while, then turned the knob.

The door, bolstered by every piece of furniture in the room, resisted. The Persian didn't force it.

"Elizabeth," he said softly.

Erzsi didn't reply. The Persian tried to open the door again, this time appearing to push his shoulder against it. The furniture gave way a little.

"Don't come in!" Erzsi shouted.

The Persian stopped, and for a moment there was complete silence.

"Elizabeth, open the door," the Persian said, more loudly.

Erzsi didn't reply.

The Persian hissed something and leant against the door with all his strength.

"Don't come in!" Erzsi screamed.

The Persian let go of the door.

"Elizabeth," he said once again, but as if from a great distance, in a dying voice.

Then, after a while, he said, "Goodnight," and returned to his room.

Her teeth chattering, Erzsi lay on the bed, fully clothed. She wept and was utterly exhausted. This was the moment of clear insight, when someone understands her entire life. She made no excuses to herself: she knew that the reason she hadn't let the Persian in wasn't because the humiliating circumstances upset her, and not even because she was an honourable woman, but because she was a coward. The secret she had always sought had been close at hand, and she fled from it. She'd been a petit-bourgeois woman all her life, and would remain one.

Oh if only the Persian would return, now she'd let him in… After all, it wouldn't be fatal, nothing truly awful could happen; oh what idiocy this childish terror had been. If the Persian would just return now, this terrible fatigue would pass, and everything else too, everything…

But the Persian did not return. Erzsi undressed, lay down and fell asleep.

She might have slept an hour or two. She awoke; dawn was already preparing to break outside. It was half-past three. She jumped out of bed, washed her face and hands, dressed and slipped out into the hallway. She didn't even think about it; she knew she had to flee this place. She knew she must never see the Persian again. She was both ashamed and glad to be fleeing with her skin intact. She was in a good mood, and when she succeeded in opening the house's great gate, which had been bolted but not locked with a key, and when she succeeded in reaching the main road through the garden without being noticed, an adolescent courage seized her and she felt that all her cowardice notwithstanding, she was the victor, the successful one.

She ran happily along the main road and shortly reached a small village. It turned out that there was a train station close by; indeed, a dawn workers' train was just setting off for Paris. It was still early in the morning when she arrived in the city.

Upon reaching her hotel, she lay down and slept – deeply, perhaps happily – until after noon. When she awoke, she felt as if she had truly awoken after some long-lasting, beautiful and frightening dream. She took a taxi and hurried to Sári, although she could just as easily have taken a bus or the metro. But now that she'd awoken, her thriftiness had also passed.

She related the entire affair to Sári with the cynical openness of women discussing their love lives with each other. Sári spiced the narrative with little exclamations and sagacities.

"And what will you do now?" she finally asked, tenderly and encouragingly.

"What will I do? Why, haven't you figured it out yet? I'm going back to Zoltán. That's exactly why I came back here."

"You're going back to Zoltán? What, is this why you left him? And do you think it'll be better now? Since you can't claim to love him very much. I don't understand you... but you're completely correct. Absolutely right. I'd do the same in your place. After all, what's sure is sure, and you weren't born to live a Parisian student's life in your old age and change lovers as if that was how you supported yourself."

"I was most certainly not born for that. And for just this reason... If you please, I finally understand what was behind last night's fear. I thought about where it would lead. The Persian might be followed by a Venezuelan, then a Japanese and maybe a Negro... I thought that once one begins there's no stopping, because what the devil would stop it? And that, after all... no, thank you. I can't be one of those, after all, can I? This was what I was frightened of: of myself, of all the things I'd be capable of and of all the things that could still happen to me. But no, not that, after all. Something has to restrain a woman. And in that case, Zoltán's the best option."

"What do you mean, he's the best option? He's outstanding. He's a wealthy man, a good man, he adores you – I don't even understand how you could have left him. Write to him now, right away, and get packed and go. My Erzsi... how wonderful for you. And how I'll miss you."

"No, I won't write to him: you'll write."

"Are you afraid he might not want you after all?"

"No, my dear, I'm really not afraid of that. But I don't want to write to him, because he doesn't need to know that I'm fleeing to him; he doesn't need to know that he's the only solution. Let him think I've taken pity on him. Otherwise, he'll be overconfident."

"How right you are!"

"Write him that you made strenuous appeals to my better self, arguing that I should return to him, and you've noticed that I appear willing, except that my pride won't allow me to admit it. That the best thing will be for him to come to Paris and try to speak to me. You'll prepare his path. Write a clever letter, my little Sári. And rest assured that Zoltán will be most gallant to you."

"Splendid! I'll write right away, right here, right away. Say, Erzsi, when you're in Pest and Zoltán's wife once again, you might send me a pair of fine shoes. You know, they're not only much less expensive than in Paris, but they're also better and more durable."

7

FOIED VINO PIPAFO, CRA CAREFO. I drink wine today, tomorrow there shall be none. The wine ran out: that mysterious inner sap – the one that woke him each morning and lulled him into the illusion that it's worth arising – ran out. And in the measure that the wine ran out, the dark sea rose from below, the lake that matches the ocean in depth, the Other Longing that opposes life and is more powerful than life.

What had been a trace of Tamás within him now grew into reality. For this thing was growing within him: his own death. It drew nourishment from the sap of his life, it thought and grew wiser from his thoughts, it drank into itself all the beautiful sights, until it became complete and the time came for it to step into the world as reality.

He wrote to Éva to tell her the time: Saturday night. Éva replied: "I'll be there."

That's all. Éva's curt, *matter-of-fact* response nevertheless dumbfounded him: was that all the whole thing meant to her? She finds death to be so routine! Frightful.

He felt some sort of coldness beginning to spread inside him, a strange and sick coldness, the way, following the application of a local anaesthetic, a body part gradually goes numb and grows alien and frightening to its own body: so did the something that was Éva slowly die inside him. Mihály was well familiar with the pauses and interruptions of love, when, right in the middle of its most burning phase, one suddenly becomes utterly indifferent to the beloved, and one gazes at that alien, lovely face, wondering whether this might be that woman… It was the same now, but he felt a more significant pause than any until then. Éva had gone cold.

But then what would become of his final minutes, if she showed him the same sweetness she had shown Tamás?

An odd, sour humour took control of him, and he established that the great act was getting off to a decidedly poor start.

That was on Saturday afternoon. He found himself faced with the weighty question of what to do with the next few hours. What does a man do when nothing has any significance any longer? "The last hours of a suicide" – this expression, now applicable to himself, astounded him still more than the one before, when he'd determined that he'd been "intoxicated by love" or that he "couldn't live without her". How horrible that the most salient moments and situations of our lives can only be approximated by the most banal expressions, and that apparently these are also, in fact, our most banal moments. At such times we are just the same as other people. Mihály would now "prepare for death", the way other men do when they know they have to die soon.

Yes, there was nothing else to do; he couldn't circumvent the rules: he was forced to conform even in his last moments. He too would write a farewell letter, as was proper. Indeed, it wouldn't be decent to leave his mother and father behind without a farewell. He'd write them a letter.

His first painful moment was when this crossed his mind. Up to that point, he had felt only a dull, tired, ill temper, a fog in which the anticipated fulfilment of the final minutes and their thoughts of Tamás phosphoresced, mysterious and greenish. But now that he thought of his parents, he felt a strong pain, strong and bright; the fog cleared, he began to feel sorry for his parents – and for himself, stupidly, sentimentally, absurdly. Overcome with shame, he took out his fountain pen to report his deed with exemplary discipline and indifference, yet with warm words, calmly, masterfully, in the routine of death.

While he sat there, fountain pen in hand, waiting for the exemplary, controlled phrases to occur to him, all of a sudden someone rang the doorbell. Mihály shuddered violently. Nobody came by for weeks: who could it be now, of all times? Indefinable suspicions ran through his mind for a moment. The landlady wasn't at home. No, he wouldn't answer the door, at this point there was truly no point, he no longer had anything to do with anyone.

But the ringing grew more and more insistent. Mihály shrugged his shoulders, like someone saying: "What can I do if they're so pushy!" and went out. He even felt a bit of relief.

To his utmost surprise, he found Vannina and another Italian girl at the door. They were very formally attired, with black silk scarves on their heads, and they had washed more thoroughly than usual.

"Oh," said Mihály, "I'm most delighted" – and he began to babble at greater length, because he not only failed to understand the situation at all, but also didn't speak Italian well enough to disguise his confusion.

"Well then, come along, *signore*," said Vannina.

"Me? Where?"

"Why, to the baptism, of course!"

"What baptism?"

"Why, my cousin's *bambino*'s baptism. Maybe you didn't receive my letter?"

"No, I didn't. You wrote to me? How did you know my name and address?"

"Your friend told me – here it is, see, written down."

She took out a wrinkled scrap of paper, and Mihály recognized Szepetneki's handwriting. "Cabbage is round," it said, along with Mihály's address.*

"You addressed it to this name?" Mihály asked.

"Yes. Strange name. Didn't you get the letter?"

"No, I swear to God, no – I have no idea why not. But do come in."

They entered the room, Vannina looked around and asked: "The *signora* isn't at home?"

"No, I have no *signora*."

"Really? It would be rather nice indeed to stay here for a while… but, well, the *bambino* must be baptized. Come, come quickly. People are beginning to gather, and we mustn't keep the priest waiting either."

"But my dear… I… I didn't receive your letter, which I regret deeply, and I'm totally unprepared today…"

"That may be, but it makes no difference. You don't have anything to do anyhow: foreigners never have anything to do. Take your hat and come along – *avanti*."

"But it just so happens that I have a great deal of work to do… An awful lot of important work."

And his expression darkened. Everything came to mind, and he saw the prosaic dreadfulness of the situation. While writing his farewell letter, he'd been interrupted to attend a baptism. All of a sudden they'd dropped in with such endearing and stupid things: the way people always used to drop in with endearing and stupid things when life was terrible and exalted, and terrible and exalted things always came crashing down on his head when life was endearing and stupid. Life is no art form – or at the least, it's a very uneven art form.

Vannina stood up, stepped over to him and put her hand on his shoulder. "What sort of important work do you have?"

"Whatnot… I have to write letters, very important letters."

Vannina stared into his face; nonplussed, Mihály turned his head.

"It will be better for you too, if you come with us now," said the girl. "There'll be a grand feast at our place after the baptism. We'll drink a little wine, and then you can write those letters afterwards, if you'll actually still be in the mood for it."

Mihály stared at her in astonishment. He remembered the girl's fortune-telling skills. He sensed that she saw right through him and understood his situation. He was suddenly overcome by shame, like a schoolboy caught in the act. Now he saw nothing exalted in the death wish. He deferred to the greater master, to everyday life, as always. They could not keep the priest waiting, indeed… He put money in his wallet and took his hat; they set off.

But as he remained alone, letting the two women walk ahead in the dark stairwell, it suddenly occurred to him: what utter nonsense it was for him to go to a baptism with Italian proles he didn't know – this too was the sort of thing that could only happen to him. He was on the point of running back and locking the door behind him. But the girl seemed to sense it, put her arm in his and pulled him out onto the street. She bundled him along like a calf towards the Trastevere. Mihály felt the same ecstasy as during his adolescent performances, when he played the victim.

The interested parties were already gathered in the small tavern, roughly fifteen or twenty people. They talked a great deal, to him as well, but he understood nothing, since they were speaking the Trastevere dialect; he wasn't paying very much attention anyway.

He only gave a start when the young mother appeared, the *bambino* on her arm. The mother's skinny, sickly ugliness and the *bambino*'s lemon-like appearance frightened Mihály. He had never liked children, whether newborn or in their later stages, being repulsed and frightened by them – and he always felt uncomfortable around mothers. But this mother and this newborn were exceptionally revolting – he sensed some satanic Madonna parody in the ugly mother's tenderness and ugly infant's vulnerability, some sardonic mockery of European man's greatest symbol. It all seemed so "last days"… as if the last mother had given birth to the last child, and those surrounding them here didn't even know that they were the last humans, the scummy dregs of history, the final gesture, full of self-mockery, of the dying god of Time.

From this point on, he experienced everything that happened, the last day and night, from a sad, grotesque distance. As they swarmed down the Trastevere's narrow streets, as they shouted here and there to the swarming acquaintances flooding into the small church, and their every movement was so strangely sprightly and small, he saw with unwavering clarity:

"They are rats. They're rats living amidst the ruins. That's why they're so sprightly and so ugly and so fecund."

Meanwhile, he carried out the godfather's functions without thinking, Vannina standing next to him and directing him. At the end of the ceremony, he gave two hundred lire to the mother, and, making a great effort, he kissed his godson, who by now bore the name Michele.

("St Michael, the Archangel, defend us in battle. Be our safeguard against the wickedness and snares of Satan. May God rebuke him, we humbly pray; and do you, O Prince of the heavenly host, by the power of God cast into hell Satan and all the evil spirits who wander through the world seeking the ruin of souls. Amen.")

The ceremony took a long time. Afterwards, they all returned to the tavern. They'd already set the tables for dinner in the courtyard. Mihály, as usual, was hungry. He knew that he'd fulfilled his obligations and should go home to write the letters, but he couldn't help it: his persistent culinary curiosity tempted him: what sort of interesting local dishes would make up the feast? "I wonder if others are hungry and curious about pasta at this point in their lives?" he asked himself.

The dinner was good; that unusual green pasta they served, tasting agreeably of creamed vegetables, was indeed a special dish deserving of Mihály's curiosity. The hosts, however, were proud of the meat dish, since they ate meat rarely in the Trastevere quarter; but Mihály wasn't much taken with it and instead set with all the more gusto to the cheese, which was a type unfamiliar to him, and a great experience, like every new cheese. Meanwhile, he drank a lot, especially since his neighbour, Vannina, was refilling his glass liberally, and because he didn't understand a word of the conversation and therefore decided to take part in the general good humour in this way.

The wine, however, didn't improve his mood but just made him uncertain, infinitely uncertain. By now it was evening, and it wouldn't be long until Éva arrived... He should get up and go home. At this point, nothing stood in his way, except the fact that the Italian girl wouldn't let him go. But by now everything was so distant, Éva and his intention and his longing were all far away, swimming, the last island on some far northern Tiber, and Mihály felt that by this point, he was as impersonal and as vegetative as that mulberry tree in the courtyard, and he was letting his leaves droop just the same way on this, his final night, which by now was no longer his own final night, but humanity's.

Night fell, and the Italian stars idled up there above the courtyard. Mihály stood up and realized that he was dead drunk. He didn't understand how it had happened, because he didn't remember having drunk all that much – although he hadn't been paying attention and it was possible that he'd drunk quite a bit – and he hadn't felt the crescendo of mood that typically preceded his inebriation. He'd become totally drunk from one minute to the next.

He took a few steps in the courtyard, then staggered and fell over. This was very pleasant. He caressed the ground and was happy. "Oh, how wonderful," he thought, "I'm already here. Now I can't fall over any more."

He sensed the Italians lifting him up and, amid a storm of talk, carrying him into the house, during which he humbly and apologetically informed them that he truly didn't want to be a burden to anyone; they should just go ahead and continue the celebrations that promised to be outstanding.

Afterwards, he lay on a bed and fell asleep instantly.

It was pitch-dark when he awoke; his head ached, but otherwise he felt fairly sober, except that his heart was pounding hard and he was uneasy. Why had he got so drunk? His psychological state when he sat down to drink had assuredly played its part, and his resistance had been much lower. He'd shown no resistance whatsoever: the Italian girl had done whatever she wanted with him. Might the Italian girl also have wanted him to get so drunk?

He became highly uneasy. He thought of the time when he'd spent the entire night wandering the streets of Rome and then wound up here, in front of this little house, and his imagination had projected mysterious and sinful things behind its silent walls. This was the house where the murders had happened. And now here he was inside the house, its walls remarkably silent: here he lay at the mercy of the darkness, just as he'd wanted.

He lay there for a while, in ever-growing unease, and then tried to get up. But his movements were laboured and his throbbing pulse pierced his head. He preferred to remain recumbent. He pricked his ears. His eyes adjusted to the darkness and his ears to the silence. He heard a thousand tiny noises: strange nearby Italian noises from every direction. The house was awake, all around him. A faint light sprang in from under the door.

What if these people were planning something... What madness it was to have brought money with him! Where had he put the money anyway? But since he was lying fully clothed, it must be in his wallet. He felt for his wallet. It wasn't in its place. It wasn't in any of his pockets.

So that much was certain: they'd stolen his money. Perhaps two hundred lire. That was not a problem... would they want something else as well? Would they let him leave and report them? They'd have to be insane. No, they were going to kill him, without a doubt.

That was when the door opened and Vannina stepped inside, with what looked like an oil lamp in her hand. She peered towards the bed and then, when she saw that Mihály was awake, she seemed to adopt a surprised expression and stepped over to the bed. She also said something that Mihály didn't understand, but which didn't sound good.

Then she set the lamp down and sat on the edge of the bed. She stroked Mihály's hair and face and encouraged him, in Italian, to relax and go to sleep.

"Of course, she's just waiting for me to sleep, and then… I'm not going to fall asleep!"

Then the frightful memory of the girl's suggestive powers came back to him, and that he'd surely fall asleep if that was what the girl wanted. And indeed, he shut his eyes as the girl caressed his eyelashes, and he suddenly fell into a buzzing half-sleep.

In this half-sleep, he seemed to hear them talking in the next room. He heard the growling of some raw male voice, and from time to time the rapid speech of another man and, in between, the girl's staccato whispers. Now they were undoubtedly discussing whether to kill him. Maybe the girl was defending him, maybe the opposite. He must wake up now, now. Oh how many times had he dreamt this: that some awful danger was approaching and he couldn't wake up, no matter how hard he tried, and lo, now his dream has become reality. Then he dreamt that something flashed before his eyes, and he awoke with a rattle in his breathing.

It was light in the room; the lamp was burning on the table. He sat up and looked around in terror, but he saw no one in the room. The murmur of speech still seeped in from the next room, much more softly now, and he could not determine who was speaking.

The fear of death was seeping through his entire being. His whole body was trembling. He sensed them approaching him with knives, these rat people. All he could do was wring his hands; something restrained him and he couldn't leap out of bed.

Only the lamp calmed him a little, the lamp that fluttered and cast shadows on the wall like those in his nursery long ago. It reminded him of Vannina's hands with their highly refined lines; he had stared at them before without noticing them, when she was holding the lamp.

"Why am I afraid?" he thought with a start. After all, what he wanted, what he'd planned, was going to happen now, now, now. He was going to die – and, indeed, he wanted to die – and there, by his side and maybe, in part, in the role of the perpetrator as well, would be a beautiful girl, carrying a strange secret, a death demon, as depicted on the Etruscan graves.

By now he was longing for it. With chattering teeth and arms benumbed by terror, but he longed for it to happen. Let the door open, let the girl step in, let her step up to the bed and kiss and embrace him, while the murdering knife carries out its task… let her step in and embrace him… if only she'd come in already… if only the door would open already…

But the door didn't open, the predawn cocks were already crowing outside, there was complete silence in the next room, the lamp also guttered out and Mihály plunged into a deep sleep.

And then it was morning, a morning like any other. He awoke in a bright room, a friendly bright room, to Vannina entering and asking if he'd had a good night's sleep. It was morning, an amiable, normal Italian summer morning. Soon it would be horribly warm, but now it was still pleasant. Only the aftertaste of the previous night's drunkenness troubled him, nothing else.

The girl said something about how drunk he'd been the evening before, but he'd been affable for all that and enjoyed great popularity during the festivities, and they'd put him up here because they were concerned that he wouldn't be able to make it home.

Mention of going home brought Éva to Mihály's mind: she must have been looking for him last night, to be with him when… What might she be thinking of him? That he'd fled, fled from himself?

That's when he realized that during the course of the entire alarming and visionary night he hadn't given so much as a single thought to Éva. The pause. The longest and most significant pause of his life.

"What an odd thing, to die for a woman who, throughout the entire night – and what a night! – didn't even cross our mind."

He straightened out his clothes more or less, then bade farewell to the few people sitting at the bar outside the room, who in turn greeted him like a dear old friend. Now that the sunlight was streaming in through the small window, they didn't resemble rats at all: they were upright Italian proletarians.

"And these were the men who wanted to murder me?" he mused. "True, it's not at all certain that they wanted to murder me. Still, it's odd that they didn't murder me; in fact they like me a great deal now that they've stolen my wallet. When all is said and done, these Italians are completely different."

His hand involuntarily felt for his wallet. It was there, in its place, above his heart, where the central European man keeps his money – not without symbolic significance. Dumbfounded, he stopped short and extracted his wallet. The two hundred lire and some small change, a few ten-lira coins, were inside; nothing was missing.

It was possible that they sneaked the wallet back into its place while he was asleep – but that would be pointless. More likely they had never stolen it. It had been there in his pocket even when he'd established that it had disappeared. Mihály accepted it. This wasn't the first time in his life that he'd taken white for black, when his impressions and beliefs had declared their complete independence from external reality.

Vannina accompanied him out the door and then carried on walking with him for a while, in the direction of the Gianicolo.

"Come again sometime. And you'll have to see the *bambino*. A godfather has his responsibilities, and he's not allowed to neglect them. Come again. Often. Always..."

Mihály gave the girl the two hundred lire, then suddenly kissed her on the mouth and rushed away.

8

HE ARRIVED UPSTAIRS to his room.

"I'll take a short rest and think it through: what do I really want, and do I want what I want – and only then will I write to Éva. Because my situation with respect to her is a bit awkward, and if I were to tell her why I didn't come home last night she might not even believe it, it's so stupid."

He undressed automatically and began to wash. Was there really still any reason to wash? But he dithered only for a moment, then washed, brewed himself some tea, picked up a book, lay down and fell asleep.

He awoke to the sound of the doorbell ringing. He hurried out, feeling refreshed and well rested. It had rained outside in the meantime and wasn't as warm as during the preceding days.

He opened the door and let in an older gentleman. It was his father.

"Hello, son," said his father. "I just arrived on the midday train. Well, I'm glad to find you here at home. And I'm hungry. I'd like you to come to luncheon with me."

His father's unexpected appearance surprised Mihály no end, but his dominant feeling was, nonetheless, not that of surprise. Nor even confusion and shame, when his father looked around the room, straining to prevent his face from betraying his disgust at the shabby surroundings. A different feeling filled Mihály, a feeling that he knew, in smaller measure, from long before, from the time when he had often been abroad. Even back then, the feeling that always seized him upon returning from a longer trip was the horror that his father had aged in the meantime. But his father had never aged this much before – no, never this much. The last time he'd seen him, he had still been the commanding, self-confident man he'd known him to be all his life. Or at least that is how he had seemed to Mihály, because he'd been living at home for several years at the time, and if some change had taken place over that period, he hadn't noticed the slow metamorphosis. He saw it all the more sharply now, not having seen his father for some months. Time had invaded the face and figure. There were signs of elderliness – not many, but undeniably present – in his father: his mouth had lost its old firmness, his eyes were tired and sunken (true, he'd been travelling all night and, who knows, in third class, as thrifty a man as he was), his hair was even whiter, his speech seemed less distinct, with some odd lisping quality in it that was frightening at first – he couldn't describe it, but the fact was present in all its horrible reality: his father had grown old.

And compared to this, everything else was as nothing – Éva and the plans for death, even Italy itself.

"Just don't let me break out crying, not now: my father would view it with utter contempt, and besides, he might figure out that I'm crying for him."

Pulling himself together, he took on his most inscrutable expression: the face which he generally used in connection to anything to do with his family.

"Very kind of you, Father, to have come. You must have had important reasons to make this long journey in the summer…"

"Of course, son, important reasons. But nothing unpleasant. Nothing's the matter. You haven't asked, of course, but your mother and siblings are all well. And as I can see, you don't have anything particularly the matter with you either. Well, then, let's go dine now. Take me somewhere they don't cook with oil."

"Erzsi and Zoltán Pataki visited me the day before yesterday," his father said during the meal.

"What's that? Erzsi's in Pest? And they're together?"

"Yes. Pataki went to Paris, they reconciled, and he brought Erzsi home."

"But, my word, why and how?"

"Son, I really have no idea and, as you can imagine, I didn't even enquire. We only spoke of business matters. You know what an awkward position your... how shall I put it... odd – although, as far as I'm concerned, not all that surprising – behaviour put me in with respect to Erzsi. An awkward financial position. To liquidate Erzsi's investment in today's world... but I should think you know this, since Tivadar wrote you all about it."

"Yes, I know. You might not believe me, but I was dreadfully worried about what would happen. Erzsi said that Zoltán... but, please, go on."

"Thank God, nothing's the matter. They came to see me precisely to negotiate the conditions under which I would repay the sum. But I can tell you they were so compliant that it surprised even me. We agreed on the instalments. The terms are not at all oppressive financially, and I hope that we'll complete this transaction without any particular difficulty. And all the more so because your brother Péter has managed to find an outstanding new customer."

"But tell me, did Zoltán – I mean Pataki – indeed behave properly? I don't understand."

"He behaved like a perfect gentleman. Between the two of us, I think this was due to his joy at having Erzsi back. And he was surely following Erzsi's intentions. Erzsi is a truly exceptional lady. It was bad enough, Mihály... oh, but I've decided not to make any reproaches. You've always been an unusual boy, and you know what you're doing."

"And Zoltán didn't accuse me? He didn't say that—"

"He didn't say a thing. Not a single word about you, which is natural enough, under the circumstances. On the other hand, Erzsi spoke about you."

"Erzsi?"

"Yes. She said that she had met you in Rome. She didn't give any details, and naturally I didn't ask, but she admitted that you were in a most critical condition, and that you thought your family had turned against you. No, don't say a thing. We've always been discreet men with respect to each other, and let us remain so. I'm not interested in the details. But Erzsi advised me that, if possible, I should come to Rome myself, and convince you to return to Pest. Or rather, the expression she used was 'take you home'."

To take him home? Yes, Erzsi knew what she was talking about, and she knew Mihály well. She understood that his father could take Mihály home like a truant pupil. She understood that Mihály had an accommodating nature, and that he'd acquiesce like a truant who had been tracked down – while making the mental reservation, of course, that, given the opportunity, he might escape again.

Erzsi was wise. He could do nothing else but go home. There would have been one other solution, but… those external circumstances from which he had wanted to flee into death had, it seemed, ceased to be. Zoltán had calmed down, his family yearned for him and nobody was persecuting him.

"So here I am now," his father continued, "and I would appreciate it if you'd immediately wrap up all your business here and come home, on this evening's train as a matter of fact. You know, I don't have much time."

"Excuse me, but this has all come a bit unexpectedly," said Mihály, shaking himself out of his reverie. "This morning the possibility that I might return to Pest was the last thing I was expecting."

"I can believe that, but tell me, what objection do you have to coming home?"

"None: just let me catch my breath. Look, it won't do you any harm either to lie down a little and take a siesta in my room. I'll order my thoughts during that time."

"Certainly, as you wish."

Mihály made his father comfortable on his bed, and he himself sat in the large armchair, with the firm resolve to think things over. His thinking consisted of conjuring up certain feelings, one after the other, and measuring their intensity. This was how he used to determine what he wanted – or what he would want if he could want anything.

Did he indeed want to die? Did he still long for a death like Tamás's? He conjured up this desire and sought its accompanying sweetness. But now he felt no sweetness; on the contrary, he felt surfeit and fatigue, the sort a man feels after making love.

Then it dawned on him, why he felt this queasiness: because his longing had already found gratification. Last night in the Italian house, in his fear and vision, he had already realized the desire that had been tempting him ever since his adolescence. It had been fulfilled in the reality of his soul, if not in the reality of the outside world. And thus the desire had been satisfied, if not for ever, then at least for a good long time: he had been freed from it, and he had been freed from Tamás's ghost.

And Éva?

He noticed a letter on the desk. It had been placed there while he was at luncheon. It must have arrived last night, but the lady from next door had forgotten to deliver it. He got up and read Éva's farewell lines.

Mihály, by the time you read this, I'll already be en route to Bombay. I'm not coming over to see you. You won't die. You're not Tamás. Tamás's death concerns only Tamás: let each find his own death. God be with you, Éva.

That evening, they were indeed already on the train. They spoke of business matters; his father related what had transpired at the firm while Mihály had been away, and what the prospects were, and what new sphere of activity he intended to entrust to Mihály.

Mihály listened to him. He was going home. Once again, he'd attempt what he had failed to do for fifteen years: to conform. Perhaps this time he would succeed. This was his destiny. He'd surrender. The facts were stronger than him. Escape was impossible. They'd always be stronger: fathers, Zoltáns, firms, and people.

His father fell asleep, and Mihály stared out the window, trying to make out the profile of the Tuscan mountains in the moonlight. He must stay alive. And he too would live: like rats amidst the ruins. But he'd live, nonetheless. And as long as one lives, something might yet happen.

Note on the Text

This translation is based on Antal Szerb, *Utas és holdvilág* (Budapest: Révai, 1937), as accessed online (Budapest: Országos Széchenyi Könyvtár, Magyar Elektronikus Könyvtár, 2015).

Notes

p. 5, *Mihály*: The Hungarian form of Michael.

p. 6, *Erzsi*: The common nickname for Erzsébet, the Hungarian form of Elizabeth.

p. 6, *Frezzeria*: The central district of Venice, between Piazza San Marco and the Rialto.

p. 6, *fiaschetterie*: Shops selling wine and spirits by the bottle or the glass; literally, "flask shop".

p. 7, *cemetery island*: Isola di San Michele contains Venice's municipal cemetery.

p. 7, *the houses of Murano in the far distance*: Murano is actually nearer the north-east shore of Venice than San Francesco del Deserto.

p. 13, *János*: The Hungarian form of John.

p. 17, *Baja... five pengős*: Baja is a town on the Danube in the south of Hungary. The pengő was the unit of Hungarian currency from 1927 to 1946, divided into 100 fillér.

p. 18, *Buda*: This always refers exclusively to the part of Budapest on the west bank of the Danube, directly opposite Pest on the east bank. Note that "Pest" can, depending on context, either refer to the portion of Budapest east of the Danube or serve as colloquial shorthand for Budapest.

p. 18, *Stonemason Kelemen's wife... fortress of Déva*: This refers to an ancient Hungarian legend – actually shared throughout the peoples of south-eastern Europe – of a stonemason, Kelemen (Clement), tasked with building an impregnable fortress. Every night, the wall he'd built that day would mysteriously crumble. At his wits' end, he consulted a seer who said the walls would only stand if he immured the very next person he saw walking down the road; but in that case, the walls would stand for ever. Kelemen agreed to the bargain. To his horror, the next person walking down the road was his wife, bringing him his meal. True to his word, he walled her in alive, and Déva fortress remains standing to this day. Déva: present-day Deva, Romania.

p. 23, *Laci, Edit and Tivadar*: Laci is the common nickname for László (Ladislaus); Edit is the Hungarian form of Edith; Tivadar is the Hungarian form of Theodore.

p. 25, *Lord Chief Justice Majláth*: György Majláth (1818–83), Speaker of the House of Lords and Judge Royal, was killed in a robbery.

p. 26, *Moral insanity*: In English in the original – further such uses of English are also indicated by italics.

p. 27, *István Tisza*: Count István Tisza (1861–1918), Emperor Franz Joseph's Prime Minister of Hungary. The only member of the Imperial Cabinet to vote against issuing an ultimatum to Serbia, he tendered his resignation, but the Emperor persuaded him that it was his duty to remain at his post. Later, he was unfairly accused of being the prime Austro-Hungarian warmonger and tool of the German Kaiser; he was assassinated days before the end of the First World War.

p. 27, *When Przemysl fell*: Przemysl, the major Austro-Hungarian fortification on the frontier with Russia, was subjected to a lengthy and bloody siege and taken by the Russians in late 1914; it was retaken, in an equally costly siege, by the Germans in 1915.

p. 27, *Ady and Babits*: Endre Ady (1877–1919), poet; the great early modernist in Hungarian literature. Mihály Babits (1883–1941), poet; the great modern classicist in Hungarian literature of the first half of the twentieth century.

p. 28, *a famous English essay... tyranny of facts*: A reference to the well-known *On the Study of Celtic Literature* (1867) by Matthew Arnold (1822–88), in which the author quotes (in translation) the French historian Henri Martin's (1810–88) phrase "revolt against the tyranny of facts".

p. 31, *Judith and Holofernes*: In the Book of Judith (which forms part of the Christian Old Testament but is not part of the Hebrew Bible), Holofernes is one of Nebuchadnezzar's generals in the Babylonian invasion of the countries of the Levant; when he laid siege to the Israelite city of Bethulia, Judith, one of the townspeople, seduced the general and when he was in a drunken sleep, she cut off his head, saving the city.

p. 33, *The eighth form*: In Hungary, four years of elementary school were followed by eight years of *gimnázium* (for those found worthy of *gimnázium*, that is).

p. 35, *March Circle*: Probably a reference to a progressive Hungarian intellectual circle named after the 1848 revolution against Austrian imperial rule, which began on 15th March.

p. 35, *Károlyi revolution*: More frequently dubbed the Aster Revolution because of the flowers worn in the revolutionaries' lapels, this was the uprising of 31st October 1918 that overthrew the last Habsburg king, Charles IV, and proclaimed Hungary as a republic.

p. 36, *Whoever puts his hands... not look back*: A paraphrase of Luke 9:62.

p. 37, *visiting brothels*: Brothels were legal in Budapest at the time, licensed and inspected; and not a few bourgeois parents sent their boys to a brothel to have a professional initiate them into the mysteries of sex.

p. 37, *pour épater les bourgeois*: "To astonish the bourgeois" (French).

p. 40, *St Thomas … St Anselm of Canterbury*: St Thomas could be any of a large number of saints, such as St Thomas Aquinas (1225–74, but who hardly needed rescue from oblivion) or St Thomas More (1478–1535, who was not well known in Hungary); Jacques Maritain (1882–1973), a French Catholic philosopher; G.K. Chesterton (1874–1936), an English Catholic writer; St Anselm of Canterbury (1033–1109), an Italian-born Benedictine monk and theologian who served as Archbishop of Canterbury (1093–1109).

p. 47, *the Sisters of Loreto*: One of two Catholic orders founded concurrently by the Englishwoman, Venerable Mary Ward, in 1609 (the other is the Congregation of Jesus).

p. 48, *At the time, Budapest… the Entente's officers*: This places the episode in immediately post-First World War Hungary, late 1918–19. Austria-Hungary, having lost the First World War, fell apart into successor states, one of which was the independent but severely truncated Hungary. As an enemy capital, Budapest was effectively run for a time by a council of Entente officers, with representation from each of the Allied countries. This tumultuous time saw, in succession, a bourgeois revolution deposing the Habsburgs and declaring Hungary as a republic (31st October 1918), the Armistice (11th November 1918) and, all in the same year of 1919, the short-lived Hungarian Republic of Soviets, occupation and despoliation by the Romanian army, and a counterrevolution that made Hungary a kingdom again, but one without a king (Miklós Horthy, leader of the counterrevolution and a former Habsburg admiral, ruled as Regent). The post-Armistice events all took place while the Entente was nominally in control of Budapest.

p. 53, *Hallstatt*: An old spa town on a deep alpine lake in Austria.

p. 55, *St Stephen*: St Stephen I (*c.*975–1038), first Christian king of Hungary, crowned in 1000.

p. 58, *unberufen*: "Unbidden" (German).

p. 61, *nichts für ungut*: "No offence" (German).

p. 69, *when he compared its acrobats… their nether parts*: A reference to Dante, *The Divine Comedy* XXI, lines 136–39. The last line cited reads "*Ed egli avea del cul fatto trombetta*" ("And he had made his arse blow like a bugle"). The original refers to runners, not acrobats.

p. 69, *the Sienese Primitives*: A reference to the pre- and early-Renaissance school of Sienese painting culminating in the work of Simone Martini (*c.*1284–1344).

p. 82, *macchia*: "Low, dense shrubland" (Italian).

p. 87, *the Battle of Skagerrak*: Better known among Anglophones as the Battle of Jutland, the major naval engagement of the First World War.

p. 89, *Fioretti*: "Little Flowers" (Italian); *The Little Flowers of St Francis* comprises excerpts from his body of work, compiled in the fourteenth century, that tell tales about the saint's life.

p. 97, *Watteau*: Jean-Antoine Watteau (1684–1721), French painter.

p. 106, *Denn da ist… dein Leben ändern*: From 'Archäischer Torso Apollos' ('Archaic Torso of Apollo'): "for here there is no place / that does not see you. You must change your life" (German; translation: Stephen Mitchell).

p. 110, *vinum ferri*: "Iron wine" (Latin), prepared by macerating an iron wire in sherry (or other fortified wine).

p. 113, *Pater Severinus from the Sant'Ubaldo cloister*: Catholic monks choose a religious name upon entering an order. Ervin chose that of St Severinus of Noricum (*c.*410–82), who proselytized to the Celts in the Roman province of Noricum, which comprises portions of present-day Austria and Slovenia. St Ubaldo (*c.*1084–1160), bishop of Gubbio, was known for his humility, self-mortification, meekness and religious fervour; he was also known for dissuading Emperor Frederick Barbarossa from sacking Gubbio during his rampage through Italy.

p. 118, *St Augustine*: Aurelius Augustinus (354–430), bishop of Hippo, theologian, Doctor of the Church, and author of the autobiographical *Confessions* with the famous line in which he recalls himself praying, in his youth: "Lord, make me chaste, but not yet."

p. 122, *Laudetur ... in Æternum*: "Praised be Jesus Christ. In eternity" (Latin)

p. 135, *crèmeries*: "Creameries" (French).

p. 137, *le patron*: "The boss" (French).

p. 137, *moche*: "Ugly" (French).

p. 148, *mondain*: "Sophisticated, worldly" (French).

p. 154, *Better to be a cotter... prince among the dead*: Homer, *Odyssey* XI, 465–540: Odysseus visits the ghost of Achilles in Hades, where Achilles rejects Odysseus's felicitations on his honoured state with the line Szerb quotes.

p. 155, *Cestius' Mal vorbei, leise zum Orcus hinab*: Goethe, *Roman Elegies*: "Lead me softly down to the underworld, next to Cestius' pyramid" (German).

p. 155, *Cor cordium*: "Heart of hearts" (Latin). This does, indeed, appear on Shelley's gravestone.

p. 159, *Incipit vita nova*: "[Here] begins the new life" (Latin). From the Introduction to Dante, *La vita nuova* (The New Life) (Italian).

p. 161, *Popolo d'Italia*: "People of Italy" (Italian).

p. 161, *Aspetti ... religione antiche*: "Aspects of Death in Ancient Religions" (Italian).

p. 165, *Doorn... the German ex-Kaiser's archaeological team*: Wilhelm II lived in Doorn, Netherlands, from his exile in November 1918 until his death in 1941.

p. 166, *Pozsony*: Present-day Bratislava, Slovakia. At the time of the novel's setting (and writing), 1937, it was already Bratislava, part of Czechoslovakia as a result of the 1920 Treaty of Trianon (part of the Versailles peace process); but Hungarians continue (to this day) to refer to it by its Hungarian name.

p. 168, *Pfarrer*: "Pastor" (German).

p. 168, *the Black Stone*: The *Lapis Niger*, perhaps the oldest shrine in the Forum, featuring the oldest known Roman inscription.

p. 171, *Sophron*: Sophron of Syracuse (fl. 430 BC), a writer of prose dialogues, and an alleged favourite author of Plato.

p. 172, *Foied vino pipafo, cra carefo*: In the Faliscan language, an ancient Italic tongue that went extinct by 150 BC.

p. 173, *Rohde's*: Erwin Rohde (1845–98), great German classical scholar.

p. 174, *Hetaerae*: "Prostitutes"; from the Greek *hetaira* (plural: hetairai). The Latin forms are *hetaera* and *hetaerae*.

p. 176, *the isle of the blessed... an irresistible compulsion*: From the *Mabinogion*, a medieval Welsh collection of stories.

p. 176, *Spenglerism*: An allusion to Oswald Spengler (1880–1936), German cultural historian best known as author of *The Decline of the West*.

p. 176, *Cluniac monastic reform*: Monastic life had fallen into corruption when St Odo (*c.*878–942), second abbot of the Benedictine monastery of Cluny in France, initiated reforms to revive the Rule of St Benedict and refocus commitment to art, contemplation and assistance to the poor. The reforms subsequently spread through much of western Europe.

p. 177, *And whereof... to think*: An ironic allusion to Austrian philosopher Ludwig Wittgenstein's (1889–1951) "*Wovon man nicht sprechen kann, darüber muss man schweigen*" ("Whereof one cannot speak, thereof one must be silent", from his *Tractatus Logico-Philosophicus* of 1921).

p. 177, *the transdanubian Hungarians*: A reference to the part of Hungary west of the Danube. The most likely reason Szerb singles this part of the population out is that they were the subject of sociological studies because of the peasants' recent habit of having only one child per family. This was done to avoid splitting their small plots of land among multiple heirs, but the concern was that this would lead to depopulation: hence, Szerb's association of the practice with a death wish.

p. 178, *what Goethe said... theory is green*: From *Faust I*, when Mephistopheles is speaking to Faust in his student's room: "*Grau, treuer Freund, ist alle theorie / und grün des Lebens goldner Baum*": "Grey, true friend, is all theory / and green the golden tree of life" (German).

p. 180, *La Belle Hélène*: An 1864 operetta by French composer Jacques Offenbach (1819–80).

p. 180, *Naconxipan... the mad Gulácsy*: Also known as the Four-cornered Circular Wood, Naconxipan was a fantastical land invented by the painter Lajos Gulácsy (1882–1932) and also made use of by the major poet Sándor Weöres (1913–89), who knew Szerb well. Gulácsy was indeed mad, spending time in a mental asylum in the 1920s and '30s.

p. 180, *Attis, Adonis*: Attis was initially a Phrygian god of vegetation, later incorporated into Greek mythology as the consort of the mother goddess Cybele, also of Phrygian origin. He was considered to possess godlike male beauty, despite having castrated himself. Attis and Cybele combine some of the attributes of the Greek Earth Mother Gaia, goddess of the harvest and fertility Demeter, and Demeter's daughter Persephone. Adonis is another Greek deity associated with vegetation (and hence with cycles of death and rebirth); he too was an archetype of youthful male beauty. In some legends, he was a consort of Aphrodite until a jealous Artemis killed him.

p. 182, *Symposium*: A philosophical dialogue by Plato (428/27 or 424/23–348/47 BC).

p. 185, *maîtresse de titre*: "Official mistress" (French).

p. 186, *Sevenal*: A Hungarian brand of anti-seizure phenobarbitol pills.

p. 187, *Szabadka*: Present-day Subotica, Serbia; at the time of writing, Subotica, Yugoslavia.

p. 187, *Krychlovác*: A fictitious figure.

p. 187, *Deutsch ist ä Weltsprache*: "German is a world language" (dialectal German).

p. 195, *A porta... defunctorum*: From the Office of the Dead: "*Versicle*: From the gates of hell / *Responsory*: Lord, deliver his soul" (Latin).

p. 197, *Pastasciutta*: Cooked pasta served with an accompanying sauce or condiment (Italian).

p. 198, *Scholastics*: Academic scholars of medieval Europe who developed influential schools of critical thought; significant figures from their ranks include St Anselm of Canterbury (see note to p. 40), Duns Scotus (*c.*1266–1308), William of Ockham (*c.*1287–1347) and St Thomas Aquinas (see note to p. 40).

p. 205, *maremme*: "Coastal marshlands" (Italian).

p. 205, *Quirites*: The earliest name given to the citizens of Rome.

p. 209, *good fortune and none other*: The personal motto of the Hungarian-Croatian general and epic poet, Miklós Zrínyi (in Croatian, Nikola Zrinski, 1620–64): "Sors bona nihil aliud" (Latin), which Szerb quotes here in its Hungarian form.

p. 210, *Navis, navis*: The nominative and genitive declensions of the Latin noun for "ship". Giving both cases identifies the noun's declension. *Navis* being a third declension i-stem noun, its nominative and genitive forms are the same.

p. 214, *aranciata*: Carbonated orange juice (Italian).

p. 223, *Consummatum est*: "It is finished" (Latin), the last words of Christ on the cross.

p. 226, *Salvator Rosa*: Salvator Rosa (1615–73) Italian painter and poet.

p. 233, *tabatière*: "Snuffbox" (French).

p. 247, *Cabbage is round*: The opening of an ancient children's song from Transylvania, which Mihály would have recognized instantly. Its opening verse reads, in translation: "Cabbage is round, its leaves are lacy, / Whoever lacks a mate, let him dance with me. / I twirl and I turn but I have no matey: / Girls and boys, who will dance with me?"

Translator's Afterword

Antal Szerb (1901–45) was a highly influential literary scholar and novelist in Hungary between the World Wars. In 1936, he published a volume that analysed recent works in the major world languages to develop a theory of the modern novel. The following year, he wrote *Utas és holdvilág* (literally, *Traveller and Moonlight*). Some critics were quick to perceive the connection between Szerb's theoretical work and his new fiction:

> In his study, *Hétköznapok és csodák* [*The Quotidian and the Miraculous*], Antal Szerb develops a theory of the modern novel. [...] Szerb fits his creation perfectly to his theory. He has written a model modern novel.[1]

What makes his novel modern? It is certainly up to date, set in the year of its writing, with most of the action taking place in Mussolini's fascist Italy. Most critics read *Journey by Moonlight* as a psychological novel about a man, Mihály, struggling not to conform to the bourgeois world of which he is part. This contemporary combination of psychology and socio-political commentary certainly forms two of the main threads in the intricate tapestry that Szerb weaves. However, Szerb sees modernity also in finding intrusions of the miraculous – the liminal and the numinous – in the everyday world. But what did

1 Miklós Kállay: '*Utas és holdvilág*' ['*Journey by Moonlight*']. In: Tibor Wagner (ed.): *Törött pálcák* [*Broken Wands 1. Reviews of Antal Szerb, 1926–1948*] (Budapest: Nemzeti Tankönyvkiadó, 2000), 304. Cited in József Havasréti, '*Egyesek és mások*' ['Certain People and Others'], *Jelenkor* 54:4, 427*ff*., 2011.

he think he was really writing about? In a letter of January, 1937, he writes to a friend: "I'm now writing a novel about nostalgia."[2]

Focusing on nostalgia opens up new perspectives on this novel. Reading it primarily in terms of rebellion against bourgeois conformism suggests that by the end Mihály, returning home to Budapest and to his position in the family firm, has lost his struggle. Reading it, however, in terms of nostalgia suggests that Mihály may not be coming out of his experience so poorly. In *The Future of Nostalgia*, Svetlana Boym distinguishes two types or tendencies of nostalgia that she terms restorative and reflective:

> Restorative nostalgia stresses *nostos* [the return home] and attempts a transhistorical reconstruction of the lost home. Reflective nostalgia thrives in *algia*, the longing itself, and delays the homecoming – wistfully, ironically, desperately.[3]

She elaborates:

> Restorative nostalgia manifests itself in total reconstruction of monuments of the past, while reflective nostalgia lingers on ruins, the patina of time and history, in the dreams of another place and another time.[4]

While Boym's focus is on public manifestations of restorative nostalgia, especially as they relate to evocation and recreation of a glorious national past, the concept can be applied fruitfully to Mihály's private, personal nostalgia for the circle of friends and

2 Letter to Dionis M. Pippidi, January 5, 1937. In: Csaba Nagy (ed.): *Szerb Antal válogatott levelei* [*Selected Letters of Antal Szerb*] (Budapest: Petőfi Irodalmi Múzeum, 2001), 96. Cited in Havasréti, *op. cit.*

3 Svetlana Boym: *The Future of Nostalgia* (New York: Basic Books, 2001), xviii.

4 *Ibid.*, 41.

activities of his adolescence. That charmed circle ignored bourgeois convention where it could and flouted it where it could not. He and his friends sought escape from the quotidian and bourgeois, finding refuge in private theatricals where death was a constant, numinous presence.

The onset of adulthood and the need to earn a living drove Mihály into his family firm and into a conventional bourgeois life. As the final confirmation of his status – and, as it turned out, in a desperate attempt to hold his nostalgia at bay – he first seduced his friend's wife Erzsi and, after she divorced her husband, married her. The novel begins with the couple's arrival by train in Venice, on their honeymoon.

The narrator observes that Mihály, although well-travelled in Europe, had always avoided Italy. Were it not for his honeymoon, he might have postponed the trip "until his death". We find out why, as his nostalgia soon looms large. It becomes clear that his nostalgia is a restorative one, seeking to reconstruct the past – perhaps innocently, at first, in touristic excursions he finds himself oddly unable to share with his bride. Eventually Mihály tries to re-establish contact, and a romantic relationship, with the lone female member of the adolescent circle, Éva Ulpius. Éva's brother, Tamás, had been Mihály's best friend, the one who'd inducted him into the charmed Ulpius circle – and who had later committed suicide rather than submit to the bourgeois order of things. Discovering how Mihály navigates a path from the restorative to the reflective form of nostalgia is one of the many pleasures of reading this magnificent novel of magical realism *avant la lettre*.

In his letter to his friend, Szerb goes on to write that his novel "has to be something like… [Cocteau's] *Les Enfants terribles*." He does not mention the novel of his Hungarian contemporary, Sándor Márai (1900–89), whose *Zendülők* [*The Rebels*] (1930) also deals with a group of adolescents graduating from high school towards the end of the First World War, just like Mihály and his friends, and likewise rebelling against their bourgeois origins. More strikingly still, Márai's rebels also act out a private theatrical experience with ominous overtones, and one of their circle also perishes. Critics have often compared *The Rebels* to Cocteau's *Les Enfants terribles*. Yet Szerb is unique in presenting youthful rebellion from the nostalgic perspective of the (surviving) characters grown to adulthood.

Mihály is not the only character negotiating a transition from restorative to reflective nostalgia. His wife, Erzsi, follows a path that sometimes mirrors and sometimes inverts Mihály's. Most obviously: where Mihály seduces, then marries Erzsi in an attempt to become fully bourgeois, Erzsi takes up with him as an act of rebellion against the upper-class bourgeois expectations of her own upbringing (and of her upper-class first husband). Where middle-class Mihály had rejected thrift as a symbol of bourgeois conformity, upper-class Erzsi indulged in thrift to a neurotic degree, rejecting the conspicuous consumption her peers considered vital to maintain appearances. The reader so inclined will enjoy observing their parallel (sometimes anti-parallel) journeys and experiences that play out like musical counterpoint in a two-voice fugue.

Hardly a single metaphor or image fails to recur elsewhere, sometimes varied; not a single thematic thread is left unwoven in its tapestry. A simple example: the book starts with a reference to a train ride; another train ride confirms the rupture in Mihály's life and sends him, both literally and figuratively, in a new direction; and the novel ends with Mihály on another train. Another example: in Part One, the inhabitants of Venice are likened to ants always following the same ant highways, whilst in Part Four, the inhabitants of Rome's poor districts are likened to rats amidst the Roman ruins. This is no mere authorial conceit: the reader may decide whether the similes reflect a significant change in Mihály's outlook.

A Hungarian literary scholar, József Havasréti, points out the many autobiographical elements in *Journey by Moonlight*.[5] These include an intense adolescent friendship that left deep psychological residues; a year after Szerb cut off the friendship, he worked out its implications for the first time in a literary fragment, *Hogyan halt meg Ulpius Tamás?* [*How Did Tamás Ulpius Die?*] (1919, but unpublished until 2000). Szerb's own trip to Italy in 1936, recorded in his philosophical travelogue *A harmadik torony* [*The Third Tower*], is an important precursor to the novel. Some incidents and observations in *Journey by Moonlight* are closely modelled on his own Italian experiences. A few passages from *The Third Tower* are worth quoting here, as they reinforce some of the larger concerns so lightly touched upon in the novel:

> ...I always travel to Italy as if it were my last time there, and when I first see one of its towns, it is as if I were revisiting it and, at the same time, also bidding it farewell. Dostoevsky writes that one should live as if every minute were the final minute of a condemned man... my own Italian impressions are, all of them, a bit like such final visions.

Szerb did not know it at the time of writing, but he had, in fact, seen Italy for the last time:

> There, at the foot of the Third Tower [outside San Marino], I understood... my uneasiness... everywhere on the trip, where I, as a solitary man, had to interact with collectivism, the happy Italian collectivism. I feared for my solitude from it, and from the European future that it symbolized to me. I feared for my solitary happiness in the face of their herd-happiness...
>
> This happiness that I feel here... I cannot hand over to anyone. Just as I cannot hand myself over to anyone or anything, to any State or Ideal.

5 Havasréti, *op. cit.*

Submergence of one's individuality, whether in the depths of nostalgia or in the ocean of a collectivist, totalitarian state, was a growing concern of the Jewish-born Catholic Szerb, as the clouds of Fascism, Bolshevism, Nazism and war gathered. These concerns show up in the novel only in the most delicate allusions, and in one passage where Mihály reads the Italian newspapers of the day. From *The Third Tower*:

> Courage: things will yet work out, somehow. Only do not give up your solitude for anything, under any circumstances. And then, in turn, nobody will be able to take anything from you. How did Milton's Satan put it, in the burning desert of the Underworld? 'What matter where, if I still be the same.' Whatever happens in Europe, trust in your personal stars. [...] And that will be enough.

In *Journey by Moonlight*, one character admonishes another that he must not seek to replicate another's death in the ultimate act of restorative nostalgia: "Let each find his own death." In the Europe of 1937, where Spain was the testing ground for a confrontation between two collectivist ideals, Nazism and Bolshevism (republican ideals having been largely swept aside), and where Szerb could foresee the continental-scale confrontation to come, the admonitions not to hand himself to any ideal, not to yield his solitude, to trust in his own stars and to seek his own death guided his work and actions. He wrote histories of Hungarian and world literature that continue to speak to both scholarly audiences and the general public; he wrote delicate, wistful, ironic and occasionally desperate novels that remain beloved to Hungarian readers today. He published an anthology of one hundred gems of world poetry in Hungarian translation at a time (1943) when Hungary, drawn into alliance with Nazi Germany, had closed itself off to the outside world and when all official means of earning a living had been deprived him. The following year, he was rounded up for forced labour; a copy of the anthology, which his biographer György Poszler characterizes as "summing up the interests and all the nostalgias of his entire career,"[6] accompanied him all the way. Still true to his own star in the Underworld of a labour camp in western Hungary, this man – who was as personally beguiling as his works – found his own death in January 1945, having been beaten to death by camp guards with no appreciation of irony.

– Peter V. Czipott
San Diego, CA
September 2015

ACKNOWLEDGEMENTS

The translator gratefully acknowledges the invaluable editorial supervision of that outstanding publisher, Alessandro Gallenzi, and his simply amazing and splendid editor, Christian Müller, whose keen eye and sense of style have rescued many passages from the perils of translatorese. The translator is solely responsible for any remaining solecisms.

English, French, German, Italian, Faliscan and Latin texts in the original appear in the original languages in this translation (original English, italicized).

6 György Poszler: *Szerb Antal* [*Antal Szerb*] (Budapest: Akadémiai Kiadó, 1973), 412.

On the
ORIGIN
of
SPECIES
Charles
DARWIN

Daniel Defoe
Moll
Flanders

CHARLES
DICKENS
CHRISTMAS
CAROL

DAVID
COPPERFIELD
CHARLES
DICKENS

GREAT
EXPECTATIONS
CHARLES DICKENS

HARD
TIMES
CHARLES
DICKENS

CHARLES
DICKENS
OLIVER
TWIST

CHARLES
DICKENS
TALE OF TWO
CITIES

The
DOUBLE
Fyodor
DOSTOEVSKY

Fyodor
DOSTOEVSKY
The
GAMBLER

The
IDIOT
Fyodor
DOSTOEVSKY
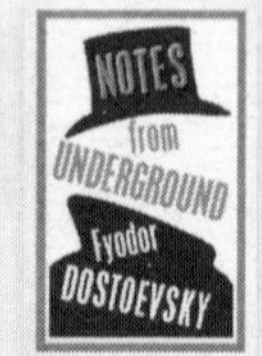
NOTES
from
UNDERGROUND
Fyodor
DOSTOEVSKY

Middlemarch
GEORGE
ELIOT
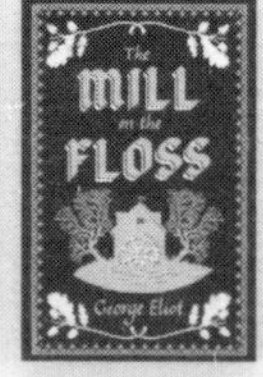
The
MILL
on the
FLOSS
George Eliot

PRAISE
of
FOLLY
ERASMUS

The
BEAUTIFUL
and
DAMNED
F. SCOTT
FITZGERALD

The
GREAT
GATSBY
F. SCOTT
FITZGERALD

TENDER
is the
NIGHT
F. SCOTT
FITZGERALD

GUSTAVE
FLAUBERT
MADAME
BOVARY

NORTH
AND
SOUTH
ELIZABETH GASKELL

THE
SORROWS
OF
YOUNG
WERTHER
GOETHE

Dead
SOULS
Nikolai
GOGOL

Nikolai
GOGOL
Petersburg
TALES

THOMAS HARDY
FAR FROM
THE
MADDING
CROWD

THOMAS HARDY
JUDE
THE
OBSCURE

THOMAS HARDY
TESS
OF THE
D'URBERVILLES

Nathaniel
HAWTHORNE
The
Scarlet
LETTER

THE
PORTRAIT
OF A
LADY
HENRY JAMES

THREE
MEN IN A
BOAT
JEROME K. JEROME

DUBLINERS
JAMES
JOYCE

ULYSSES
JAMES
JOYCE

FRANZ
METAMORPHOSIS
AND OTHER STORIES
KAFKA

FRANZ
KAFKA
THE
TRIAL

LADY
CHATTERLEY'S
LOVER
D.H. LAWRENCE

SONS
AND
LOVERS
D.H. LAWRENCE

Mikhail
Lermontov
A Hero of
Our Time

ALMA CLASSICS

ALMA CLASSICS aims to publish mainstream and lesser-known European classics in an innovative and striking way, while employing the highest editorial and production standards. By way of a unique approach the range offers much more, both visually and textually, than readers have come to expect from contemporary classics publishing.